The Mystery of the Tiger

The Mystery of the Tiger

by
Maurice Magre

Translated, annotated and introduced by
Brian Stableford

A Black Coat Press Book

TABLE OF CONTENTS

Introduction

This is the fifth volume of a twelve-volume set of translations of Maurice Magre's prose fiction. It contains translations of the novella *Le Roman de Confucius* (1927), as "The Story of Confucius," and the novel *Le Mystère du tigre* (1927), as "The Mystery of the Tiger."

Volume One, *The Marvelous Story of Claire d'Amour and Other Stories*, contains translations of early short stories, including the contents of the collection *Histoire merveilleuse de Claire d'Amour suivie d'autres contes merveilleux* (1903) and six other stories from various sources published between 1901 and 1913.

Volume Two, *The Call of the Beast and Other Stories*, contains translations of his first three works of prose fiction in volume form, *Les Colombes poignardées* (1917), as "Stabbed Doves," *La Tendre camarade* (1918), as "The Tender Comrade" and *L'Appel de la bête* (1920), as "The Call of the Beast."

Volume Three, *Priscilla of Alexandria and Other Stories* contains translations of the original version of the story collection *Vies des courtisanes*, first published in *Oeuvres Libres* 23 (1923), as "Courtesans' Lives" plus the additional story added to the version published in volume form in 1925, and the novel *Priscilla d'Alexandrie* (1925), as "Priscilla of Alexandria."

Volume Four, *The Angel of Lust*, contains translations of the novella, *La Vie amoureuse de Messaline* (1925), as "The Love Life of Messalina," the novel published as *La Luxure de Grenade* (1926), as "The Angel of Lust," and the chapter from *Magiciens et illuminés* (1930) entitled "Christian Rosenkreutz et les Rose-croix," as "Christian Rosenkreutz and the Rosicrucians."

Volume Six, *The Poison of Goa*, contains translations of the novel *Le Poison de Goa* (1928), as "The Poison of Goa," and the prose poems contained in *Le Livre des lotus entr'ouverts* (1926), as "Lotus Blossoms."

Volume Seven, *Lucifer*, contains a translation of the novel originally published under the same title in 1929 and the novella *La Nuit de haschich et de l'opium* (1929), as "The Night of Hashish and Opium."

Volume Eight, *The Blood of Toulouse*, contains translations of the novel *Le Sang de Toulouse* (1931), as "The Blood of Toulouse," and the chapter from *Magiciens et illuminés* entitled "Le Maître inconnu des Albigeois," as "The Secret Master of the Albigensians."

Volume Nine, *The Albigensian Treasure*, contains translations of the novel *Le Trésor des Albigeois* (1938) as "The Albigensian Treasure," and the collection of vignettes "Communication avec la nature" from *La Beauté invisible* (1937), as "Communication with Nature."

Volume Ten, *Jean de Fodoas*, contains translations of the novel *Jean de Fodoas: aventures d'un Français à la cour de l'empereur Akbar* (1939) as "Jean de Fodoas" and the chapter from *Magiciens et illuminés* entitled "Le Mystère des Templiers," as "The Mystery of the Templars."

Volume Eleven, *Melusine*, contains translations of the novel *Mélusine, ou le secret de solitude* (1941) and the collections of vignettes "Le Côté d'ombre des âmes" and "Révélation des mondes invisibles" from *La Beauté invisible*, as "The Dark Side of Souls" and "The Revelation of Invisible Worlds."

Volume Twelve, *The Brothers of the Virgin Gold*, contains a translation of the novel *Les Frères de l'or vierge*, first published posthumously in 1949.

The first edition of *Le Roman de Confucius*, issued by Fasquelle in 1927, adds a superscription to the title, "La Lumière de la Chine" [The Light of China], which is sometimes mistakenly cited as if it were the title. The story was probably written and published before *Le Mystère du tigre*, issued in the same year by Albin Michel; publication of the latter book is dated internally as 30 September, whereas the list of the author's previous publications in the former does not include *Le Mystère du tigre*. At first glance it might seems that the two texts have very little in common, but in fact they are united by overlapping concerns as well as the common narrative device of employing an extremely unsympathetic protagonist, which Magre had not done previously and was never to do again.

The introduction to the previous volume in the present series suggested that the particular enterprise undertaken in the violent erotic melodramas *Priscilla d'Alexandrie, La Vie amoureuse de Messaline* and *La Luxure de Grenade* has run its course, and that there was no point in its further extrapolation. The time had come to move attention away from the hazards and deleterious effects of carnal lust, in order to look more closely on the possibilities of a constructive development of a life-enhancing philosophy and spirituality.

Magre knew, however, that such a quest was by no means a straightforward matter, in spite of the guidance provided by the great philosophers and religious founders of the past. Indeed, he was all too well aware of the fact that there were conflicting approaches to the development of a virtuous philosophy, whose contention had frequently become murderous. He was very conscious of his conviction that some of the competing systems were, at best, sterile, and at worst damaging, as dangerous in their own way as the urges of the inferior self fiercely stigmatized in the triptych of erotic melodramas.

In order to dramatize the competition between rival philosophical approaches to the problem of how human life ought to be organized and orientated, Magre selected the contrasted approaches of two famous philosophers, one of whom, Confucius, was well documented, and whose life could be dated with reasonable accuracy, whereas the history of the other, Lao-Tsu, was so uncertain as to render his real existence dubious, but who might, if he had actually existed, have been the contemporary of the former.

In his non-fictional writings, Magre speaks of Confucius in vaguely complementary terms, as befits his reputation, but for the purposes of his fictionalized reconstruction of the opposition between Confucius' quintessentially rule-bound and dogmatic ideas and Lao-Tsu's meditative mysticism, he exaggerates the great man's faults to the extent of making him not merely a villain but a monster. The result is undoubtedly dubious as history, but as poignantly dramatic fiction it is highly effective. Its deft detailing of the manner in which Confucius casually crushes the spirit of his unfortunate wife and devastates the life of his luckless half-brother, by virtue of his obsession with rules and regulations, is heart-rending, and the account of the rise and abrupt fall of the "utopia" he creates when given the political opportunity to put his philosophy into action is a clever exercise in deadly serious comedy. As a Voltairean *conte philosophique*, *Le Roman de Confucius* has few twentieth-century peers.

The story also takes advantage of the greater coincidence that Lao-Tsu, if he did exist, might not only have been contemporary with the Buddha but also with the pre-Socratic philosophers of Greece, including Pythagoras, if he too actually existed. Lao-Tsu's heroic role is therefore not limited to finding the supposed truth to which Confucius is blind; he is also credited with an attempt to join forces with his analogues in order to found the organization of Secret Masters who, in the secret history that Magre had borrowed from Madame Blavatsky for constructive reshaping, would become the guardians of the true wisdom and the patient guides of future illuminati.

Magre's biographer Jean-Jacques Bedu, author of *Maurice Magre: Le Lotus perdu* [Maurice Magre: The Lost Lotus] (1999), was unable to establish exactly when Magre began to investigate the occult underworld in earnest, although it must have been in the years immediately following the end of the Great War. He had been introduced to it before the war by Gabriel de Lautrec, who had similarly begun is career as an affiliate of the Decadent Movement, and still was when he took Magre to an exotic séance, although he eventually developed an outstanding reputation as a humorist. That encounter is described in the opening chapter of the first of his autobiographical texts, *Pourquoi je suis Bouddhiste* [Why I Am a Buddhist] (1929), and is summarized the introduction to volume 2 of the present series. Although his stern skepticism had been abolished by 1920, Magre still seems to have launched himself into his exploration of that underworld more as a fascinated tourist than a would-be initiate. Always likely to be carried away by surges of enthusiasm, however, he rapidly allowed himself to be convinced, or at least to take the notion seriously, that there must be something behind the manifestations he saw in spiritualist séances. He was equally quick to be convinced, however, that many of the specific assertions being made by his interlocutors were nonsensical.

As with his marriage and his infection with syphilis, although not as ruthlessly, Magre mostly left his intercourse with the occult underworld out of his autobiographical writings, with the result that slender clues to the nature of his interactions with it mostly have to be gleaned from his fiction, the most revealing of which are perhaps contained in *Lucifer*, especially in the chapter in which, desperate for expert assistance in his psychological struggle against apparent demonic possession, the narrator hires a cab and has the driver take him to all the unorthodox churches in Paris, one after another, but cannot find the succor he needs anywhere. Bedu, however, ascertained that Magre was the pseudonymous author of *Magie à Paris* (1934), signed "René Thimmy," a distinctly tongue-in-cheek survey of the occult underworld in the early twentieth century, which cites Magre as a well-known client of various strange organizations. "Thimmy" followed it up, however, with *La Magie aux colonies* (1935), which must have been based entirely on hearsay, and it is probable that much of the earlier volume was also more a product of reportage and rumor than first-hand observation.

In any case, by 1927, Magre had certainly investigated many of the occult resources available in contemporary Paris, with varying degrees of fascination. He had certainly attended séances by several celebrated mediums, and had attended meetings of self-styled Rosicrucians, although the only group that seems to have captured his serious allegiance for a while was the Theosophists, to whom he was attracted after stumbling across Madame Blavatsky's account of *The Secret Doctrine* (1888). What impressed him most about the neo-Rosicrucians and other practitioners of ritual magic was their flamboyant and far-reaching revisions of history, and at that game Madame Blavatsky, the inventor of Theosophy, had been a past master. Although he must have taken due note of the contradictions between the various reconstructions of history embraced by different sects, the fundamental endeavor of discovering or inventing an unorthodox history in opposition to the one that was generally accepted obviously appealed to Magre greatly.

Magre's infatuation with Theosophists, which was probably at its peak in 1925, did not last long, and he was direly unimpressed on the one occasion when he attended a lecture by Annie Besant, whom he considered to have betrayed the principles of the movement's founder. He always retained a sincere, if slightly wry, admiration for Madame Blavatsky, sometimes writing about her as if he had known her personally, although he could not possibly have met her, given that she had died in 1891. She is the subject of the last chapter of *Magiciens et illuminés* [Magicians and Illuminati] (1930), effectively book-ending his history of the alleged secret wisdom with Apollonius of Tyana. The sheer ambition of Theosophist scholarly fantasy, as applied to human history, obviously had a considerable impact on him, and when he built his own fantasized history, it was probably inevitable that it would be Madame Blavatsky's that he used as a fundamental template rather than the one that contemporary magicians and would-be Rosicrucians had inherited from "Éliphas Lévi" (Alphonse-Louis Constant).

The notion of an ancient wisdom known to various seers of antiquity, including Plato and Hindu sages, and still preserved by "secret masters" resident in Tibet, became central to

Magre's own unorthodox history, as mapped out, episodically but with an uncommon coherency, in *Magiciens et illuminés* and further elaborated in the *La Clé des choses cachées* [The Key to Hidden Things] (1935). When he began to develop works of fiction celebrating and popularizing that secret history, therefore—into which *Le Roman de Confucius* was slotted along with *Priscilla d'Alexandrie* and *La Luxure de Grenade*—he orientated their direction by means of a narrative compass pointing in the direction of Tibet. That is where Lao-Tsu heads, however improbably, in the conclusion of *Le Roman de Confucius*, and it is the region from which the enigmatic peripatetic sage featured in *Le Mystère du tigre* is said to originate.

An earlier translation of *Le Roman de Confucius* was published in London by Thornton Butterworth in 1929, as *Confucius and His Quest*, but it seemed worthwhile to make a new translation for the benefit of present project.

Even if one sets aside the narrative device of employing an unsympathetic protagonist, *Le Mystère du tigre* was not entirely a new departure for Magre. It deliberately picks up and elaborates a theme introduced in an extraneous sub-plot in *L'Appel de la bête*, which includes a character-sketch of the sadist Jean Lathème, an obvious precursor of the animal-tamer Rafaël Graaf. In addition to its connections with *Le Roman de Confucius*, *Le Mystère du tigre* also has thematic overlaps with *Pourquoi je suis bouddhiste*, and it is the version of the Buddhist philosophy outlined in that work of which the protagonist of *Le Mystère du tigre* is the incarnated antithesis, until the machinations of the plot, with the aid of the effects of opium, pave the way for his spectacular expiation and redemption.

The narrative strategy of *Le Mystère du tigre* might seem odd and a trifle risky—many readers find antipathetic protagonists direly uncomfortable—but it is entirely appropriate to the nature of the project. The Buddhist sage encountered by chance in an opium den and intricately entangled with Graaf's destiny requires an extreme antithesis just as Lao-Tsu required an exaggerated Confucius in *Le Roman de Confucius*, because without such caricaturish opposition there were would be little or no scope in the story for dramatic incident or any kind of robust story-line. The story told in *Le Mystère du tigre* is undoubtedly peculiar, but it is certainly not lacking in incident or narrative strength, nor is it lacking in effect. Although it is not one of the author's better-known works, Jean-Jacques Bedu does not hesitate to describe it in his bibliography as a masterpiece.

Although *Le Mystère du tigre* partakes of the same narrative fervor as most of Magre's prose works, it must have been a difficult book to write, because of the decision to use first person narrative to account for the protagonist's motives and actions and then to describe the phases of his psychological metamorphosis. Because Graaf's opinions and character are the complete opposite of Magre's own—he is an archetype of the kind of person who has absolutely no sympathy with everything for which the author stood, especially by virtue of his hatred of books in general and poetry in particular—it must have been much harder for the author to step into his shoes imaginatively than it was for him to identify with his previous and subsequent first-person narrators, who are much closer analogues of his own personality. Then again, give the nature of Graaf's conversion, the problem of mapping it out in documentary form and getting the presumed document into recoverable circumstances in a plausible fashion was by no means trivial. Whether Magre's solutions to those various problems are entirely satisfactory from a logical viewpoint remains debatable, but they certainly demonstrate considerable ingenuity, and add an extra dimension of drama to an extraordinary story.

The particular subject-matter of *Le Mystère du tigre*—the relationship between humans and animals, and between humans and their own animality—gives the story a particular dimension of interest. It was a theme further developed in some subsequent works, and it is worth noting that the central image of the release of the caged captives—which had been used before, in *La Vie amoureuse de Messaline*, of all places, and was to be employed again, with similar incongruity, in *Le Sang du Toulouse*—must have had a particular resonance in Magre's imagination that went far beyond the specific requirement of the plot of *Le Mystère du Tigre*. The image of the strange ruined temple featured in the novel had also cropped up, quite arbitrarily, in *Priscilla d'Alexandrie*, and was to do so again in one of the most striking vignettes in *La Beauté invisible*, and that too must have had a particular personal significance.

Another feature of *Le Mystère du tigre* worthy of attention is the deliberate peculiarity of Magre's natural history, as exhibited in the highly improbable account of all the animals gathered in the protagonist's menagerie. That enumeration strays into the fringes of surrealism in its variety and calculated inconsistency, and its eccentric implausibility cannot be an error. Similarly bizarre and impossible juxtapositions of species are contrived elsewhere in Magre's work, notably in the subplot featuring Noël Alga in *Les Frères de l'or vierge*. The enigmas contained in the novel thus extend much further than the Buddhist sage's deliberately gnomic utterances. The final sequence of the novel is by no means the only episode in Magre's work to be calculatedly reminiscent of an opium dream, nor to use such a fictitious dream to attempt a symbolic analysis of one of the issues dear to the author's heart, but it is perhaps the most personal, as well as the most poignant and bizarre.

The novel is, therefore, exceedingly eccentric—a judgment meant entirely as a compliment—and there is nothing else like it even within Magre's own *oeuvre*. That whole endeavor was too varied and too imaginatively adventurous ever to gain him the kind of popularity that thrives on repetition and easy comprehension, or the kind of critical attention that prefers consistency and is deeply suspicious of the fantastic, but *Le Mystère du tigre* offers one of the most obvious examples of his stubborn defiance of convention. Although deliberately awkward in its employment of an alien viewpoint, and somewhat disconnected as the viewpoint character gradually slides from unrepentant unpleasantness into a kind of remorseful divine madness, it is a truly remarkable work.

The translation of *Le Roman de Confucius* was made from the copy of the 1927 Fasquelle edition reproduced on the Bibliothèque Nationale's *gallica* website. The translation of *Le Mystère du tigre* was made from the copy of the 1927 Albin Michel edition reproduced on the same website.

Brian Stableford

THE STORY OF CONFUCIUS

To the Men of the Occident

Men of the Occident, listen to me. I have traversed millennia; I have seen planets that have disappeared and I made the first harvest when the earth was muddy and had scarcely emerged from the primitive waters.

Men of the Occident, I learned to write and the art of composing books with bamboo tablets when you were walking on all fours and eating the flesh of your dead.

Men of the Occident, I have searched for the truth and I have loved it with a thousand times more ardor than you, and if there are harp players, men who count the stars and others who trace figures in stone, it is because of the sweat that I have poured out.

Men of the Occident, you who are proud of your ships and your machines, your inventions and your God, for a very long time I have been transforming matter in a thousand fashions, and when I knew God, I remained immobile.

Men of the Occident, you do not know all of me, because my science is secret and my wisdom is silent. Beware of the woe caused by the man who reveals too rapidly that which ought to remain hidden.

Men of the Occident, do not hurry. On the mountain of Tai-Chang I am sitting and waiting. I can see you coming from afar. The sand rises and falls. All peoples are dispersed. The word of sages remains.

Men of the Occident, listen to the sages, the great sages of ancient China. In their lifetime they were petty and no one

17

knew that they were sages, for such is the law. The truth is invisible and we aspire to it without knowing it.

Men of the Occident, the truth is invisible but it was born in the yellow earth, it ate grains of rice and slept under the blue mulberry, and we transmit it there modestly. Men of the Occident, listen to the sages, the great sages of ancient China.

The Youth of Sages

The Garden of the House of Confucius

In winter, at the second moon of the twenty-first year of the reign of Ling-Wang, in the mountainous kingdom of Lou, under the flat roof of a little bamboo house, Khoun-Fou-Tseu was born, whom the barbaric men of the Occident call Confucius.

Tchang, the guardian of the little bamboo house, was occupied in sticking on the door the paper images of the tutelary deities of thresholds, when a maidservant confided the infant to him, in order that he should be held up toward the nascent light of the sun.

And Tchang, who attained an extreme old age and watched over Confucius, recounted later to pilgrims that the marvelous child, on appearing in the world, had a cranium in the form of an amphitheater, and that he inclined it several times, with a calculated solemnity, to express his precocious love of prescribed reverences and obligatory rites.

Tchang also recounted many other prodigies, but he recounted them while laughing because, in spite of his simplicity, Confucius had taught him the principal truths that he held. Tchang therefore knew that reason is superior to everything, that the world transforms itself without prodigies and without divine intervention, by the logic of connections.

For many years, he had heard the devils walking on the wooded hills, and the aquatic serpent, Wei, respiring sadly on the river bank. He was freed from those dreads. No more amulets against evil spells! No more supplications addressed to errant souls! A long time ago, he had thrown away the cumbersome talismans that ward off maladies. What a joy it was, after having been reckoned stupid for hundred years, to be a sage liberated from superstitions! Truly, what a great joy!

And because of that, his face, which resembled in spite of its age a large lunar pumpkin, sometimes took on an expression of emptiness and despair. For he also knew that he would not be a guardian of a little bamboo house in the unknowable realm of the dead, and that he would never see his beloved master again, now rotting between the four planks of his double coffin beneath a tumulus covered with narcissi.

Plum-Ear

Fifty-four years earlier, in the mountainous realm of Thsou, a poor aging peasant woman had become the wife of an uncouth peasant. They only knew one another for one night, the one when the great comet appeared over the mountainous realm of Thsou, putting red and blue flames into the mica of the rocks and caused long luminous steaks to flow in the rivers.

They loved one another in the hollow of a furrow during that resplendent night, and when the comet disappeared in the morning, the uncouth peasant yielded up his soul.

The poor aging woman went along the roads, knocking on doors, hiring herself out as a maidservant. But when her pregnancy was visible, the master for whom she pulled up weeds in the rice-fields was discontented and dismissed her. She wandered at random for a long time, miserable and without nourishment. And on the night when the great shooting star divided the sky in two—the sky of the realm of Thsou—she sat down under a plum-tree and brought a son into the world.

The hair and eyebrows of the infant were as white as snow and his gaze had a strange profundity because of the light of the shooting star that had remained there.

The mother gave her son the name of the tree that that had sheltered him, but she perceived subsequently that he had very long earlobes and called him Plum-Ear. She walked with pride, carrying the child in her arms and showing him to pass-ers-by.

And it was people astonished by the child's white eye-brows and hair who named him Lao-Tsu: old-man-child

Certainly, all infants are reminiscent of old men by virtue of their grimaces and wrinkles, but only that one had the signs of wisdom, only that one had the light of the shooting star in his eyes, for he was Lao-Tsu the divine, the unique, the indi-vidual charged with bringing the secret verity of the earth to reasonable and child-like, laborious and timid, superstitious and positive human beings, in the immemorial land of China.

The Two Sages of China

Two sublime men had come almost at the same time into China the color of rice, and one was the man of the white pop-py and the other the man of the black poppy. Why had two sublime men arrived at almost the same time? It would be more rational to ask why there were millions who arrived de-prived of all sublimity.

Alas, the human race is like a snail that has been ordered to go around an immense mountain ten thousand times. The end of the journey is so distant that it seems logical that the snail should take it easy and travel without haste, leaving its trail of slime behind it. But no, a singular law obliges it to torment itself in order to advance ever more rapidly.

In China the color of porous clay, there were two masters at that moment because there are two verities, once that is launched directly toward the heavens and another that seeks its aliment in the earth, an ideal verity and a verity of life, a verity of the wild swan and a verity of the faithful dog.

And that is why Lao-Tsu is sitting on a mountain and looking into himself profoundly, and why Confucius makes his words heard by princes and seeks honors in order that, thorough him, the virtue that he represents might be hon-ored—the virtue that he believes he represents, for it is not certain that the meditation of the sage is not merely a philosophical form of egotism.

In China the color of crushed oats, two verities have been heard. The buds continue to burgeon, the vapors continue to rise in the channels of the rice-fields, the kingfisher still smoothes its feathers in the willow, but more than one literate man has dropped his brush and gazed at the sky with astonishment.

For there was an impenetrable mystery in day and night, good and evil, wisdom and folly, spring and winter, heads and tails; an impenetrable mystery in China the color of saffron, the man of the white poppy and the man of the black poppy.

The Mother of Confucius and the Unicorn

Rational minds try in vain to remove the marvelous from terrestrial events. They say that great men are born in the same way as other men. But to begin with, is it not the case that everything is marvelous, even simple birth?

The sub-prefect of the town of Tseou, having wanted a male child, married a well brought up young woman in order to have one. From that loveless union Confucius was born. People do not reflect on the strangeness of the phenomenon that causes a living child to be born of the conjunction of two beings in a marital bed, but they are astonished by less astonishing things.

On the morning of the conception, Tcheng-Tsai, the well brought up young woman, went down a little path under cinnamon trees, prey to the typical thoughts of surprise and resignation that wedding nights inspire.

A unicorn emerged from a juniper bush and approached Tcheng-Tsai. It came so close that she wrapped a silk ribbon around the animal's unique horn. Then she tried to caress it, but the unicorn fled lightly and Tcheng-Tsai then perceived that it had deposited a little jade tablet at her feet. On the tablet was written: *A child will be born as pure as crystal, who will be a king but without a kingdom.*

And, while carrying away the tablet, walking beneath the cinnamon trees, Tcheng-Tsai marveled at that presage and drew pride from it.

However, as she had common sense, she marveled far less at that than what had happened during the night, when she had lain down beside the sub-prefect of Tseou.

And when, nine months later, she learned that two winged dragons had enlaced over her house while she was suffering the dolors of childbirth, and that the five sacred Elders, the spirits of the five heavenly planets, had descended into the courtyard in order to discuss celestial matters, she turned her head away, and considered her abdomen as the symbol of a vulgar but immense mystery, a mystery more mysterious than the presence of two winged dragons and the five planetary Elders.

Mong-Pi

The sub-prefect of Tseou said, with pride, force and gravity: "I have only been given one son."

But he knew full well that he had two.

The town of Tseou was perched on the side of a hill. The most beautiful houses were higher up and, as one went down, the gardens were smaller and the roofs, instead of being slate, were made of woven thatch. In accordance with a rigorous prescription, all the streets had a painted paper lantern every hundred and twenty tche. There was only one that had no lantern, and that was the one that had the most need of light, an ill-famed street at the bottom of the town, which petered out in the valley.

With regard to that street, the sub-prefect of Tseou neglected his own ordinances, for regularly, when the moon was new, he slipped down there furtively and descended it at a rapid pace. He preferred not to be seen then, and he had given secret orders to the functionaries of his police that no lantern should be lit there.

"Sin," he said, "ought to remain secret."

By favor of that darkness, bad men assembled and drank rice wine in smoky shops, women squatted on thresholds, and poverty, immobile during the day, agitated and suffered more in seeking joy in the dark.

The sub-prefect was ashamed of himself, but, for the satisfaction of his desire, a blind force drove him to go to the house of a poor creature name Lu, who gave him a pleasure as humble as her own soul.

And after a long sequence of the sub-prefect's visits. Lu brought a child into the world. He was slightly deformed, ugly of face, with a certain expression of stupidity, but Lu loved him immensely. Under the veil of apparent ugliness, the pure soul of a mother perceived the real beauty, which is independent of the facial features.

"O sub-prefect of Tseou," she said, the new moon following the birth, "this is the child born of you, and whom I have named Mong-Pi."

And the sub-prefect was very indignant at those words and went away, never to return. It was from that day on that the ill-famed street at the bottom of the town had painted paper lanterns.

The child's face became less stupid because of his mother's love, which was reflected there. All day long Lu held him in her arms, and when she had been drinking she placed him on the ground. And as the single room in which she lived was at a place where the street sloped steeply, the child, whom she had placed on the elevated side, rolled toward the lower side and bumped into the bamboo wall. She replaced him immediately, but the more frequently she replaced him, the more frequently he rolled. He rolled so often that in the end he was more deformed than before, and he could not take a few steps without limping on the right or the left side. But the gods who protect poor children from death with a greater solicitude than rich children always preserved his life.

Lu was a humble woman. Mong-Pi was a humble child. The sub-prefect of Tseou turned away angrily when he crossed their path in a street. Mong-Pi never dared approach him, but sometimes he followed him at a distance when he went for a walk in the country, and in the evening, he stood outside his house and watched the windows light up.

And the sub-prefect of Tseou was very irritated by the infantile shadow that followed his own shadow.

On the night when Confucius was born, the night when the winged dragons hovered and the five Elders descended, Mong-Pi was sitting in the road; but he did not see either the dragons or the Elders. He perceived that Tchang, on the threshold, was raising a child toward the sky.

"May that child," he said, "be placed on very flat ground!"

And he ran away, very quickly. He never followed the sub-prefect of Tseou on his walks again.

The Salutations of Confucius

Throughout his childhood, little Confucius saluted. He saluted the ancestral tablets in the shadow of Miao impregnated with incense; he saluted his mother emerging from her room at dawn, impregnated with lavender. He lay in wait for his father outside the door in order to salute him when he came home, impregnated with the dust of the streets; he observed, in order to imitate them, the reverences that aged people made to one another; in the street he saluted the people passing by when they had embroideries on their robe; he saluted his comrades while playing with them and taught them salutations; he saluted the old cypresses for their majesty and their rectitude, the young roses for their perfume, the stones for their solid character, and the sky for its fluidity. And when he was conscious of the pure qualities with which his soul was filled, he would have liked to salute himself, to honor that nascent virtue.

His father, the sub-prefect, died; he saluted his tomb. Difficult days came; he saluted poverty. Then it was necessary to be educated; he saluted the school.

Modesty, application and mildness were his quotidian attributes. Politeness appeared to him to be a sublime expression of human perfection. All its forms were dear to him, and the mere resonance of the word politeness filled him with an ideal delectation. He found all customs respectable because they were customs. All rites were to be celebrated because the rites formed a chain that ought not to be interrupted. All worship was legitimate because it was ancient. But he honored above all propriety and moderation, with the reservation that they were only to be honored in an appropriate and moderate fashion.

When he was fifteen years old, a habit of prostration had given his body a slight forward inclination. His skull had lost its strange amphitheatrical form and was modeled normally. He had regular features, slightly slow gestures and a slight unction in his voice. A mist veiled his eyes and he often lowered his eyelids in order to attenuate that treason of the gaze, from which sincerity sprang, for he already knew how inconvenient and ludicrous an excessive sincerity can be in human relationships.

A renown for filial piety, love of study and respect for respectable things had spread round him, and, as for all those who are renowned for a quality, that quality was augmented by the idea that people had of it. He sometimes interrupted his meals to throw himself at the feet of his surprised mother. The consumption of incense in the altar of the ancestors became so great that, in order to have a sufficient supply, he went to sell certain jewels that he judged wretched because they did not have a sacred character. He acquired the habit, when someone came to see him, of launching himself from the threshold of the house to meet him with open arms, agitating them like wings, in order to show him that, in the intoxication of his politeness, he was flying toward him.

He fell ill and was obliged to lie down the first time he saw a comet in the sky, because that luminous singularity, contrary to habit, troubled order and interrupted harmony…but on the third day of his illness he got up precipitately, left the house in spite of his mother's pleas and climbed the hill above Tseou at a run, in order to salute the comet solemnly. It had disappeared, and Confucius meditated that celestial irregularity, that whim of the divine, for a long time.

The Supreme Book

While Confucius saluted, Lao-Tsu stood up very straight, as straight as a growing cypress, as straight as a rising thought, as straight as the bony conformation of a human being.

He had been poor in his childhood; he had guarded flocks in the desolate plain of the kingdom of Thsou; he had wandered the roads, and waited at the gates of towns for the guard to fall asleep in order to go in. He always stood up straight.

He had walked in deserts with his little boy's legs, walked for long days without eating or drinking. And he had perceived in the sadness of the sands the silent forms of Koei, which had fixed him with their milky pupils and tried to seize him with their insectile antennae. He had looked those demons in the face and, under the descending clouds, in the midst of the rising sands, he had always stood up straight.

A merchant of buffaloes had started to hate him because of the benevolence of his soul and had attached him to stake by a chain in order not to be separated from him and to make him suffer at his ease. For if the good attract the good and the bad attract the bad, the perfect attract the worst and exasperate the evil within them. Before the merchant of buffaloes and beneath the strokes of his bamboo, however, he always stood up straight.

With adolescence he had known the greatest human suffering, which is the desire for learning, sensing that one's mind is like an interior flower ready to bloom, and not having books, the books in which knowledge is enclosed, and of being cast out among inferior men, far from what is beautiful and what one loves. But even when looking over walls, behind shaped gardens, at literate men with broad foreheads raising their brushes and discussing divine things, he had prevented his heart from breaking, and he always stood up straight.

For, since the beginning of the world there has been an inexorable law. The man who is to rise very high, the one who is to go very far, begins his ordeal in the lower depths. It is necessary for him to cleave through the earth like a grain of wheat, after having taken on its substance. It is necessary that he travel the inferior cycles of humanity without a father and mother to protect him. He must recognize for himself, with the touchstone of his soul, what is pure and what is impure. In the changing world of reflections, he must seek the true light, which, when it is found, is no longer extinguished. It is necessary that he learn without a master, and that he find his road without a guide. It is necessary that ugliness be his spouse, that he has lice like beggars, eruptions of the skin like the mangy.

Always, he must stand up straight.

By dint of desiring to read the books of men, he came to read another book that was before him. Innumerable were its characters, but they could be deciphered without study. He read the text of the clouds in the sky. In the antiquity of mountains he raised the dust of origins. In the fresh youth of grass he caused the ode of awakening to crackle. While walking in the water of rivers he understood that the world is nothing but a mirror in movement.

He learned secrets that can only be learned when one is not blinded by the deceptive science of men. In the gaze of animals there are some of the great thoughts that form the foundations of the unique verity. The aspect of certain vegetables and certain ways that stones have of being sad informed him that there only differences of form and that all lives have the same essence, at different points in an immense spectrum.

And he read so much in that great illuminated book whose pages have no need to be turned, that when he had the leisure to pore over the bamboo tablets attached by a silken thread, in order to read the science of the ancient sages therein, he perceived that he had already read that science, traced in vaster characters, and that the only true wisdom is what one discovers oneself.

The Palace of Delightful Thoughts

At Lo-Yang, the Emperor King-Wang of the Tcheou dynasty possessed an ancient palace of stone, which he thought too old and too sad to serve him as a residence. That palace was called the Palace of the Spirits of the Earth. At its four cardinal points there were four great blocks of black marble on which the name of Fo-hi was engraved. It was surrounded by a garden in which nothing grew but box-trees and cypresses.

On the other side of the Huang-Po river, facing the Palace of the Spirits of the Earth, the Emperor King-Wang had the Palace of Delightful Thoughts constructed, the roof of which was made of blue tiles, the exterior wall covered with colored faiences and which had five superimposed terraces in white marble veined with azure, with colonnettes as light as he stamens of flowers.

The Emperor had the Palace of Delightful Thoughts surrounded by a garden containing all the varieties of flowers known in China and even singular flowers brought back from the Occident by voyagers.

He had the garden strewn with delicate summer-houses for reverie, and jade ponds with crystal beds for the reflection of the face. And that garden was entirely composed of silver birches and gilded lemon trees.

The Emperor King-Wang had dreamed in his youth of bringing back to obedience all the feudal kings of vast China and restoring the powerful Empire, as in the times of the first Tcheou, his ancestors. By virtue of an inexplicable evolution, however, his intelligence had become futile, a little more futile every day, and he could no longer occupy himself with anything but insignificant things and futilities. He was passionate about quarrels and female lute-players, the quality of the paper of fans and a new kind of sheath for the fingernails. He had begun to have headaches at the mere sight of the great sheets of bamboo on which on which the instructor kings had traced ceremonials, religious hymns and the chronicles of wars and endeavors. And he went to lie down whenever, by mistake, his fingers had encountered a book on a shelf, because of the fatigue communicated to his body by the occult influence of the book.

He had the archives of the Empire, the sacred books and the works of ancient philosophy transported to the other side of the Hoang-Po River, into the Palace of the Spirits of the Earth, behind the somber files of cypresses and the accumulation of box-trees, in order no longer to see them or hear mention of them. But the great literates of his entourage declined the title of Guardian of Literary Treasures, thinking that if they accepted it they would incur a sort of disgrace and would no longer be admitted to discuss futilities with their master.

The Emperor King-Wang knew the suffering of hesitation. That suffering was particularly cruel for him. It was aggravated by the persistence that certain mandarins put into obtaining an audience with him promised long ago. It was a matter of receiving a man of great wisdom who lived wretchedly at Lo-Yang and whose name was Lao-Tsu. That man, who did not have the culture of the official schools, professed personal ideas of a great profundity on the origins of the world. The mandarins in question often went to hear him and admired him greatly. In their zeal, they thought that the Emperor could not ignore such a remarkable person and be deprived of the pleasure of hearing him.

King-Wang was futile, but did not admit it. He knew that a sovereign is only great when he favors intelligence among his subjects. Thus had acted the Tcheou, and before them the Tchang, and before them the Hia, and all those who had governed China since Hoang-Ti. Thus he acted himself. Had he not installed the books in the ancient Palace of the Spirits of the Earth? He could not, for the moment, accord an audience to the remarkable man called Lao-Tsu. A collection of caterpillars occupied him entirely. However, he wanted to honor a mind that had developed far from the schools. The post of Guardian of Literary Treasures was vacant. He gave it to the sage in question. The audience was unnecessary. He would visit him in person at an indeterminate time.

O joy of occupying oneself with caterpillars, after having warded off the threat of two annoyances!

The Palace of the Spirits of the Earth

When Lao-Tsu went into the Palace of the Spirits of the Earth the sun was beginning to rise. It gilded the crowns of the cypresses, the circle of box-trees, the water of the river, and, on the other bank, the Palace of Delightful Thoughts, in the midst of its flower-beds, its jade basins, its jasper footbridges and its towers of sculpted silver. Further away, the city reposed, like an ocean of colored toys bounded by ramparts, with its flat temples with five facades, its large empty spaces for religious ceremonies and its hump-backed bridges like stone camels.

Lao-Tsu considered the profound rooms where the leaves of polished wood knotted with cords had been piled up; he opened the catches of the caskets that contained the most precious tablets, touched the scrolls of bark amorously and respired the sacred dust. An odor of mildew and antiquity rose up, which seemed to him more intoxicating than the odor of the most aromatic valleys or the spring that causes vegetal saps to seethe. His dream was belatedly realized. The secrets that he had desired so much to find in books he had already glimpsed in the mist of his meditations. Now, he knew internally what he was about to learn; for dreams are only realized when there is no longer any need for their realization.

He was in the presence of signs of the grandeur of humankind, of the transmitted word, of the intelligence of ancient China. He was no longer his own master. He opened his arms to seize materially that which is spiritual. He took armfuls of tablets. He hugged them to his breast, caressed them with his wrinkled face and his bony hands. He let them fall on to the floor. He scanned one book, then another. He would have liked to read them all at the same time.

There were millenary annals in ancient characters and annals of peoples anterior to the Chinese, in characters that he did not know. The sacred books of Yao and Chun were composed of plates of virgin gold so numerous and heavy that he had difficulty lifting them. He perused the book in which the relationships are explained that exist between our planet and the other celestial globes, the books of the five immutable rules and the five duties, the book of Ta-Nao in which the principles of arithmetic and geometry are set out, and the book that the Empress Loui-Tsu, the one who was nicknamed the Spirit of the Mulberry Bushes and Silkworms, wrote about the art of spinning and dressmaking.

He read the narratives of the ten sages who had accompanied the Emperor Mou-Wang in his voyage to the Kuen-Lun Mountains, which the Indians call Merou, which confirmed him in his hypotheses that all science comes from the Occident. He touched a jade plaque on which the Emperor Fo-Hi had traced with his own hand the eight primal diagrams, and the ivory sheets on which were designed the dances named Ta-Vou, instituted by the fiftieth Emperor to perpetuate the beauty of the human form. And there were also the ephemerides of cities, enumerations of meteorological phenomena, reproductions of moons and comets, maps of the islands of the Oriental Sea, lists of genii and spirits, and certain books made with mysterious metals, so thin that they were translucent and the characters gave the impression of being alive, like armies of intelligent insects.

The mildness that only the sentiment of gratitude brings descended over Lao-Tsu's features, hardened by privations and solitude.

He stood up, went to the threshold of the palace and, looking beyond the city, at the circular hills where the blue mulberry-bushes were ranged and peach-trees covered in pink flowers, he said:

"I thank the first-born of ancient races. With patience, they each brought a seed of knowledge to the exceedingly poor spiritual granary. They have constituted a great treasure. I can touch it, I can see it, and I possess it. But the precious, ineffable stone can only be contemplated by looking inside. With my lidless eyes I shall search for it among the innumerable characters of books. Perhaps I shall find it. If I do find it, I shall not be able to bequeath it. Everyone must seek it and find it. May men receive the benediction of man.

Then he had the confused sensation of numerous presences around him. It seemed to him that in the avenues of cypresses there was a slow procession of sages in meditation. He could not distinguish their faces or their exact form, but he was certain of a grave passage of individuals who were clad in robes and stood up as straight and pensive as the cypresses, and who were marching, invisibly, with their arms folded. Those individuals made no sound as they trod the sand, and their respiration was inaudible, but they left behind them a wake of thought.

Lao-Tsu stood for a long time with his eyes fixed on the garden, where drops of dew were shining like thousands of pearls. Then the noises of the city rose up, and the sun, in spreading a warmer light, dissipated the illusion.

At the same hour, clad in a white silk robe, the Emperor descended through the flower-beds of his gardens and arrived at the river bank. He had not been able to sleep, because he knew that at dawn, two domesticated ibises fought playfully in the reeds, and since the previous day he had dreaded missing the moment of their frolics, from which he obtained a puerile joy.

Between the box-trees and the cypresses he perceived the silhouette of Lao-Tsu standing on the threshold of the Palace of the Spirits of the Earth. Lao-Tsu also saw him, and for a few seconds the sage and the Emperor, separated by the river, considered one another in the light of the rising sun.

The Emperor turned away rapidly, annoyed. Contrary to the most elementary ceremonial, however, Lao-Tsu did not prostrate himself in order to touch the stone with his forehead. As he had always done, he continued to stand up straight, before the Spirits of the Earth, and the invisible brethren who haunted the old palace of Books.

The Marriage of Confucius

The Burial of Humble Lu

As Confucius was standing at the door of his house one day, he saw a strange funeral cortege coming toward him, up one of the sloping streets that climbed the hill of Tseou.

Two porters were marching at the head with a wooden coffin on their shoulders. That coffin could not contain a very heavy corpse, for the porters seemed to be carrying it effortlessly, and even agitating it, as if it were only a light box, quite empty. The porters were followed by a group of women who had colored combs in their hair and who, in the plaster of make-up and the carmine of lips, seemed to be wearing white masks stained with blood.

Confucius recognized creatures of sinful life, inhabitants of the lowest street of the city.

And he also recognized, in their midst, two tightrope-walkers, an old beggar who had been holding his hand out for years at the northern gate, and a grave master of Feng-Shui, who practiced the divinatory arts for a few coins. He thought that it was a prostitute who was being buried, for the only mortuary ceremonies that could take place at night were those of prostitutes. Furthermore, he distinguished on the coffin the emblematic thread from which a copper disk was suspended bearing the imprint of the royal seal and the sort of diploma that he had often seen drafted by his father the sub-prefect in which it was certified that the holder exercised the profession of prostitution.

He was about to go back inside hastily and slam his door when he was retained by the enormity of the impropriety that struck his sight.

A caricaturish and deformed individual was marching behind the coffin and leaning on the arm of one of the tightrope-walkers. He was clad in a white mourning robe, but that robe, too long and too large, had visibly been lent to him, and was a woman's robe, a kind of indoor chemise. That individual, in whom Confucius did not immediately recognize the scorned Mong-Pi, had red eyes and a face covered in tears. Sometimes however, he stopped uttered a sort of frightful burst of laughter and sketched a grotesque caper while limping behind the coffin. Then he turned toward the rope-dancers, the master in divinatory art, the beggar and the other women, and incited them with a wink and a gesture to imitate him.

The dancers made a leap, the beggar raised his crutch, the grave master of Feng-Shui bobbed his head to the right and he left, and the made-up faces showed the ivory of teeth and widened their eyes in a humorous and dramatic fashion.

Confucius was motionless on his threshold, like a statue of disapproving virtue.

On perceiving him, however, Mon-Pi seized the hem of his white robe and, deploying it, launched himself to very edge of the coffin and stated shouting: "Don't look that way! Don't look to the right!"

And he seemed to want to hide the scandalized Confucius and his house from the light corpse that the porters were swaying. As he was walking backwards and was not solidly balanced on his unsteady legs, he slipped and fell into a deep puddle of rainwater, splashing water around him. The splash spattered the porters of the coffin with mud, and one of them received some in his face. He recoiled, and the coffin slipped from his shoulder and fell.

Cries ensued, and great confusion.

The dancers picked Mong-Pi up, his white robe soiled with mud. The women surrounded the coffin, the nails of which had been dislodged by the fall.

And then, for a few seconds, Confucius was witness to a singular apparition. Very thin, almost ethereal, there was a little woman, straight and stiff, between the disjointed fir-wood planks. Death had ornamented her face with the purity of marble and the pride of statues. Everyone was impressed by the grandeur that her narrow form radiated. It was he prostitute Lu, who, having been a humble creature all her life, found in that twilight, among the puddles of rainwater, the unique regal attitude that men would know in her.

Night was about to fall. The cortege resumed its route. Confucius remained motionless on the doorstep of his house. On the subject of that incomprehensible scene he interrogated a man he knew and who was passing along the road.

"That's poor Mong-Pi," said the latter, "who is burying his mother Lu. She lived on prostitution and was very poor. She had no greater joy than seeing her son make grimaces and joke with other good-for-nothings like him. So Mong-Pi, who loved his mother, wanted her spirit to be cheered up one last time before she reposed under the ground. When your father was sub-prefect he would not have permitted such a scandal. Everything is worse than it used to be."

Confucius raised his eyes to the heavens. He saw the star Ki shining through thick storm-clouds. Thus, like the star Ki, filial piety could shine in the midst of the clouds of vulgarity, in the heavens of the soul.

The Blue of the Star Ki

One night, Confucius woke up with a start. He sat up and wondered what had caused that awakening, for he usually slept profoundly, like those who are healthy and have nothing for which to reproach themselves.

There was a tempest that was making the roof groan, and engulfing noisily in the sloping streets of the town of Tseou, but it was not the thunderclaps and the streaming rain that had woken Confucius. It was a bizarre human voice that was coming from the upper part of the hill, above his house.

Confucius thought about the impropriety there was in shouting at such an hour on the hill might be caused by some distress that it was appropriate to relieve. He therefore got up, got dressed, picked up a lantern and went out.

The voice was coming from a place on the road where, between wild junipers,. Confucius had noticed the mount of a new grave a few days earlier. He had stopped in front of that grave and had read the text engraved on the wooden tablet in which the spirit of the deceased was supposed to come to perch:

Lu the very gracious, very humble, very disinterested, who loved everything and everyone.

Confucius distinguished a silhouette near the mound and, by its limping gait, he recognized Mong-Pi. His white chemise was so tightly stuck to him by the rain that he seemed to be naked. He was waving a stick in a threatening manner and shouting in a terrible voice: "Go away! Further away, or woe betide you!"

And he made the gesture of striking invisible beings. Then he precipitated himself on all fours before the tablet and, in a tone imprinted with softness and tenderness, and a hint of consolation, he murmured: "You no longer have anything to fear. They've gone. In any case, I'm watching. Go on, sleep in peace now."

Confucius felt trickles running down his water and chilling him, but he had warmth in his heart. He guessed why Mong-Pi was there, the meaning of his cries and his solicitude. Doubtless, when she was alive, his mother had been frightened by storms in her little house in the low street. So he had thought that she might be even more frightened, alone beneath the melancholy mound, near the junipers. He had come to protect her from the evil spirits that circulate with the winds.

Confucius had an irresistible impulse of sympathy for the young man whose filial virtue redeemed his bad existence. He advanced toward him, raised the lantern in order to be recognized and then, extending his arms, he said to him: "Mong-Pi, from this moment on, I want you to be my brother."

Mong-Pi looked at him in surprise, scratched his streaming head and replied: "Brothers? But we always have been."

And he resumed striking the air with his stick, threatening the downpours of the rain, to reassure the wooden tablet where the humble maternal presence ought to be shivering.

Confucius remained perplexed by that response, the meaning of which was mysterious to him. And as he went back down the hill to go inside, soaked to the skin and suddenly frozen, he thought that the manifestation of virtue is sometimes as incomprehensible as the blue tint of the star Ki.

Ki-Keou's Lute

Ki-Keou was a young woman who bore a close resemblance to the songbird Tong-Hou-Fang. She was the daughter of noble but poor parents who lived some distance from Tseou in a dilapidated dwelling.

In imitation of the bird Tong-Hou-Fang, which flutters from one branch to another for no reason, she ran hither and yon in the house full of dust or the garden full of weeds and seemed to be very occupied with trivial things of no importance. She loved to play the lute before dawn, and when she was reproached for waking everyone up without reason, she said that music is only truly sublime shortly before daybreak—a theory that seemed absurd to musicians consulted on the subject.

There was, however, someone who thought the same. At the hour when the summer nights commenced to blanch slightly, Ki-Keou, who was playing the lute in her garden, heard another lute resonating and drawing nearer in the direction of the hill of Tseou.

On the road, where peach-trees alternated with willows, Mong-Pi advanced limping. He came to play before the tablet where his mother's spirit posed in order to listen to him. And he went as far as a ruined wall where he knew that through a breach he could see the beautiful face of a young woman illuminated by the mystery of music.

Sometimes, Ki-Keou accompanied him with her lute. At other times she listened, motionless, and gazed from a distance at the strange individual in the white costume, who stood motionless and played the lute sweetly. For Mong-Pi never budged. He hoped that the young woman would not find out that he limped when he walked. And he waited for the contours of things were designed and the young woman had gone back into the house in order to depart along the peach trees and willows.

For a long time Ki-Keou thought that the lute-player was a benevolent spirit of the familiar countryside.

But one morning, when she lingered, she distinguished Mong-Pi's face more clearly and saw a tear shining there. Then she thought that he was a man. From that day she felt remorse, but she applied herself more to playing the lute.

The Marriage

Ki-Keou's father summoned his daughter to his presence one day and spoke to her solemnly.

"The time has come when you must cease to be like the songbird Tong-Hou-Fang and when you ought to marry. Doubtless you have heard mention of Confucius, the young man of Tseou who has already acquired a great reputation by his virtue and his knowledge of history and the canonical books. To be sure, he has no fortune, but he belongs to a noble and ancient family and it is even claimed, without it being verified, that there is an Emperor among his ancestors. He has just obtained from the King of Lou the employment of administrator of the public granaries, which is not a very elevated position, but indicates that he has a knowledge of expenses and receipts, the production of the land and its monetary return—knowledge that your father always lacked, since he is ruined and has made his daughter a being similar to a bird. Confucius has come to ask for you in marriage and I have replied that you will probably accept.

"He has already sent the note of eight characters designating the year, the month, the day and the hour of his birth, and I shall send him the note of eight characters designating the year, the month, the day and the hour of your birth, in order that they can be presented to the diviner, as is customary. For Confucius holds customs in respect essentially. He recommends scrupulous obedience to the three hundred prescriptions of the ceremonial and the three thousand rules of decorum. Personally, I have always thought that those rules were excessive and too numerous, but he must be right, since he is the administrator of the public granaries and we live poorly in this solitary house. In any case, you will end up becoming accustomed to those rules over time. Have you any objection to make to this proposal of appropriate union?"

Ki-Keou remained silent for a long time.

"Will I be able to play the lute before dawn?" she said, finally.

"Undoubtedly," her father replied, shrugging his shoulders.

And the marriage was decided.

Ki-Keou was brought nenuphar lilies and sunflowers, water-melons and pomegranates, which are the flowers and the fruits that it is appropriate for a fiancé to offer to his fiancée. And she ran hither and yon with her young woman's wings; she smoothed her plumage; she formed a thousand puerile projects, and the days passed, and they arrived at the seventh moon of the Year of the Hare, during which the marriage was to be celebrated.

Ki-Keou learned from her fiancé's mouth the number of canonical books and the principal verities they contained. In the Chou-King there are fifty chapters relative to the epochs of Yao, Choun and Yu. In the Chi-King there are hymns by the hundred, odes by the thousand. In the Y-King there are all the modes of divination employed by the ancient thaumaturges. In the Li-Ki are the precious rites, the inestimable rules of ceremony. But to the rules it was necessary to add others; it was necessary to multiply the rites, to codify and recodify the ceremonies. It was necessary to make a compilation of all the books, to excise carefully that which was not in conformity with propriety and equity, to add the traditions to the traditions, to build a monument of precepts, to edify a fabulous code of all the prescriptions and all the laws, and to erect a gigantic mountain of historic and moral texts.

Ki-Keou was very frightened to learn that that task belonged to Confucius. She smiled, and approved everything her fiancé said, and was filled with admiration; but afterwards, she had a headache. It seemed to her that the sacred Books were placed on her breast and stifling her, and when she played the lute, her fingers were not as light, and her music was not as beautiful, as if a hidden genius that had been her companion had flown away from her atmosphere.

"What is that noise in the street?" asked Confucius in the middle of the marriage feast.

And Tchang, the guardian of the house, advanced, laughing, and said: "It's the cripple Mong-Pi, who is so happy about your marriage that he is making a thousand astonishing pleasantries, which the children are enjoying.

"Have him come into the courtyard," replied Confucius, "and give him something to eat and drink."

There was so much talk of happiness around Ki-Keou that she criticized herself for not experiencing more of it. She also criticized herself for a sort of apprehension, a desire to get away, analogous to the one that birds must experience when they sense that they are trapped in bird-lime.

And she reproached herself for experiencing that again when, alone with her under the wisteria in the garden, Confucius said to her with a tender solemnity:

"There are three joys that marriage procures, which we are going to know at our leisure: the sweetness of mutual love"—and he clasped her hand tenderly—"the nobility of familial virtues"—and he raised a finger toward the heavens—"and the beauty of conjugal duty"—and he lowered his eyes modestly.

How many noble qualities his face reflected: natural goodness, love of parents, respect for family, the desire to perpetuate the race, and the desire to inform men of the good. Ki-Keou sensed all that, and thought that her heart must be deeply, irredeemably wicked to experience the desire to flee. Oh, the solitude before dawn, in the old garden full of weeds, where the dewdrops covered the trees with stars! She would never see all that again! An ineluctably virtuous life awaited her; but the first nocturnal hour seemed to her to be very difficult to live.

Help, however, arrived.

She was lying on the bed; she had parted her robe and had put the most docile smile possible on her face. Outside, cries and laughter could be heard, and the light of lanterns illuminated the room sadly.

Then Confucius had undressed, as was appropriate, and made a genuflection, in accordance with the rite, before the bed where he was about to join his spouse and accomplish the essential familial act.

Ki-Keou, her eyes closed, heard a familiar lute resonating somewhere, a fraternal lute that brought her a petty aid, almost nothing: all that irrational fantasy, futile dreams, and the camaraderie of poets who do not know one another, can do against the conquering gods called social order, virtue and family.

The Hidden Gift of Music

That year was a year of abundance for the harvests. As the administrator of the public granaries, Confucius was called upon to create a supplementary grain depot that would serve as a reserve for times of famine.

Taking advantage of the full powers he had received from the King of Lou, he decided to establish that depot in a part of the houses of the low town, whose inhabitants he would compensate. He would thus purify, by means of the healthy presence of grain, the quarter that was the shame of Tseou.

The house that Lu had inhabited, and where Mong-Pi now lived alone, was one of the houses that was due to be transformed. When Mong-Pi discovered what had been decided, he declared that, rather than abandon his old sloping roof, he preferred to be buried under the grain, and he threw away the silver taels that were brought to him on behalf of the administrator of public granaries.

"I am in the presence of a conflict of duties," said Confucius, when he was informed of that.

He meditated for some time.

"The reason of State must take priority over the reason of an individual, even if the latter is based on the most noble sentiments, since the State is the sum of all individuals, and hence of all noble sentiments."

And he gave the order to expel Mong-Pi, making sure that he did not precipitate himself under the grain in order to be stifled, in accordance with his promise.

Henceforth, Mong-Pi slept under the beautiful stars. All he had taken from his house was a piece of wood that he had sculpted crudely, and which represented his mother Lu. And he continued to accomplish many irrational acts, to sing and laugh without reason, and sometimes to weep when he was at the top of the hill, beside the mound between the junipers.

And Confucius grew in wisdom, virtue and knowledge. His renown was soon such, in spite of his young age, that many people came from afar to hear him speak and to study history and morality with him. In the end, he was obliged to open a school, and he had his disciples.

He perceived one day that he had acquired a strange love for music. He did not know how, but it was certain that harmonious sounds developed in him the appetite for virtue. He went to study the lute with a great musician named Siang, and soon became a consummate artist. However, he established a great difference between music that was correct and that which was not: music that enables a tendency toward perfection, and music that develops the deregulated passions.

Because of that difference, he was obliged to forbid his spouse Ki-Keou to get up before dawn to go and play the lute in the garden, firstly because it was not appropriate to make music when everyone was still asleep, and secondly because there was a certain languor in the tunes that she played, something winged and magical that was not appropriate to the wife of an administrator of the public granaries.

In order that she could play the tunes that he indicated at normal hours, he bought Ki-Keou a whole variety of new lutes, which he obtained from the capital of the kingdom of Lou.

But Ki-Keou only knew how to play before dawn and on her old lute, that of a young woman. She was resigned, because caged birds have never been seen to revolt. In any case, she was enveloped by Confucius' goodness as if by a net of white silk. She admired him and she said:

"He has completed me. I owe him everything. And I can give him nothing of what he loves, neither sacred texts, nor religious hymns, nor the words of ancient emperors. How can I ever acquit my debt?"

She did not know however, that she had given him the most inestimable of gifts. It was with the harmonies of her lute that the love of music that he esteemed so highly had insinuated itself into Confucius' soul by means of subtle invisible vibrations. And he was unaware of it too, for men cannot believe that the best part of their soul, the seed of their wisdom and their art, is brought to them by ignorant women.

One day, when Confucius was conversing, while walking in the country, with Tsu-Lou and Tsu-Kong, rich young men who had come to install themselves in Tseou in order to listen to his teaching, he saw Mong-Pi appear on the road.

Mong-Pi was limping more than usual and seemed very weary. He knelt down before Confucius.

"Since you have taken everything from me," he said, "take my soul as well and transform it. Teach me wisdom. I want to be your disciple."

"I would like nothing better than to educate and reform you," said Confucius, "but why do you say that I have taken everything from you?"

Mong-Pi remained silent.

Confucius reflected and, turning to Tsu-Lou and Tsu-Kong, he added: "Perhaps he is right. The substance of wisdom is made with the substance of folly."

Tao

There was a light breeze, a breath, that palpitated close to Lao-Tsu's face. He got up and he followed something invisible that preceded him.

The Palace of the Spirits of the Earth was deserted and the dusk that was about to fall was weighing upon the trees in the garden. Lao-Tsu headed without hesitation toward the great block of black marble that sustained the palace in the direction of the rising sun. There was an ancient paving stone there and he thought immediately that it was under that stone that it was necessary for him to look.

He fetched a gardener's spade and began to dig, but he soon perceived that the stone pivoted. It covered a space in which there was a bronze casket eroded by time. On the casket was the name of Fo-Hi.

Trembling with emotion, Lao-Tsu took the casket in his arms and transported it piously into the palace. In that casket, no doubt, Fo-Hi had deposited the secrets of the destiny of humans before birth and after death. The man who had replaced the language of knots tied in strings by writing, and had domesticated the six kinds of domestic animals, was about to transmit to him the supreme knowledge from which all knowledge flowed.

Lao-Tsu opened the casket and looked inside.

As immaculate as truth, clouded like the mystery by which it is enveloped, there was a block of azurean jade in the bronze casket soiled by earth. In its softness was the benevolence of the race and its excellent qualities. In its polish shone the intelligence of the first emperors, in its compactness their firmness, in its uniform hue their rectitude. And that jade was resplendent, in the certainty of its blueness amid the veils of exquisite nuances, like the divine spirit of human being under the terrestrial rind of form.

A word—one single word—was engraved on the jade.

In vain, Lao-Tsu turned it in all directions, admiring the spiritual fluidity of the essential stone that the mineral realm produces like the drops of its soul, in the hope of finding another complementary text.

There was only the unique word, which was sufficient in itself, the word of the beginning and the end; and that word was:

Tao.

Lao-Tsu placed the block of jade on the ground and knelt in front of it.

The sun was setting in the distance and light rose up on all sides.

"O unnamable," he said, "you who are without form, you who are not measured with time, you who are not limited by space, whom the word does not design, I am you, I have emerged from your breath, I have been measured by time and limited by space, I am expressed by the word and I aspire to disappear in your unknowable aspiration.

"I was already born before the manifestation of any corporeal form. I appeared before the supreme commencement. I have acted at the origin of simple and organized matter. I was present at the development of the primal mass. I stood on the cliff of the great primordial ocean and I floated in the middle of the void and the darkness. I have entered and I shall emerge thought the portals the mysterious immensity of space.

"I have been projected into the innumerability of lives. Millions of times, I have been modeled differently. Rejoicing in and afflicted by my separation, I have turned in the circle. But now the guiding light has been transmitted to me. I know the perfect initial perfection to which I ought to tend and, born of the unique essence, I shall finally sleep in the estate of wakefulness in the unique essence."

Confucius and Lao-Tsu

The First Carp

The important administrator of public granaries was installed in the capital of the kingdom of Lou and it was there that Ki-Keou gave birth to a child. That child was born with a strangely restricted stature, nature wanting to mark by that the insignificance which the son of a great man retains all his life.

Confucius rejoiced in that, for it is in the common order to bring children into the world by the pious means of marriage. Thus races are perpetuated, and there is no action more recommendable than the one that consists of augmenting the number of living creatures under the sun.

On the occasion of that birth, an event of extreme importance occurred that threw into Confucius' heart a joy almost as great as the joy of the birth itself.

In order to mark the sympathy he felt for the excellent functionary of the public granaries who had become a father, the King of Lou sent him as a gift a carp, a beautiful river carp, on the day of the ritual meal.

Confucius was conversing with Tsu-Lou and Tsu-Kong in the courtyard of his house when the messenger bearing the carp arrived. First, Confucius made a genuflection before the fish, and then his face lit up and he allowed a joy to burst forth, which was measured, but which seemed to come from the source of veritable delights.

Tsu-Lou and Tsu-Kong thought at first that there was an irony in that, because of the derisory modesty of the gift. For themselves, they considered it as an offense, and they were about to show their indignation at the ingratitude of the sovereign, but they stopped just in time. Their master's joy was sincere. For the more powerful men are, the lighter their gifts

49

can be. Those who venerate power are content with the little it accords, because that little comes from power.

Confucius sent Tchang to issue more invitations to the ritual meal. Was it not necessary to enable as many friends as possible to take advantage of a meal give by the King? And in order to commemorate the favor he had received, he called his son Pe-Yu—which is to say, the first fish—the carp being the first of fish, since it was a gift from the King.

But on that day of satisfaction, on the occasion of the meal and the carp, an event of extreme importance occurred that threw into Confucius' heart a sadness almost as great as the joy of the reception of the carp.

Either because she did not realize the honor received, or because she did not like the flesh of the fish in question, in spite of her husband's order, Ki-Keou refused to eat the carp. Thus women sometimes reveal the savage instincts of revolt and disorder, and do not honor that which ought to be honored.

Confucius knew that his wife Ke-Kiou did not have to the humblest degree the sentiment of hierarchies; he had the revelation of her inferiority.

The disciple Mong-Pi had not been invited to that meal, because he ate poorly.

The Exercise of Filial Piety

Like the tradition of filial piety in the Empire, the health of Confucius' mother declined. She died in the year Koci-Yeou and Confucius, who had loved her tenderly, mourned her. But the fate of great men is rigorous; it is necessary that even their grief serve as an example to other men.

The ancient ceremonial dictated that on the death of the father or the mother all function is forbidden to the son, that he shut himself away for three years without going out once, in order to devote himself to his grief. That redoubtable tradition, which often caused the ruination of the voluntarily captive families, was only observed rarely.

When his mother was buried in accordance with the rites, her feet to the south and her head to the north, sheltered from carnivorous animals in a coffin coated in varnish and four inches thick, Confucius declared that he intended to observe the rigorous mourning of the ancients, that he made it an obligation to resign from his employment, and he passed through the door of his house not to emerge again for three years, in order to dwell with the spirit of his mother.

The rites prescribe that the wife and the son of the wife had to act as the husband did, and Ki-Keou was therefore imprisoned along with Confucius with the spirit of her mother-in-law.

The house was at the extremity of an outlying district and was vast enough for one to meditate in tranquility there, but small enough for one to know limitless tedium. The paving stones of the interior courtyard were somber and worn by the feet of ancient inhabitants of Lou, and when Ki-Keou had counted them a thousand times she no longer had the courage to do it again. The garden expired at the foot of the ramparts of the city and those ramparts, made of massive blocks, extended over the garden a shadow so heavy that, when Ki-Keou traversed that shadow, she remained penetrated by it internally, as if a shadow had also invaded her soul.

Confucius' mother had been a devoted ewe, of the species of those who march in their thick wool with their eyes obstinately turned toward the ground, and do not see the birds flying around them. She had scarcely seen Ki-Keou, but she had been importuned by her flight and had shown it by looking obstinately at the ground with the disapproval of silence, giving the impression of being unaware of her existence.

When Ki-Keou was a prisoner in the house bordered by the ramparts and the heavily shaded garden, she began to hear the voice of the woman who had hardly every addressed a word to her while alive.

"Bad daughter-in-law, you are not saddened by my death!"

Syllables without inflection falling from the unique mulberry bush in the garden. which the shadow of the rampart could not attain, and next to which Ki-Keou loved to sit.

"Bad mother, your son Pe-Yu is not sufficient for your happiness!"

Verbal breath that slid over the painted wooden balcony from which she sometimes watched the water-carrier pass by, and the donkey-drover leading a donkey laden with rice.

"Bad wife you are unable to console your husband!"

That rose up from the paving stones of the courtyard. In the room at the back, there was the altar of the ancestors and a lamp provided a ruddy light there in the dusk. Before the altar, Ki-Keou perceived Confucius in his yellow robe, prostrate, praying or meditating. His back seemed enormous and thickset, powerful enough to carry the weight of the house, and even that of the city with its ramparts.

Oh, no! She was not able to console her husband! That altar of the ancestors was terrible, with its lamp that stared at her like a unique eye. It was not a matter of consolation, of being a good mother and a pious daughter-in-law. It was a matter of not being afraid, of no longer living with a dead woman who talks to you, of getting out of that icy temple, of being somewhere where one has a little warmth in the heart.

That evening, Ki-Keou stated running in all directions, running in circles in the garden and the house, to escape the invisible accuser and reach the region of human life. Her wings bumped into the entrance door and it was there that she fainted, to recover herself again in the arms of the guardian Tchang under the saddened eyes of Confucius.

"Mutual love entails duties," he said. "But obedience to one's duty procures, at length, the purest joy. It is merely a matter of becoming accustomed to that obedience."

And the next day she found, in the place in her room where she had the habit of sitting, a copy of the Yi-King, the most abstract of the canonical books, an affectionate attention on her husband's part to distract her.

Ki-Keou tried to become accustomed. But one can become accustomed to anything, except fear. She could no longer sit under the mulberry bush; she could no longer walk in the courtyard or watch the water-carriers and donkeys from the balcony, because of the toneless voice, because of the occult presence, because of the faceless companion who accompanied her in the house.

She did not become accustomed, but she obeyed. Her blood no longer flowed through her veins with the same ardor, her cheeks paled, her eyes became hollow. The beauty of the body quit her, as an angel quits you who has not been given the azurean aliment by which he is nourished.

Poring over the sacred books, Confucius said, when he thought about Ki-Keou:

She is not intelligent, but she practices the second virtue, which is obedience.

The Broken Lute

One morning, at the hour when the sun had not yet risen, Ki-Keou, who was not asleep, resolved to struggle against the enemy shadow. And she went to fetch her weapon, the old lute with which she had once played in the garden of weeds.

She went downstairs stealthily, traversed the silent courtyard, went past the altar of the ancestors without prostrating herself, advanced through the tenebrous garden further than the mulberry bush, and then started to play.

She played light tunes, old tunes in which there were dances and gusts of songs and vagabonds' refrains. She knew that the shadow was prowling around her with its accusations and maledictions, and she defended herself with her tunes, dealing it musical blows, enveloping herself in the dream of her youth as if in armor of ethereal crystal.

"Bad daughter-in-law! Bad mother! Bad wife!"

Yes, she was all that. She knew it well, and it was of knowing that she was so bad that she was perishing a little more very day and the delightful sweet expression of her features had disappeared. But for once, she savored the spiritual intoxication of the pre-dawn twilight in the light turbulence of music.

Rapid footfalls resounded in the garden. She stopped playing. Confucius was before her.

He sensed the gravity and the extent of his duty, the duty of directing a weak soul toward the good, that of repressing impropriety. He experienced a sincere sadness in perceiving that Ki-Keou had not understood his teaching, did not possess the sole virtue that he attributed to her: obedience.

"This is how you honor the spirit of my dead mother," he said, severely. "You do not hesitate to violate the majesty of the mourning, and to contradict by a nocturnal scandal the fine example that I want to give. To act thus, you cannot have loved my mother."

Ki-Keou looked at Confucius, as terrified as she would have been in the presence of the judge who weighs human actions in Hell.

"No," she murmured softly.

Confucius' eyes plunged with horror into the innocent eyes of Ki-Keou as into the monstrous abyss of Chaos in the distant days when evil was born from matter in disorder. He seized the lute, the emblem of the revolt, of incomprehensible actions, of insensate art in conflict with virtue, and he broke all its strings with a single blow. Then he threw it on the ground, angrily.

Ki-Keou uttered a feeble cry, like that of a dying bird, and crossed her tapered hands over her thinned breast.

Ashamed of that gesture, unworthy of a sage, Confucius was already drawing away with long strides.

Insensibly, the garden was brightened by a light as confused as the consciousness of a bird. The ramparts began to extend their heavy shadow. In the distance, the hand-bell of a bonze resounded.

At that moment the head of the wandering Mong-Pi appeared above the wall of earth that surrounded the garden. It had been such a long time since he had seen Ki-Keou! He knew that she was imprisoned in the house of mourning. He wanted to see for a second the beautiful face from which had emerged, like a vapor rising from a blue lake, the first dream of his youth.

He saw the emaciated features, the thin body, and the broken lute. In that joyless garden there was the phantom, despoiled of beauty, of the woman he had loved. Confucius' back was disappearing in the direction of the house, rounded like politeness, crushing like virtue.

Mong-Pi let himself fall back into the street. Crouching at the foot of the wall of earth, he wept for a long time.

What a terrible human law! The man who seeks wisdom simultaneously loses beauty. Was folly not better?

The Three Sages of the Earth

In those days, China, the color of alabaster at sunset, was traversing a period of decadence. Its monuments were allowed to crumble, its administrations were disorganized, and the Empire was fragmented. By a singular coincidence, all the sovereigns were born incapable, or with some flaw that corroded their intelligence. The Emperor King-Wang was futile, no longer interested in anything but insects and the plumage of birds. The King of Tsi was cruel and killed for pleasure. The King of Lou only liked art.

And outside the frontiers of China, beyond the western deserts, in the immense hot regions of India the color of emerald, where the Ganges descends between the jungles and virgin forests, the peoples were unhappy because of the captivity of their souls. The priests, under the menace of the gods, had enclosed them in narrow castes and the sky of India was low above them, and death did not liberate them because of the eternal recommencement of lives.

And beyond the River Indus, and beyond the River Oxus, on the shores of Greece the color of marble at sunrise, over all the lands bathed by the sapphire-colored sea, the sea of Phoenician barks and Carthaginian triremes, there was, in the bright eyed men with curly beards, an anxious expectation of the new word that renders thought more apt: the word that creates, in consequence, the love of the enlightenment of explanation.

Lao-Tsu was born in China. At Kapilavastu, in the land of Cakia, Prince Siddartha was born, who was called the Buddha, and from the island of Samos, Pythagoras departed in order to go from city to city and from temple to temple. Thanks to him, beautiful forms latent in stone mutated into statues, scattered speculations became philosophical systems, sparks of intelligence were ignited under the porticos of agoras from Memphis to Corinth, from Syracuse to Athens.

The voices of those three sages resonated at the same time. When the spiritual treasure of humanity is in peril, those who must save it appear. Perhaps there was a secret peril, and that is why the most elevated beings in the human hierarchies, the lords of the worlds, sent those three messengers full of love and science.

But they did not know one another. They only sensed one another. They appealed to one another in the silence of meditation. They did not triumph over the solitude imposed on prophets, the limitation of their physical form. Each one had to accomplish his task alone, submit to the slowness of childhood, support difficulties and labors, ingratitude and hatred, and to pass through the portal of death without having had the recompense of the result.

For the law is the same for everyone, for the greatest as for the most insignificant.

The Disciple Siu-Kia

In the Palace of the Spirits of the Earth, Lao-Tsu lived with a single servant named Siu-Kia. An increasingly great solitude surrounded him because, in imitation of the Emperor, as much by virtue of flattery as natural inclination, the entire court had become futile. The literates went with increasing infrequency to converse with Lao-Tsu, no one desired the acquaintance of books, and the old palace reposed in an atmos-phere of neglect.

The servant Siu-Kia was a simple and taciturn man, Lao-Tsu did not instruct him. But even when he does not speak, the wise man, by his proximity, gives a secret instruction that has no need of writing or words. Siu-Kia, the guardian of books, the companion of hours of study, became more of a disciple than a servant.

He ceased, gradually, to repair his master's old robe, to sweep his room and to shake the mat on which he slept. The garden around the palace became unkempt because Siu-Kia was meditating. He was no longer susceptible of any effort but that of going across the river in search of rice for nourishment and cooking it. Lao-Tsu had acquired the habit of fetching water from the well himself in order not to interrupt his serv-ant's meditation.

Dust accumulated in the palace. Nocturnal birds filled the rooms with the flutter of their wings and made their nests on the jasper columns. Plants sprang forth between the paving stones of thresholds and obstructed the doors. A cypress fell in the great avenue as if to forbid the route to the last visitors. There was a denser pullulation of vegetation in the garden, as if nature wanted to give the sage and his disciple a more per-fect solitude.

And, seated on the shaky stones or under enlacements of bamboo, the archivist of the Empire benevolently explained the mystery of the Tao to his servant, and his own ideas be-came clearer by virtue of the magic of expression. Siu-Kia learned that the Tao is the supreme reason, the primordial es-sence, the path that the moving spirit travels, and he learned that the Te is the second aspect of the Tao, the supreme virtue, the ideal perfection, love in motion, which permits the human spirit to be absorbed by the Tao, the divine essence.

The more Siu-Kia penetrated the truth, the more he be-came motionless, for, according to his master's teaching, it is by meditation that one arrives at knowledge of the Tao—with the result that Lao-Tsu, who did not want to impede his disciple's development, departed at dawn in search of rice on the other side of the bridge, cooked it for the meal and sometimes repaired Siu-Kia's robe when it was too badly torn.

And one day, Lao-Tsu said to Siu-Kia:

"It is reported in the Books that a long time ago, the Emperor Mou-Wang made a voyage to the Kuen-Lun Mountains situated in the west. There he met the woman he called the daughter of the Occidental King, and they went sailing together on Lake Yao, taking turns to sing to one another in order to give one another pleasure. Mou-Wang had taken twelve philosophers, who brought back the knowledge of magical arts and hidden sciences.

"I have always thought that in the lands of the West, beyond the Kuen-Lun Mountains, there was an inaccessible place where men of a perfect wisdom live, inheritors of the lost secrets of ancient races, who are no longer submissive to the transformation of death and who strive to direct humankind in the way of the spirit. Now, last night I had a dream. I saw a man with a radiant face, imprinted with a ineffable benevolence, sitting under a fig-tree, meditating. I rediscovered in his gaze an expression that I have often seen in my own eyes when it I have seen its reflection in the water of a pool.

"The landscape surrounding the fig tree and the radiant man enabled me to deduce by its luxuriant richness that it is that of a land beyond the mountains of the West. I am too old to go so far, but perhaps you, who are young and strong, would like to go out there and enquire about the teaching of that marvelous man who, I am certain, belongs to a group of marvelous solitary sages who direct humans mentally and have been sent to them."

Scarcely had Lao-Tsu spoken those words than Siu-Kia was on his feet.

"Master, I shall depart straight away. I shall reach the Kuen-Lun Mountains and the realms that are to the west of them. I shall see the marvelous man and I shall bring back his words."

He took a staff, made a ball of boiled and pressed rice, and knotted it on his back. But he hesitated.

"Who will take care of you? Who will prepare the food in my absence?"

Lao-Tsu smiled.

"That is very little. My needs are diminishing every day. You are going a long way to search for a divine nourishment for me."

And many days went by. Every morning, under the aspect of a very poor man, the archivist of the Empire went to the market to buy a few vegetables. No literate visited him any longer. He only saw, every full moon, the functionary charged with paying his salary. He rejoiced in his solitude. Increasingly, for the inhabitants of Lo-Yang, the Palace of the Spirits of the Earth was as tedious as science, as redoubtable as the truth.

Very often, Lao-Tsu interrupted his meditations and gazed anxiously at the great avenue of the uncultivated garden, with the hope of seeing the silhouette of his disciple Siu-Kia appear there.

The Travels of Confucius

The celebrity of Confucius spread throughout the Empire by means of word of mouth, as the waters of the River Hoang-Ho spread into the crop-fields by means of irrigation channels.

When the time of his mourning was terminated, Confucius said to Tsu-Lou and Tsu-Kong:

"I cannot devote to a wife who has no filial piety a wisdom that would be useful to the whole empire. Because my soul is as inaccessible to a bad thought as a piece of jade is to the bite of an ant, princes are summoning me to them in order to ask my advice. I intend to respond to their appeal. Perhaps one of them will choose me as a minister, in order for me to restore the reign of virtue among his people."

Then the travels of Confucius commenced. He made them slowly in a cart covered by canvas and drawn by an ox, for wisdom travels without haste. Few disciples accompanied him, and it was Mong-Pi who prepared the meal when they stopped in a meadow on the bank of a river, and who pushed the cart when the slopes were too steep.

The King of Tsi received Confucius magnificently, and made a semblance of consulting him on various matters of politics, but he was a cruel man who only believed in evil and cherished it. He was amazed to learn from the mouth of Confucius that goodness is innate in humans and that the duty of a prince is to develop it in himself and his subjects. He would have liked to put the sage and his disciples to death, but he dared not, and contented himself with sending them away.

The King of Wei offered Confucius a palace as a dwelling and conversed with him several times, but he was a timorous man, so opposed to novelties that he was even frightened by a sage who only showed himself an innovator in making a profession of banishing novelties and returning to the customs of the ancients. After a while he assigned Confucius a palace more sumptuous than the first but in a mountainous region far from the city, which could only be reached by a sunken road that rain rendered impracticable. Confucius was obliged to depart in the autumn under penalty of being blockaded therein for months.

The King of Thsou came to meet him and stood in order to welcome him on the bridge that marked the frontier of his kingdom, but he was a limited man who did not understand any of what Confucius said to him. He was timid in his presence and did not know what to reply to him. In order not to have the painful sentiment of his inferiority any longer he refused a further conversation had sent word to him that the conversation in question would not take place until he had fully digested the information of the first conversation and assimilated its substance. In the meantime, he offered him a spacious palace as a habitation and sent him abundant nourishment every day.

From all directions young men came running who wanted to be the disciples of the sage and listen to his lessons. Mandarins held meetings in his honor, and when he traversed a village, the people assembled along the roadside in order to see him.

Confucius decided to visit the capital of the Empire, where many literates were demanding him. Lia-Yu, the son of a great man of the kingdom of Lou, who possessed one of the largest fortunes in China and who came to enroll among his disciples, offered to pay the expenses of the journey.

The King of Thsou was delighted by that decision and sent a new cart with horses as a gift. He also decided that an escort should accompany Confucius, for the roads were infested by brigands.

On the eve of that departure, Confucius deliberated with Tsu-Lou and Tsu-Kong as to what course of action it was necessary to follow in regard to Mong-Pi. Mong-Pi frequented ill-famed places and had recommenced getting drunk. He was vulgar and sordid in appearance. He did not seem to have made any progress in wisdom and virtue since he had been admitted to listen to Confucius. In sum, he was scarcely more intelligent that the King of Tsou. Many respectable men were astonished that such a creature lived in the wake of such a great sage.

"He practices filial virtue," repeated Confucius, hesitantly.

"But he practices it contrary to the rites," replied Tsu-Lou, "while making contortions and grimaces before a piece of wood that he plants in the ground. That is dishonoring filial virtue rather than practicing it. Lia-Yu, who is a delicate young man, is sickened by the manners and the costume of the eternal mendicant that Mong-Pi is. Now, we are about to have obligations to him. If wisdom is always on the side of propriety, I believe that propriety dictates that Mong-Pi be expelled from the company of sages."

It was decided thus.

The departure of Confucius was an apotheosis. All the literates of Thsou were grouped outside his door; speeches were made and flowers were strewn in his footsteps. His disciples filed behind him in the midst of cheers.

In order to participate in that splendor, Mong-Pi had cut a brand new staff, on which he leaned, and on which he had left a green branch covered in foliage. He thought by mean of that hint of spring to compensate for the sad appearance of his costume and to figure honorably in the last rank of the master's disciples. But Tsu-Lou informed him of Confucius' formal orders. The practice of virtue involves good conduct in life as well as respect for propriety in exterior appearances. So much the worse for Mong-Pi, who had forgotten that, and was content with a little foliage at the end of a staff. He would not be making the journey. He had to stay with his peers.

It was a long time after they had emerged from Thsou, and the cortege composed of carriages and cavaliers had climbed a hill, when Tsu-Lou, on turning round, saw the limping form of Mong-Pi in the distance, running along the road in the dust.

He told Confucius, and the later whipped his horses with a certain ill-humor, which probably came from the remorse he was experiencing.

Then he murmured: "Virtue has an exterior image that constrains our heart to certain sacrifices. Thus, one is sometimes obliged to get rid of a faithful but poorly trained dog."

The Conversation of Confucius and Lao-Tsu

Lao-Tsu was standing up straight at the end of the avenue that led to the Palace of the Spirits of the Earth. As he did every day, he was waiting for his disciple Siu-Kia. He was surprised to see a troop of men in the process in climbing over the cypress that blocked the breadth of the avenue with its fallen trunk. The former Minister of State Tchang-Houng was guiding that troop, and in the person around whom everyone was crowding in order to help him over the cypress trunk, Lao-Tsu recognized, from the descriptions that had been given to him, the celebrated Confucius.

The man of solitude advanced toward the man of life.

"He's scarcely better dressed than Mong-Pi" said Tsu-Kong in a low voice.

But Confucius was already making the ritual genuflections that are owed to Masters. He was honoring in Lao-Tsu the man whom the Emperor had honored with the title of Guardian of the Archives of the Empire, the man who lived face to face with the monuments of Chinese thought, the man who had acquired a great renown or philosophical wisdom and who loomed above the futility of the court of Lo-Yang like a tower of pure intelligence.

When he got up he could not prevent himself keeping his head slightly inclined forward and suddenly regretted having put on a robe of fine silk and wearing several insignia given to him by sovereigns around his neck. He took off and slipped into his belt, covertly, a family sapphire that he always wore on his little finger.

The former minister Tchang-Houng and the disciples stood aside in order to let the two great men discuss sublime things.

Confucius spoke. He talked about his projects of bringing men back to the good, of resuscitating old traditions, of making the old doctrine of purity of Yao and Chun live again.

Lao-Tsu listened in silence.

But how could good and justice be enabled to reign? Confucius thought that if the princes and, in default of them, the ministers, were good and just, the world would be rapidly ameliorated.

Lao-Tsu still remained silent.

"As one who loves the good and wants to spread it, am I not right," said Confucius, in the tone of a man justifying himself with regard to an accusation that has not been formulated, "to seek the confidence of a prince and to want to become his minister?"

Lao-Tsu shook his head negatively.

What was it necessary to do, then? Witness with folded arms the decadence of the Empire, where morality was crumbling, where virtue was falling into dust? What, according to Lao-Tsu, was the goal of life?

"To attain the perfect way."

And how did one succeed in that?

Lao-Tsu pointed to the stone where he was accustomed to sit.

"By immobility."

Confucius had difficulty in not shrugging his shoulders.

Oh, yes, meditation! But what was the use of that sterile flight toward an inexplicable sky? Meditation did not prevent evil from extending and men from suffering. "I have spent days without nourishment and nights without sleep in order to devote myself to meditation, without the slightest utility. Study is much preferable."

Lao-Tsu smiled. "Not all souls have the subtlety necessary for meditation."

Oh, well! Confucius agreed; he had a vulgar mind, down-to-earth. But the down-to-earth has its good points, for the man who lives on earth. He advised his disciples not to occupy themselves with the incomprehensible heavens, but the excellent earth on which their feet rested with certainty. Was he wrong?

Lao-Tsu made a gesture with his head to indicate that he was wrong.

Confucius felt a great surge of discontentment rising within him. Nothing could attack the rock of his rational certainty. He found himself in the presence of another rock-hard certainty and he judged it insensate. What would become of the world if sages sat down to gaze at the inaccessible heavens and neglected to give average instruction for the use of average men?

"What is, then, in your opinion, the foundation of morality?" he said with a certain impatience.

"There is no morality," replied Lao-Tsu, "since there is neither good not evil."

"What about familial duties?"

"They are harmful."

64

"And the sacred rites of the ancients?"

"They are useless."

"And respect for sovereigns? The sentiment of hierarchies? The immutable regulation that engenders order?"

Lao-Tsu's gaze became more heavily charged with scorn. Confucius sensed it posing on the insignia of which the kings had made him a gift and he bowed his head as if the plaques of gold and sculpted jade had suddenly become heavier.

The conversation was concluded. Confucius thought that it was appropriate to pronounce one last modest word as he withdrew.

"O Master," he said, "Give me an advice regarding the work I have undertaken."

"It is vain," relied Lao-Tsu.

"I am wrong, then, to want to govern men in order to make justice reign?"

"It is not men that it is necessary to govern but oneself."

"However, I feel myself animated by the passion of the good."

"All passions are bad, including that of the good."

Confucius bowed down to the ground in order to salute. When he raised his head again. Lao-Tsu was already moving away. He only saw his thin back, where a rip in the wool of his robe affected the form of a star.

Climbing over the fallen cypress seemed more difficult going back. It seemed to Confucius that he would breathe more freely when he was out of the unkempt garden that surrounded the Palace of the Spirits of the Air.

All the disciples surrounded him and wanted to know his impressions.

"The fish swims," he said, "and I understand its movement in the water. The bird flies, and I can see how it cleaves the air with its wings. The quadruped runs on the ground, and I know that it is pushing the ground with its feet. But if the dragon of legend, borne by a magic cloud, launches toward the fabulous sky, I am incapable of studying its nature. Lao-Tsu is like the dragon."

Prayer to Mediocrity

That evening, as the stars were lighting up, Confucius advanced on to the terrace of the pavilion where he was residing in the gardens of the former minister Tchang-Houng. It was the first day of the full moon of spring and the Festival of the Lanterns was being celebrated in honor of the Spirit that presides over celestial power.

The murmur of incantations was a kind of musical mist above the houses. In the immensity of narrow streets accumulated to the right, Confucius saw the temples with their crown of painted glass lanterns, which gave the impression of luminous hearts in which the blood of prayers was beating. To his left was the mass of the walls surrounding the Palace of Delightful Thoughts. Those walls had lanterns at the top and they extended in a circular fashion like pathways of stars.

Songs of delight were coming from the Emperor's gardens, mingled with the muffled music of drums and kins. In front of him, the river carried innumerable junks decked with flags, which had double sails like a butterfly's wings. Processions were going toward the temples, others were emerging from them. In the popular quarters, a multicolored, joyful, moving, undulating, densely-packed crowd displayed on ten thousand faces the human bliss from which the mask of cares has been removed.

Confucius did not feel at ease. The capital was too vast, too noisy. He missed the ordered calm of provincial towns. There were too many boats on the excessively wide river. He had found Lao-Tsu too sublime a few hours before. He was embarrassed in sensing his silent presence behind the mass of somber cypresses that he perceived on the other bank. And even the sky, in the radiant moonlight, had never appeared so profound, so full of mystery and so unlimited.

Having folded his arms over his breast, as if to clasp his unshakable conviction more narrowly, he formulated this prayer:

"O mediocrity, dry bread of the soul, aliment that is not in short supply, it is you on which I am nourished. Wine without alcohol, which does not procure inebriation but one can drink at leisure, it is you on which I get drunk. Poetry without verve, strophe that does not take wing but is familiar, song that demands no enthusiasm, it is you that I sing.

"O mediocrity, you have made me love the average life into which I was born, its hills without altitude, its temperate climate, and its slightly veiled sky. You have given me the mental neutrality that permits me to comprehend all ideas and the coldness of heart that is the natural armor against the excess of instinct. You have taught me that it is necessary neither to approve nor disapprove, nor embrace, not reject, and to avid the initial ardor of desire as well as destructive despair. It is you to which I owe rectitude of mind, love of order and equilibrium, and the divine benefit of regulation. You have driven away from my path the shadow of mysterious death and you have suppressed mystery in teaching me never to think.

"Thanks to you I have neglected the distant heavens for the earth on which I live and where I have savored the happiness that comes from self-satisfaction when one has respected the rules, cherished customs and practiced virtue. I walk the middle way with the purity of a man who is ignorant of impurity. O mediocrity, I love you, as I love mediocre men, my brothers."

The Perfect Way

At the same moment, standing under a cypress whose thrust gave the impression of wanting to traverse the nocturnal sky, Lao-Tsu said:

"O perfect way that I have glimpsed in the interior abyss of my mind, carry me in your invisible current, roll me on the wave devoid of moisture, all the way to the threshold devoid of a door, by which one penetrates into the colorless palace that contains ten thousand rainbows.

"Let me no longer desire anything in this world except the water that I can draw into earthenware jars, the rice that I can boil in the iron cooking-pot, the air that I breathe, the light with which I fill my eyes, and the night that covers me with its peace.

"O perfect way, grant me the quotidian ecstasy by which I reenter the Ineffable and plunge into the protection of the divine.

"Preserve me from the instinct of the beast and the curiosity of humans, and permit me to gaze with indifference at the succession of lives and deaths, the mutations of beings in their eternal movement.

"May my inferior soul fall out of me like a stone into a lake.

"May my superior soul rise up into the region that is neither on high nor low, neither to the right nor the left, in the abode without dimension in which there is neither purity nor impurity, neither wisdom nor folly, neither verity nor deceit, and where the light of the sun is confounded with the human heart."

Confucius the Minister

Prince Tin

The city of Lou was built around a lake that it circled with its multicolored houses, with the consequence that the lake gave the impression of a large mirror in a frame of lacquer and porcelain.

In the lake there was an island in the form of a diamond, which enclosed another, smaller lake. It was there that Prince Tin had built his five palaces, where he lived with his musicians in a nostalgic solitude.

Prince Tin scarcely saw his minister, to whom he delegated the affairs of the kingdom. He did not see his musicians, who played behind curtains or, by night, on errant junks on the little lake in the heart of the diamond. He only saw the form of Queen Wen-Kiang, who had been very beautiful and had died a century before.

Queen Wen-Kiang had been regent during her son's minority; she had loved the arts as Prince Tin loved them; she had loved amour as no human being had ever loved it. No portrait of her remained that Prince Tin could contemplate; and yet he lived with her image.

He had had the walls and ceiling of the palace in which he lived entirely covered with bronze mirrors, because it is the indefinite half-light of mirrors that the apparitions of the dead come toward the living when one burns certain secret perfumes and when one makes certain magical instruments resound.

At every sunset he went out with the invisible Queen Wen-Kiang and he followed, as she had had the habit of doing during her lifetime, the avenue of cinnamon trees that bordered the diamond-shape of the island. On the way he picked narcissi, deliberately sown, because he knew that she had cherished those flowers, and he raised them to the height of her face, her face devoid of a carnal oval and terrestrial tresses. Sometimes he stopped in order to watch her walk, and then he ran to catch up with her. When the sun had disappeared and he returned to the palace of the mirrors, Queen Wen-Kiang went away through a door that did not lead anywhere, and she never took the narcissi with her.

Then Prince Tin began to suffer. He suffered from jealousy, because of all Queen Wen-Kiang's past amours. Tradition had reported the story of her liaisons. He knew that she had loved vigorous warriors for their vigor, delicate literates for their delicacy, functionaries, sculptors of ivory, polishers of jade, and a mute slave for his silence, a man named Tai-Fou with a monstrous face because he resembled a donkey, and a clown from a troop of strolling players because he had a gangling body. The faces of all those dead lovers came to grimace in the mirrors; they displayed obscene bodies, they pursued ten thousand Queen Wen-Kiangs, ten million naked and swooning queens with open arms and drowned eyes.

And sometimes, when the moon was full and filled the palace with its wan gold, there was only one Queen Wen-Kiang in the mirrors, who emerged from the region of immaterial enchantments pink, smiling and naked, advanced through an empty corridor of crystal as far as the pace where Prince Tin was reposing, showed the ivory of her teeth very close to his, brushed him with her amber-tinted and phosphorescent skin, and disappeared when he tried to seize her, leaving nothing beneath his fingers but the cold of polished bronze, the temptation of the desert metal.

When he was not thinking about Queen Wen-Kiang, Prince Tin was only interested in the shade of lacquers or the fabrication of colored porcelains. He loved to mix pig bile and pulverized red sandstone himself, with a small Sun-chi ebony plaque. He polished and thinned resins with tea-oil and the charcoal of deer-antlers. He supervised the furnaces where clay was baked in which he had mingled the ashes of chalk and ferns, and spread gold powder. He said that he wanted to rediscover a certain violet that he had only seen once, in the water of a certain pool illuminated by a stormy sky, and that the violet in question was the same as the violet of Queen Wen-Kiang's eyes.

"It is better that the singularities of a King are exercised on the substance of porcelains and the varieties of their cooking than on the affairs of the kingdom," said his minister Yung-Lo.

Now, Yung-Lo died and, to everyone's surprise, it was the sage Confucius that Prince Tin called upon to replace him.

The Broken Mirrors

Leaning over the prow of the junk that was taking him to the island of the five royal palaces, Confucius frowned.

"If one wants to suppress evil," he murmured, "It is necessary to suppress its cause."

The desire for virtue had entered the soul of Prince Tin and had invaded it entirely. Henceforth, he obeyed his minister Confucius.

And as, that evening, he wanted to consult with him about the reforms to be accomplished, he invited him to walk a little along the edge of the calm water.

"We won't take that path," said Confucius, mildly. "The perfume of narcissi is too penetrating and invites reveries. The shade of cinnamons is too soft and invites idleness. The promenade of kings ought to be devoid of shade and perfume."

And during the night, by the light of lanterns, servants cut the narcissi and pruned the cinnamon trees, to such an extent that in the morning, nothing remained but the trunks, like melancholy stakes.

"In order to liberate the sovereign's soul in torment, I shall break a mirror every day," Confucius had said to his disciples. "Thus, the illusion will die and the verity of life will appear."

71

And every day, in the palace of mirrors, Prince Tin saw one of the facets of his dream shatter into smithereens. For him, the face of Queen Wen-Kiang gradually took on a dolorous and weary expression, and her form became more vaporous and tenuous. It seemed that she was having trouble appearing; she glided sadly, having become timid and fugitive.

When the last mirror was broken, Prince Tin saw in one of the fragments a Queen Wen-Kiang who was no larger than his finger and who faded away in a mist of bronzed crystal.

"How glad I am," he said, sadly, "finally to see things as they are."

He still pleased himself listening to concerts of his musicians, who played in the evening on the little lake between the five palaces, in a junk hung with silk.

Confucius gave the order that behind the silk of the junk, there should be one musician fewer every day. The concert gradually weakened. Standing on the terrace of his palace, Prince Tin listened to the manner in which beauty of the world sings when it is about to die.

The moon was resplendent and spring had never been as beautiful as on the evening when there was nothing on the junk but the shrill voice of a single lute. Confucius had come to take account of the effect on the Prince's mind of the last sigh of the music.

The tones of the unique lute were particularly strange, such that their like had never been heard before.

The mandarins of the court, the guards, and the pilots of junks ran to the edge of the lake and arranged themselves between the trimmed trunks of the cinnamons in order to hear more clearly. Boats were detached from the city, which gathered around the diamond of the island and remained motionless, as if fixed on the blue waters by the mystery of harmony. In the distance, the shores of Lou were populated with attentive forms, as if avid to collect the crumbs of sound.

Between the five palaces, in the middle if the diamond of the little isle, the solitary flute-player, invisible behind the extended silk, sang the sadness of beautiful faces that fade, great ambitions that do not have the courage to go on to the end, amours to which one is unfaithful in spite of oneself. And in that music there were the echoes of a bizarre and violent gaiety, a slightly insensate dance, which permitted the belief that the plaint was only a game.

Prince Tin was shaken by sobs, and Confucius could not explain at first why he saw once again images about which he no longer thought, which he had voluntarily set aside. And suddenly, he recognized the music. He recalled a chilly dawn in his garden, he saw once again his wife Ki-Keou violating the rule decreed by him, disregarding filial piety, trying to make her whim triumph, to turn to derision the sanctity of familial custom. In that music there was fantasy, free delight, the spirit of revolt, all that was dangerous and hateful. It was that tune that Ki-Keou had played, at the intermediary hour when a wife ought still to be reposing beside her husband.

The musician had already fallen silent when Confucius thought of giving the order to have the junk stopped.

"Summon that musician to appear before me," he said to the steward of the orchestra.

But he could not be found. He had already regained the shore of Lou.

"I had engaged him recently," said the steward of the orchestra. "He doesn't observe any of the prescribed rules, and yet there's a singular beauty in his manner of playing."

"There is no beauty without the observance of rules," said Confucius, severely.

The steward lowered his head.

"Who is he?" asked Confucius.

"He's a certain Mong-Pi, who is lame and very ugly."

Confucius lowered his head.

"Should I have him found and beaten on the soles of his feet?" asked the steward.

Confucius remained silent. He reflected.

"Have him found and taken to the frontier of the realm, after giving him some money."

The Reign of Virtue

Confucius verified the force of regulation with innumerable rules that he decreed and which he spread through the kingdom of Lou like a flood of bitter but vivifying water.

Recompenses ornamented the rules with an appearance of joy, and punishments gave them the authority necessary for them to be respected.

Confucius created a great administration composed of hundreds of functionaries for the publication of regulations and the surveillance of their execution.

Everything was regulated: the hours of work and those of rest; the time that ought to be devoted to meals and that permitted for sleep. Everyone, in accordance with his fortune, had to burn a certain quantity of incense on the altar of the ancestors. Everyone, according to his aptitude, had to devote himself to a certain art, but only at a certain hour. Music was rigorously proscribed after sunset because of the influence it had on the sensual passions. For the same reason, there were considerable taxes on spices and certain herbs to which aphrodisiac effects were attributed.

From sensuality, according to Confucius, a host of evils were born: forgetfulness of filial duties, the incapacity to understand the sacred books, a slowness of intelligence and certain passionate movements that threw disorder into the family and deflected the virtue of adolescents.

Dances were censored. The heads of families received a list of faults that the shadow of the hearth covers, and the description of the dangerous familiarities of brother and sister, and cousins of different sexes, that were to be forbidden. Young men and young women did not have the right to walk in company along the roads, and even spouses, when they went out together, had to leave a gap between them wide enough for a chariot to be able to pass through. A committee of scholars fixed or conjugal embraces a number that conciliated the desires of human nature, the necessity of reproduction and the concerns of the legislator, who feared sexual excess as the most dangerous excess of all.

The kingdom of Lou was measured, channeled and administered from one end to the other. A complicated hierarchy of functionaries covered it, supervised it and organized it, and at the summit of that hierarchy stood Confucius, as exact as justice, as cold as morality and as inexorable as ennui.

And under that regime, the kingdom of Lou prospered materially. More regular labor produced more abundant harvest; the more efficient police gave security to travelers; life was less expensive for the poor because of the penalties imposed on the speculation of merchants. General honesty increased. If an object was lost in the street, no one dared pick it up for fear of being accused of theft. No kiss was exchanged outside marriage, and even when a marriage was consummated, the spouses hesitated to bring their faces together, and remained chaste for a long time afterwards, so accustomed were they to considering their desire as culpable.

The delicacy of features was attenuated; men grew fat. Everyone diverted to nourishment, which remained a permissible pleasure, the faculty of enjoyment. Happiness diminished in proportion to wellbeing and the narrow reigning morality. Ennui, lack of initiative and the absence of high hopes engendered stupidity. Virtue reigned in the kingdom of Lou.

Confucius' Dream

Confucius had a dream.

Beside his bed, between the two screens that formed the principal furniture of his bedroom, Lao-Tsu was standing.

On his face there was a more benevolent expression than when Confucius had seen him on the threshold of the Palace of the Spirits of the Earth. He seemed to be unsupported by the floor and to be floating bizarrely. There was a sort of commiseration in his voice.

"So, you are a minister! But do you not know that a saintly man ought not to attach himself to his merits and ought to consider glory as an ignominy? Are you not ashamed to be a minister of a king, commanding the police and preparing for war?"

Confucius replied that he was not ashamed.

"Too bad! That is because you see things from below. It is because you are troubled by the passions that you want to repress in others and you are not conscious of the ambition that is devouring you. You have not developed the power of the soul's perception that permits the contemplation of the double aspect of things. Oh, if you could only elevate yourself a little!"

Then Confucius perceived that what he had believed to be the two screens of his bedroom were immense wings, which Lao-Tsu had on his back, and which were palpitating gently.

And he perceived by a little noise behind him, that he also had wings, but infinitely smaller than Lao-Tsu's: the stumps of wings, which were beating in a rather ridiculous fashion.

But he did not have time to be astonished. Lao-Tsu had made a sign and Confucius was now flying behind him in the twilight that precedes the dawn.

His first thought was that the sage had justly chosen for the extravagant exercise into which he was drawing him the hour at which Ki-Keou once liked to play the lute in her garden.

Lao-Tsu's huge wings were making a mysterious noise, and Confucius was out of breath behind him.

"I'm afraid of falling," he murmured.

They had surpassed the clouds. They brushed icy peaks, inaccessible summits where there was a livid snow.

"We're too high," said Confucius.

"One is never too high," said Lao-Tsu. "The sky is immense."

They surpassed those summits and went along others, more jagged and more desolate, devoid of vegetation, as naked as pure intelligence.

"I'm afraid of bumping into those needles of stone," said Confucius.

"Can you not see that they are not rocks, but ideas?" said Lao-Tsu. "It is sufficient not to be afraid to traverse them easily, and render their solidity empty."

And Confucius saw him, with amazement, pass through an enormous mountain with as much facility as he would have passed through a light mist.

"Come and join me," cried Lao-Tsu.

"How can I?" replied Confucius. "I can't suppress matter."

"Climb, then."

Confucius saw that Lao-Tsu was flying high above him in the blue-tinted air.

"It's impossible; my wings can scarcely carry me."

"Be animated by the desire for elevation and your wings will become immense," said the voice of Lao-Tsu, enfeebled by distance.

"I sense them becomes smaller with every passing minute." And, looking over his shoulder, Confucius saw that his wings were indeed diminishing more and more, and no longer had any but a few stunted pinions.

The nascent dawn illuminated the celestial space with all the colors of the rainbow.

"Renounce the earth and you will find the divine path," said Lao-Tsu, from very far away.

But those words were not lost.

"Never! I can't renounce the beloved earth," proclaimed Confucius, with all his might.

And then he fell. He fell with a vertiginous speed through the clouds that the rising sun colored with a bright red; he fell all the way to the uniform, compact, protective earth.

He found himself, bathed with sweat, in his bed, that of a man without wings. He looked round with anguish, but nothing lifted up his linen night-shirt. His back was as flat as was appropriate. He uttered a great sigh of relief and got up in order to feel the pleasure of feet on the ground.

"To each his task," he said. "I don't fly. I walk, and I'd rather crawl than fly. I'm only the poor sublime man of ordinary men. That's sufficient for me."

The Beautiful Miao-Chen

The kingdom of Lou communicated to the west with the kingdom of Tsi by means of an ancient paved road that dated from the reign of Wou-Wang. A stone bridge over a river was the limit of the frontier, and a numerous guard was stationed there to prevent entry to the kingdom of virtue by the elements of disorder and immortality. Those impure elements presented themselves one evening at the entrance to the bridge in the picturesque form of a troop of traveling actors.

It was the troop of old Yan-Yu. His actors, the sons of slaves that he had instructed, belonged to him, and he had a great deal of difficulty nourishing them. Yen-Ying, the minister of the kingdom of Tsi, who did not protect the arts, had recently indicated to him an order to leave the territory of Tsi. He was unaware of the transformations wrought by Confucius in the neighboring state and was counting on the benefits that the favor of Prince Tin ought to procure him

His troop was unique. It consisted of twenty individuals, to whom he had taught the texts of very ancient plays recorded in his prodigious memory, and the barbaric Lai-Y dances, performed with flags and sabers to the sounds of wild music and concluded by a frenetic ecstasy of the dancers. Yan-Yu had the art of grouping around his performers amateur singers recruited among the people of the country he was traversing, with the consequence that his coming was the signal for great popular rejoicing.

He threw himself at the feet of the Tai-Fou, the guardian of the frontier of Lou, begging him to let him pass. But the latter was pitiless, for Confucius' orders were formal.

As night had fallen, Yan-Yu's troop camped on the other side of the bridge.

The next day's sun illuminated surprising events.

In the same way that a diamond is sometimes swept into a pile of rubbish, the young marvel of beauty Miao-Chen had been projected into Yan-Yu's ambulant troupe by a thrust of the broom of the gods. She was sixteen years old and her body was inhabited by the genius of dance, her fingers were animated by the spirit that teaches the knowledge of lutes and her lips were the expression of the god of evocative and harmonious words.

But in the same way that a diamond, when it is uncut, is easily confused with a shiny pebble by those who do not have a sense of rare substances, a young marvel of beauty is mistaken for a vulgar creature by the vulgar creatures in whose midst she lives.

Yan-Yu's traveling troupe was woken up that morning by the beautiful Miao-Chen's cries of despair.

As usual, on waking up, she had extended her right hand to cress the face of the lame Nieou, the troupe's clown, who slept alongside her and to whom she accorded the simulacra of her child-like amour. The clown Nieou was old and ugly and he made her laugh. Every morning she woke him up by pulling his nose. But the nose she pulled that morning was strangely icy. Nieou had died during the night, without moving and without manifesting his sadness at quitting life, doubtless in order not to trouble the slumber of his young companion.

The entire troupe emerged from the tents that had been extended along the river bank and ran to Mao-Chen's cries. Lamentations rose up toward the early morning sky. In despair, Miao-Chen tore her robe, and her thin body appeared like a trembling flower in which the dew made delicate pearly glitter.

In accordance with the ancient customs, Yan-Yu, the dead man's master, who represented his father, turned toward the rising sun and called to Nieou by his name several times to exhort his already wandering spirit to return to its corporeal form. The actors and musicians repeated "Nieou!" in chorus to give more power to the appeal.

And a cry sprang from all breasts.

From the direction of the rising sun, over the bridge that gave access to the kingdom of Lou, a limping individual advanced who had almost the same facial ugliness and waddling gait as the dead clown.

It was Mong-Pi, who was quitting the kingdom from which he had been exiled.

For a few moments, in the half-light of the morning, they all believed that Nieou, resuscitated and rejuvenated by the mystery of death, was advancing toward them. The cries of grief were replaced by a clamor of joy.

At first, Miao-Chen remained immobile, arms open and eyes wide. Then, light and naked, she launched forward, climbed the slope of the bridge at the summit of which Mong-Pi had just arrived and clasped him against her, tenderly.

Fortunate welcomes are sometimes thus reserved for travelers when a certain folly guides them.

Explanations were made. It followed from that event that Mong-Pi would be able to learn Nieou's roles and perform them in very little time. Yan-Yu engaged him in the troupe immediately as a free actor. But his arrival retained a certain supernatural character that was sufficient to earn him the amour of Miao-Chen.

Nieou's grave was dug immediately. The lamentations had cased. They suddenly resumed, for it was written that that morning would be fertile in events for the players.

Cavaliers appeared in the distance on the road to Tsi. They surrounded a chariot drawn by four horses, and Yan-Yu recognized by the azure standards embroidered with gold that were floating to the right and left of the chariot that it was the minister Yen-Ying in person, in the process of inspecting the frontiers. What would he say on seeing the troupe that he had ordered to quit the territory of Tsi? On the other hand, the Tai-Fou of Lou was standing on the other side of the bridge. In the middle of his soldiers, as pitiless as the order he was carrying out.

All foreheads touched the dust. The minister Yen-Ying's chariot had stopped. The cavaliers' pikes were straight and there was nothing n the air but the rustle of flapping banners. In that pause, the beautiful Miao-Chen dared to raise her curious and puerile head.

A cry resounded.

The minister leapt from his chariot and came to look at the young dancer at close range.

"She has violet eyes!" he exclaimed. "The violet eyes of Queen Wen-Kiang!"

And s twenty stupefied heads turned toward the minister, the latter perceived Mong-Pi and burst out laughing.

"And there's the donkeys head that I need!"

He made a sign to Yan-Yu to get up.

"You re henceforth the King of Tsi's chief of entertainments. You will follow me to Tsi-Nan-Fou with your actors, but it will be necessary for you to learn a play for which I shall furnish the theme, and of which these will be the two heroes."

He pointed at Mong-Pi and the beautiful Miao-Chen, in whose eyes the rising sun reverberated, and which resembled two celestial violets.

The Conference in Kia-Kou

When the King of Tsi sent an ambassador dressed in blue, as a sign of amity, accompanied by cavaliers similarly clad in blue, to invite the King of Lou to an amicable conference, Confucius immediately anticipated a trap, for he possessed the clairvoyance of human things. As he cultivated courage as well as the other virtues, he decided to accompany his master to the amicable conference, which was to take place at Kia-Kou on the territory of Tsi. And as he also cultivated prudence, he gave an order to the Tai-Fou of war to follow the royal chariot with a troop of well-armed cavalry.

The two sovereigns and their ministers were to confer on the subject that had divided them for a long time, which was the possession of three towns in the kingdom of Lou of which the King of Tsi had taken control, to the scorn of all justice. The conference was to take place at sunset because of the performance that was to follow and to which the shadow of night would give more beauty.

In a large meadow, a stage had been set up in the midst of clumps of bamboo and cinnamon trees, and he two sovereigns took their places there with their ministers.

Immediately, Confucius spoke with the firmness of a man whose claim is just and who knows that he is able to support justice with strength.

Night had fallen during the ceremony of welcome, the initial polite formulae and the hypocritical protestations. Prince Tin, his eyes lost in the evening sky, seemed uninterested in the debate. Confucius was speaking, but the force of his reasoning permitted him to follow what was happening around him and the event of which he read the design in the faces of the King of Tsi and his minister Yen-Ying.

Lantern-bearers emerged from the bamboo clumps and surrounded the stage on all sides. A triple rank lined up on each side of the stairway that linked the stage to the meadow. Confucius noticed that the lanterns, instead of being blue like amity, were red, like violence, and that all the bearers had put on armor and had the sabers of warriors in their belts.

The minister Yen-Ying had stood up. He was about to discard the mask. Confucius did not give him time. He seized the gong that a servant was holding and struck several precipitate blows on it.

At that signal the Tai-Fou of Lou and his cavalry emerged from the nearby wood where they were waiting and raced across the meadow toward the stage, which they surrounded, with a great clink of weapons. A few lanterns fell, a few sabers were drawn. There was a moment of confusion. The men of Lou and those of Tsi waited for the order to come to blows. Yen-Ying advanced to shout that order.

Confucius forestalled him again.

"I thought the time for the play had come," he said. "I wanted these few men of the escort to witness the amusements that are in preparation."

Yen-Ting evaluated the forces in presence silently, and bowed. He made a sign to Yan-Yu and his troupe to come forward.

Prince Tin had not interrupted his reverie.

The music that immediately resounded was more unusual, more voluptuous and more extraordinary than anything commonly heard. There were explosions of drumbeats that collided with reason and plaints of flutes that lacerated the sense of decency.

But before Confucius was able to become indignant at the impropriety of such harmonies, the actors had begun the performance of the play.

Now, that play depicted the amours of Queen Wen-Kiang with a ridiculous warrior wearing the head of a donkey. The beautiful Miao-Chen was so delightful in the role of the Queen that when she appeared there was a frisson in the audience, and all the lanterns oscillated in the air as if the bearers were drunk.

Confucius had the presence of mind to deploy his fan before the face of Prince Tin in order to hide the gleam of the violet eyes, while talking to him in a low voice about the three towns whose restitution he was demanding. Thus occupied by the movement of the fan, he only listened with one ear to the play, which had almost finished when he perceived the scandalous insult it constituted, by virtue of its subject, at the same time as a perfidious appeal to Prince Tin's dementia.

He stood up in order to interrupt it. But tumultuous laughter drowned out his voice. Mong-Pi, the wearer of the donkey's head, mimed in such a humorous fashion the joy of a caricature warrior favored by the amour of a divine creature that the spectators sat down on the ground in order to laugh at their ease and the cavaliers of Lou let themselves down from their horses, guffawing.

Then a silence suddenly fell and the indignant words froze on Confucius' lips. Miao-Chen danced. She danced almost naked with a slight movement of her breasts and her narrow hips. She had put an expression of the most perfect purity on her face at the same time as her body expressed the quiver of desire and the expectation of sensuality. And as that sensuality grew in her, as if it had emerged from the most profound depths of her slender body, her eyes, like the water of a pool on a stormy evening, became more intensely violet and more ingenuous, and she fixed them, as she had been commanded to do, on Prince Tin.

But in vain. Confucius' fan passed back and forth, and throughout the time that the dance lasted, the sage minister talked to his sovereign about the gravest subjects, and occupied his attention.

Now, faults ought to be followed by punishments, and the strong ought not to support insults without becoming weak. The Tai-Fou of Lou was now standing to Confucius' right, ready to avenge the insult, and the breastplates of the cavaliers were sparkling in a circle. Scarcely had Confucius let his anger burst forth than the King of Tsi uttered confused apologies and the minister Yen-Ying wrung his hands in despair. They had nothing to do with all that. The play had been performed without their knowledge. It was all the fault of the worthy actors.

Confucius did not consent to withdraw without a visible and immediate reparation. Yen-Ying offered to put the entire troupe of comedians to death immediately, on the very spot where the insult had been committed.

Confucius thought, in his love of humanity, that such a massacre was exaggerated and unnecessary. He only demanded the death of the immodest woman who had danced. He knew that he would thus destroy one of the adversaries of virtue, one of the forms of evil in its most tempting, most mysteriously attractive and most detestable aspect.

When they came to fetch her, the beautiful Miao-Chen was laughing, sitting in the meadow with a donkey's head on her knees, and she sometimes placed her head on the shoulder of her companion Mong-Pi. She thought it was a matter of recompenses and felicitations, and she fell to her knees with delight, very small before the enormous power of royal hypocrisies and official proprieties.

A little later, Confucius having made the King of Tsi sign the restitution of the three towns and taken leave of him with a thousand salutations, he heard heart-rending cries and he stopped as he was about to mount his chariot.

"It's nothing," said Yen-Ying. "It's the clown Mong-Pi mourning the woman he loved."

Mong-Pi's Three Heads

That night, Confucius had a dream.

Mong-Pi was standing next to his bed, but Confucius noticed with surprise that he had three different heads, which he placed on his shoulders alternately.

The first head was that of the beautiful Miao-Chen. She was even more beautiful than when she danced; she gazed at him with her violet eyes and Confucius knew with certainty that the amethyst hue of her irises really was the rare gleam that rises from a pool where dead vegetation is rotting, when a stormy sky is reflected therein. But he did not have time to reflect on the mystery that made a beautiful radiance emerge from the putrefaction of waters, because the head of Miao-Chen was replaced by the head of a donkey. A donkey! The hateful stupidity, the incongruity, the vulgarity! But he did not have time to reflect on something strangely faithful and amicable that was disengaged from the beast. It was Mong-Pi's true face that was positioned close to his own.

And Mong-Pi said to him:

"I am the beauty of the courtesan, the folly of the man who lives outside of any rules; I am laughter, I am your victim, Confucius. You will always persecute me, for there is a force in you that makes you believe that your verity is the sole truth and that it is necessary to force others to adopt it. Morality is your essence and you are prepared to make me suffer a thousand tortures for my greater good. I escape you incessantly, but you dominate me because you are order and you command the guardians of gates and those who close the grilles separating the quarters in the evening. A courtesan, I strip naked in spite of you in order to trouble adolescents; a musician, I play insensate hymns that procure people forbidden dreams.

"I will be your despair eternally, O son of the subprefect, master of reverences, perfect magistrate, model of ministers. You will have on your side fathers of families full of common sense, venerable matrons, sane men, virtuous men, and all of organized society. I shall continue to live with poor people, dividing my time between prison and the highway, but, in spite of the scorn you have for me, you will suffer from never having succeeded in forcing me to make honorable amends before your sane reason.

"You can break the lute, cut off the head of Miao-Chen, rip the heart out of my breast, but I will never perish, for I am eternal and I shall be reborn in the form of the idle cricket or the futile nightingale. Of the two of us, O sage, you doubtless believe yourself to be the better, but I have one superiority over you of which you are unaware, which is that I cannot hold a grudge against you, because I am your brother, O Confucius!"

The Eighty Young Women

Confucius ate little, scarcely slept and worked enormously. In vain his disciples exhorted him to rest. He replied to them that the prosperity of the kingdom demanded all the hours of his life. In the end, however, he yielded to them. He consented to stay at home for one day, a single day.

And it was on that day, while he was asleep, that the magnificent presents sent to the King of Lou by the King of Tsi arrived.

They arrived via the northern gate in the middle of a guard of eunuchs on white horses, and they were eighty young women with skin as milky as young almonds, loins as supple as palm leaves and lips as red and moist as carnal pleasure.

They came from Yang-Tcheou, a town renowned throughout the Empire for the lascivious character of its inhabitants. There were schools of dancing and music there, and the art of sensuality was taught to women at a very early age. Yen-Ying had gone there in person and had bought with the treasure of Tsi the most beautiful creatures he could find, knowing full well that he would recuperate the treasure of Tsi by the downfall of the kingdom of Lou.

The eighty young women traversed the city like a voluptuous dream, and Prince Tin, who was strolling on the shore of the diamond-shaped island, heard the music of their lutes and saw the pale forms aboard junks that were advancing over the waves. In several places at once, the young women disembarked; they ran, laughing, to the five palaces; they filled the pathways of the gardens; they accosted the guards at the doors; they climbed the marble stairways; they caused an immense gust of joy to rise up toward the sky.

And they all replied to Prince Tin, when he questioned them:

"We are the followers of the marvelous, the mysterious and the splendid to behold."

And they designated the most beautiful among them, who had the bearing of a young queen, an amethyst in the form of a star on her forehead, and was clad in a mauve tunic sufficiently transparent to allow a perfect body to be seen.

Prince Tin finally advanced toward that creature of election and asked her name.

She moved aside the veil that hid her face, fixed her immense violet eyes upon him, and said, modestly: "I am Queen Wen-Kiang and I have come back to live on my island."

Prince Tin suddenly perceived that spring had enabled the branches of the cinnamon trees in the avenue to grow back, and that narcissi were emerging from the soil forcefully, as if the musical substance scattered in the air were giving them life. He saw that he was at the center of the immense blue mirror of the lake and that he was walking alongside the woman about whom he had thought for such a long time.

As they walked he collected a bouquet of narcissi that he held out to her, and as Queen Wen-Kiang showed herself to be strangely provocative, he had no scruples about drawing her gently toward his apartments and she had no hesitation in following him. She even put an urgency into it that would not have seemed regal if Prince Tin had not been blinded by desire.

Night fell. Lanterns lit up like irises of pleasure. A pale farandole extended along the avenue, along the lake, and seemed to envelop the five palaces with a voluptuous crown.

The soldiers had abandoned their weapons, the literates their books. Boats furrowed the lake and a song rose up from them that rose toward the stars like a long crystal branch. Sometimes, a venerable mandarin returned to the land, carrying a precious young woman toward his house like a fragment of white jade, the symbol of essential purity.

By the communication of the rhythm of dances the intoxication that had taken possession of the island reached the entire city. Everyone rejected the excessively heavy yoke of an excessively perfect morality. Closed windows opened. The forms of women avid for furtive things and forbidden rendez-vous slipped through hidden doors.

Functionaries were seen who, while going to accomplish a ritual ceremony at the Pagoda of the Imperial Ancestors on a nearby hill, threw away the sticks of incense and the jugs of milk and ran at a fast pace toward the ill-famed quarter of the city.

On the threshold of the Tribunal of Rites, the Grandmaster of Punishments stopped, uttered a sigh and retraced his steps, saying: "Where are my twenty years?"

In a single night, the work that Confucius had edified over years collapsed. For the man who takes human morality for the foundation of society, who takes no account of the hidden beauty of passion, the virtue of disorder and the creative force of pleasure, and who does not know that there is no more magnificent aliment to nourish and elevate the soul than amour, the simple amour of man and woman, builds on sand.

The Triumph of Joy

An ironic skylark fluttered its wings against the window and Confucius finally woke up. The persistence of the skylark in making little irregular holes with its beak in the mica of the panes caused him to sense that something had changed around him in the respect of that which ought to be respected.

He got dressed in haste. His guards and his bearers were not waiting outside the door around his palanquin. In the street he was nearly knocked over by a drunkard. Then he rubbed his eyes, having a singular dream. The august director of ritual ceremonies was walking in front of him without an escort and he was embracing a svelte and immodestly clad creature who sometimes tickled his nose playfully with a peacock feather.

I've slept too long, thought Confucius. *The dream is continuing in reality.*

When he reached the shore of the lake the continuation of the dream was manifest thus:

Half-lying in a boat on a heap of rose petals was the Tai-Fou of war. He was visibly drunk. A painted paper lantern was swinging over his head and he was oscillating with it laughing stupidly. A very small woman was on his knees and he occasionally threw a handful of rose petals into her hair.

That lantern, lit in broad daylight, and the disproportion there was between the enormity of the Tai-Fou and the smallness of his companion were for Confucius the material symbols of debauchery in its most hideous aspect.

At that unreal image, he could not help making an imperious sign.

The Tai-Fou responded to it by negligently throwing a handful of roses at him, and, as the boat was very close to the shore, one of them touched Confucius' forehead, and a little thorn pricked him lightly. He perceived, by means of that veridical thorn, that what he took for a dream was a reality, and he sensed the extent of the catastrophe that had struck the kingdom of Lou.

On the threshold of the palace he had himself announced to Prince Tin, but the latter sent the response that he could not receive him. He waited in vain. He was never to find himself in his presence again.

The authority of Confucius died mysteriously in all souls at the same time. The workings of the administrations he had created only operated sluggishly and ended up breaking down. The dignitaries of the kingdom no longer came to request his orders. People ceased to obey him. He could not refer the matter to the invisible sovereign. A lute-player received, without him being informed, the title of Grand Organizer of the Festivals of the Kingdom, with discretionary powers. The eunuch from Tsi who had escorted the eighty young women and who was reputed to be a man of detestable mores, became governor of the five palaces of the diamond-shaped island, and gardeners sowed innumerable narcissi there and transported cinnamon trees with long flowery branches.

Yan-Yu came with his troupe to install them in the main square of the city facing the Temple of Immaculate Perfection. He had lost his two principal artistes, because Mong-Pi had disappeared after the death of the beautiful Miao-Chen, but in accordance with the methods familiar to him he instructed local people in the art of singing, and organized immense choirs that filled the city with an immense song of joy.

There had been no precise royal order. Confucius sensed that he had been rejected and eliminated, by virtue of the natural play of things, along with his moral rules, his virtuous laws and his implacable love of the good. He decided to quit the kingdom of Lou and arranged a rendezvous at six o'clock in the morning for the few disciples who had not yet swapped their black robes for gala costumes.

He insisted on not taking anything with him, and going away poorer than he had arrived, for he was sincerely disinterested.

But Tsu-Lou and Tsu-Kong were the only ones who came to the rendezvous. Confucius waited for a long time, fruitlessly, in the matinal melancholy of a deserted street. In the end, he set forth with his two faithful companions.

A stray dog, a miserable yellow dog, started walking behind his horse, and did not want to quit him. Confucius knew it well. The dog had selected the threshold of his house as a domicile. He saw it every day and was obliged to use a stick to prevent it from getting into the house, for he estimated that possession of a dog is contrary to domestic cleanliness.

He threatened it uselessly. The dog seemed to have given itself to him. It stopped, looked at him with large sad eyes, and then, when Confucius set off again, it resumed walking behind him, faithfully.

In the end, Confucius let it do so, and said to Tsu-Lou and Tsu-Kong: "There isn't a single one of the inhabitants of Lou whose well-being I wanted so passionately to accompany me, but that dog, which I've always chased away from my threshold, is giving me evidence of the most veritable attachment. How mysterious that is!"

The Old Age of Sages

The Return of Siu-Kia

When the disciple Siu-Kia appeared on the threshold of the Temple of the Spirits of the Earth, with his hair gathered up and knotted behind his head in the Hindu manner, Lao-Tsu extended his arms to him but did not manifest an extreme surprise. Siu-Kia was astonished by that absence of astonishment, but Lao-Tsu said to him:

"Some time ago, I acquired a singular fashion of seeing, on closing my eyes, those to whom my soul is linked. I distinguished you on the roads. I saw the crook of your staff in the snowy squalls of the Loung Mountains, and the desert sands whipped up by the wind did not succeed in hiding your shadow. But tell me what you have seen in the lands that are beyond the frontiers of China."

"O Master," said Siu-Kia, "the moon has swelled and then thinned many times above my head. I emerged from the Empire through the Hang-Kou pass and I have traversed regions where there is nothing but savage wolves, and I have climbed very high mountains where eagles were flying in hundreds and brushed my head with their wings. The wolves respected me because of my thinness and the eagles did not peck out my eyes because my desire for knowledge gave my irises a resemblance to the sky.

"I have traversed the River of Sand where one dies if one encounters certain burning winds that are genii with robes of fire. I have passed through the kingdom of Chen-Chen, and, marching north-westwards, I reached the kingdom of Oui, whose inhabitants are inhospitable, and the kingdom of Yu-Thian, whose inhabitants are welcoming and kind, but not very numerous, and where there are square monasteries of black stone at the summits of conical mountains.

"I always headed westwards. The vegetation changed around m, the sky took on an indigo color that I had never seen; I descended the slopes of Tsoun-Ling and I arrived in valleys so pleasant that one cannot look at them without weeping. There are trees there that are reminiscent of young women amicably leaning over rivers whose waters are as pure as jade at sunrise. Finally, having crossed the River Aciravati, I reached the land of the Cakias. There, there was no talk of anything but the incomparable wisdom of the son of a prince, named Siddartha."

"A son of a prince!" Lao-Tsu interjected. "I thought that only very poor men could arrive at incomparable wisdom."

"Not at all, my Master. This Siddartha is the son of Souddhodana, a powerful sovereign who has war chariots, slaves and elephants, and who commands in the city of Kapilavastu. But Siddartha has quit all of his father's wealth, his palace and his wife, for meditation and solitude in the forest, among the wild beasts."

"His wife!" Lao-Tsu interjected again. "I thought that only a man who had been chaste all his life could arrive at incomparable wisdom."

"Not at all, my Master. A son named Rahoula has even been born of this Siddartha. Now, Siddartha experienced to an extreme degree the suffering of humans condemned to malady and death. The pity he experienced for their ignorance and their misery tore his heart. He sat down under a Pei-lo tree and remained there until illumination came to him and he knew the secret of deliverance. Then he got up and has walked among men in order to inform them of the fruit of his meditations and the verity that is proper to him."

"Have you succeeded in reaching him and seeing him?" Lao-Tsu asked. "Can you tell me whether his visage is splendid, and whether a radiant light escapes from his eyes, like the man I have seen in my dream?"

"Not at all, my Master. Doubtless the dream transforms and embellishes. The man whose renown extends across the plains of the Ganges and into mountainous Tibet, and is called the Buddha, has the appearance of an ordinary man. No sublime grandeur radiates from his person, and if I dared, I would say that he resembles you, my Master. I was able to approach him with a few monks from a monastery in the land of Kie-Tcha who had accompanied me for a part of my journey.

"He was standing in the sunlight near a small hut of latanier branches under the branches of a tree in the form of a vault, and he was about to pour water from a jug into a cup in order to drink. Beside him, on a stone, he had a barley-cake that he must have cooked himself, and which he was about to have for a meal. Yes, that great sage eats and drinks like all men, as you are obliged to do yourself, and I don't know why that fills me with emotion. When he saw us, he put down his jug with a movement of affectionate delight and smiled at us benevolently. He always smiles benevolently and I must say that a little later, his teachings appeared to me to come from higher up and further away and to have more beauty because they came from an ordinary man who smiled benevolently."

"What are these teachings that come from so high and so far?" asked Lao-Tesu, impatiently. "Doubtless you have been struck by them as if by a thunderbolt and you remain amazed by the revelation of that which was hidden from you?"

"Not at all, my Master—for those teachings, I knew them. They are those that you taught me with few words a long time ago, and which you teach to the small number of sages who have come to seek instruction from you. The verity that, thanks to your words, is circulating an ancient China is the same as the one that the Buddha is spreading in India. You inform everyone that it is necessary to vanquish desire in oneself in order to escape the recommencement of successive lives and reenter the bliss of the perfection that is above good and evil and in which one savors immutable amour. You inform everyone that one can succeed in that by the simplicity of mores, the absence of pride, solitary meditation and the search for the divine in oneself. So my joy is great in having terminated my journey in order to sit down by your side and seek the ecstasy that you prescribe."

Lao-Tsu had uttered a great sigh of relief. The truth has no need of confirmation, but the human mind is so lacking in certainty that even the greatest sage is glad to know that there is another sage far away who thinks like him.

The Departure of Siu-Kia

When Siu-Kia had told the story of his journey in detail, when he had eaten and drunk, he sat down to mediate. But Lao-Tsu said to him:

"I have mentioned to you the singular power that enables me to see at a distance those to whom I am linked by a spiritual affinity. Now, for some time I have had the vision of a marvelous man who has a radiant face, imprinted with an extraordinary curiosity and eyes that shine with the desire for explanation. He is sitting on the shore of a sea the color of sapphire strewn with triangular sails; there is a white temple behind him and I see numbers fluttering around his head like mathematical birds. The landscape that surrounds the man full of curiosity enables me to augur, by the clarity of its atmosphere, an abundance of bright marble and the whiteness of women's skin, that it is the landscape of a country beyond the mountains of the West, beyond the kingdoms that are after the mountains of the West, in a region where no man born in China has ever reached. I am too old to go so far, but perhaps you, who are young and strong and are accustomed to traveling, would like to go there and enquire about the man with the mind as luminous as the sky that shines over his head and the science of numbers in which I suppose he is well-versed."

Scarcely had Lao-Tsu spoken those words than Siu-Kia picked up his staff and got to his feet.

"Master, I shall depart right away. I must hurry, for the country about which you are speaking seems to me to be very distant. I've never heard mention of it and it might be that my entire lifetime is insufficient for me to reach it."

"Perhaps, in the way," said Lao-Tsu, "you can obtain some information about the perfect sages, the inheritors of the lost secrets of ancient races, who live in the vicinity of the Kuen-Lun Mountains, the central point of the earth, in a hidden community, and direct humankind by the effort of their intelligence. I do not know whether it is possible to recognize them. I do not know whether, like the sage of India, they smile benevolently, or whether, like the seeker of numbers beyond the lands of the West, they have a gaze full of curiosity. If it is given to you to see them, however, return to me in haste, for it is in their midst that the heart of the true light exists."

Siu-Kia left the Palace of the spirits of the Earth and drew away rapidly, for he had thousands and thousands of tchang to travel, and his first journey had enabled him to glimpse the immensity of the world.

"I am very old," Lao-Tsu had said to him, while accompanying him as far as he fallen cypress.

"See you soon!" Siu-Kia had shouted to him, from a distance.

But he was never to return.

Mong-Pi and the Dog

Confucius traveled. He went from country to country, retaining the hope of gaining the mind of a king with his ideas and moralizing the kingdom by that means, and then the entire Chinese Empire. But the kings only listened to him distractedly. As he had grown older he had become more rigorous in the principles of his morality, more demanding in regard to the manifestations of an obligatory virtue. He had a concern for justice o the highest degree, but he only conceived it clad in a girdle of ennui. He professed the most sincere love for his neighbor, but that love had an armor of chastity, obligations and rules that rendered it almost as redoubtable as hatred.

The king of Soung received Confucius with great honors. He was a fat man who thought of nothing but pleasure and nourishment. He was at table finishing his meal while Confucius spoke. The sage had reached the rules of abstinence that rendered the spirit freer. The King went to sleep just in time to avoid hearing an indirect reprimand addressed to him. Confucius was offended by his slumber and quit the kingdom of Soung.

The King of Tcheng was a great hunter. He received Confucius in his garden. He was holding his bow in his hand and his horse was beside him, because he was about to leave for the hunt.

Confucius nevertheless explained to him in the slightest detail his method of government. The King gazed obstinately at the wild geese that were flying in a circle overhead. He interrupted Confucius to ask him what the significance was of that unaccustomed circular flight of wild geese, which, at that time of the year, should have been heading northwards.

Confucius replied dryly that he occupied himself with the mores of humans and not those of geese. The King of Tcheng leapt on to his horse and departed. Confucius was obliged to do likewise.

The years passed. He had numerous disciples in the towns through which he passed. He spread his doctrine with an untiring perseverance. It was easily understood by all the average and educated men who collected it respectfully. But that was not enough for Confucius, who dreamed of the foremost position in the Empire, not by virtue of personal ambition but in order to enable his moral concepts to triumph. He became somewhat embittered. In the end, he became discouraged. He blamed the decadence of the times. He decided to return to his homeland.

In the mountainous massif to the north of the kingdom of Lou, his chariot, drawn by an ox, and the little troop of his disciples, mounted on donkeys, were stopped by a troop of brigands who held travelers to ransom. But the brigands recognized Confucius, whose celebrity was immense and whose poverty was legendary. They did not demand anything of him and those who accompanied him, but they obligingly gave him information regarding a short cut that permitted the avoidance of the slope of a sheer mountain.

Just as the two groups were about to separate, Confucius almost uttered a cry of surprise. He had just recognized one of the brigands, who was particularly ugly and ragged, as Mong-Pi. Laden with weapons of ridiculous grandeur, Mong-Pi was staring at him intensely, and there as a mixture of joy and extravagance in his gaze. He burst out laughing and took a few strides toward Confucius, his arms extended, and causing the two large sabers hanging from his belt to clash.

"I can't let my brother pass by without hugging him in my arms," he said.

Confucius shivered. He did not know fear, but what was scandalous seemed to him to be worse than death.

His disciples were about to rush forward, but Mong-Pi, having reached Confucius, bent down, seized in his arms the wretched yellow dog that had become Confucius' faithful and beloved companion, kissed its soiled muzzle several times, with a fraternal tenderness, and then set it down again.

Instead of growling, the yellow dog yapped amicably, and when Confucius' chariot was on the point of disappearing around a bend in the road, it turned round several times toward the silhouette of Mong-Pi, who made it a sign as if he were regretful.

A little later, Confucius leaned toward Tsu-Lou, who was beside him in the chariot and sad to him, sighing: "I'm saddened by having seen Mong-Pi among those brigands. That's where the deregulation of passions and the disorder of life lead."

He remained silent for a long time and then said:

"I don't know why Mong-Pi called the dog his brother and why the dog didn't bark when he took him in his arms. There is, in truth, a similarity between those two stray creatures, but what is entirely inexplicable is that such creatures can attach themselves to me, and that I have a weakness for them."

The Death of Ki-Keou

On the hill that overlooks Tseou, holding in her hand the skeleton of a lute devoid of strings, an old woman was running through the snow. It was Ki-Keou, the patient, solitary spouse of Confucius.

Because of her lack of filial piety, she had been relegated to Tseou and she had grown old there in the lightless dusk of simple souls who have lost their ideal.

She was running quickly because she knew that her life was short. Confucius had announced his return a long time ago. She had hoped for that return and had dreaded it. Then she had ceased to believe in it. But this evening, there could no longer be any doubt. A disciple had come to bring the news. Confucius was sleeping scarcely a hundred li from Tcheou and would be there the next day.

For years, Ki-Keou had no longer had a clear consciousness of things. Everything was confused in her mind: the travels of Confucius, the departure of her son Pe-Yu, the face of the old guardian Tchang—but she knew that it was necessary for her to play one more time with her dead lute in the uncultivated garden of her father's abandoned house. By virtue of her own timidity and absence of will she had put off its realization incessantly, and now a great terror had seized her of no longer being able to find herself again in the pathways of her youth at the intermediary hour in which the sun has not yet risen.

In the white, cold night, past the cedars and frangipanes, she moved as if in a dream, sometimes bumping into funerary stones that protruded from beneath the snow along the route. Finally, in the depths of the valley, she saw a little dark patch.

Since her father's death the old house had been uninhabited. The wind had taken possession of it and had dispersed the roof. The rain and the sun had accomplished their slow work. The open windows were like punctured eyes, and a flapping door uttered a perpetual groan.

Ki-Keou had no difficulty getting into the garden, because the enclosing wall, which had already had breaches in the days of her childhood, was now almost completely destroyed. But she recognized neither the silhouettes of the trees nor the contours of the bushes. The garden had changed, as she had. The years had brought the exuberant folly of nature into it.

At every step that Ki-Keou took, searching for the place where she had once sat, a thorn caught her robe as if a nocturnal demon were tugging at it. She knew that the Tao-Niu, sorceresses associated with the spirit of weasels, had the custom of haunting solitary houses and lying in wait for passers-by in order to drag them through secret corridors into subterranean halls where they drank their blood. She remembered that on winter nights, an enormous frog of terrifying aspect emerged from a nearby pond and strode through the valley on legs like those of a wading bird. Only someone who possessed the Che-Kan-Tang stone and threw it at it had the power to make it return under water. She watched to see whether she might perceive before her the old man Fong-Pe, who has an ermine robe and two waterskins made of mouse-hide behind his back and is attached by a silken thread to the star Ki; his breath is filled with icicles as sharp as darts which transpierce anyone he encounters. And she put her arms in front of her face because in every flurry of snow there is a fantastic heron that punctures the eyes of humans with a dull porphyry beak.

There was a howl in the distance, and then another in a different direction, and then many howls much closer. Among the stones of the wall Ki-Keou saw the red eyes of a pack of wolves that were forming a circle around her.

Then she began to play, to make the absent strings of the lute vibrate, because she thought she had perceived an auroral tint in the snow, which was only the reflection of the moon wandering vaguely in the depths of the horizon. Passionately, she played the music that had no sounds, and she ended up forgetting the Tao-Niu, the terrifying frog and he old man Fong-Pe at the end of his silken thread. She played for a long time in the snowy darkness, until her fingers were numbed by cold and he contact of invisible strings.

Perhaps the music that is only dreamed by an insensate soul has an action on wild beasts. The wolves with red eyes remained motionless behind the stones, and listened to what they could not hear.

With an inexorable slowness the sun insinuated a diffuse light into the snow. A light breeze shook the tall cedars like wads of tinder. The wolves glided with felted steps. A human shadow advanced along the road.

And in the hyperborean enchantment of the landscape, the lute with true strings of the musician Mong-Pi made the icy air of the past vibrate. Had he come to find in memory the first image of beauty? Had he heard the music of the soul at a distance? He was there. He played while the globe of the rising sun emerged from the milky mists, pouring its violet blood into the fleecy sky.

Then, by force of habit, he leaned toward the garden suddenly painted with flames, and he saw, leaning in a tree trunk, a beautiful frozen corpse, as white as a crystal statue.

The Death of Confucius' Dog

Confucius had the funeral of his wife Ki-Keou celebrated in accordance with the most ancient and most complicated ritual. He installed himself in Tscou. But bad days had come. Successively, he lost his disciples Tsu-Lou and Yan-Yuan, whom he cherished infinitely, and experienced great grief in consequence. He lost his confidence in the duration of his doctrine and suffered even more from that. He had just completed his compilation of the canonical books and his redaction of Spring and Autumn, but with the end of his labor he saw his faith in his eternity die.

He had found on arrival the house in Tseou in a disorder so great that he had not succeeded in triumphing over it. The garden, in particular, saddened him by virtue of the wild character that it had taken on for lack of care. Camphor trees, which once grew there in small numbers, had multiplied with an extraordinary exuberance; they caused their white flowers to rain down on him, and, as their wood has the property of giving off sparks by night, Confucius saw singular gleams when he went for a walk, which he found shocking. There were also rubber plants with excessively thick foliage, whose stems exuded an overabundant milk, bamboos that cleaved the pathways like lances, and a sycamore that had developed in a fashion so unexpected that there was a sort of insolence in the enormity of its trunk.

So, though Confucius, *nature presents herself thus under the aspect of disorder; disorder is her intimate substance and triumphs as soon as once ceases to struggle to limit it. Perhaps my work will be like this garden. I have laboriously rediscovered, reorganized and reconstituted the four sacred books of the Empire of China. In the vegetation of the poetry of the ancients I have cut down the weed of enthusiasm, and torn out the nettle of metaphysical reverie. I have hoed the poetic and moral field of the old masters of the times of Yao and Chun. But when I am dead, foolish exaggerations and parasitical lyricisms will doubtless grow everywhere, and people will no longer recognize the straight paths that lead to the good.*

Confucius had a further chagrin. His dog died. He was accustomed to that companion, which, with the years, had become mangy and lame. He mourned it and wanted it to be buried with honor, as the rites prescribed, with its feet turned in a westerly direction. He chose a sheltered spot in the garden and had Tchang wrap the body in a thick rush mat, sewn up in order that the earth would not touch it.

The garden was only separated from the road by a lattice fence and while Tchang was next to the hole, sewing the lame dog into the mat, Mong-Pi went past and stopped to look.

It was only a little later that Confucius recognized Mong-Pi leaning on the fence. Tchang and Tsu-Kong, who had participated in the funeral rite with surprise, had already returned to the house.

Confucius sometimes thought about Mong-Pi, as the shepherd thinks of a stray lamb when there is a storm. He felt pity for him; he would have linked to bring him back to the good road, which was his own.

He approached him and exhorted him with all his power of persuasion. He would like nothing better than to do something for him. He would take responsibility for obtaining an honorable and appropriate position if Mong-Pi promised to mend his ways. He would strive to forget the company in which he had found him in the mountains of Lou. He would not think about the horrible actions that he might have accomplished. It is never too late to behave well. From the bottom of his heart he forgave him.

But Mong-Pi was visibly distracted. He was following his own train of thought. He seemed to wake up at the mention of forgiveness. His eyes moistened.

"Oh yes," he said, "I forgive you, because you loved your dog and had him buried like a man."

The Death of Confucius

Having killed a creature of bizarre form in a nearby forest, peasants brought it to Confucius, and he recognized it as a unicorn. As he examined it curiously he saw that there was a silk ribbon attached to the animal's horn. That ribbon seemed very old. Confucius recalled that his mother had often told him that on the morning of his conception, as she was walking on her own, a unicorn had emerged from a juniper bush and she had wound a silk ribbon around its horn.

As those rare and very shy animals do not often wear ribbons as ornaments, Confucius thought that the unicorn that had just been killed was the one that had once approached his mother, and he saw it as a presage of his imminent death.

But he was not frightened by that. He was seventy-three years old; he had never feared death. The regularity of death in striking all men without exception, the quantity of ceremonies, genuflections and rites with which the ancients had enveloped it, and the mystery that it had been able to retain regarding its origin and its goals, all rendered death respectable. And the perfect order that obliged all the living to lie down in tombs in an ineluctable manner appeared to him to be full of grandeur and necessity.

He judged nature to reasonable to prepare for humans, when life had ceased, the surprise of secret and unmerited suffering; but he could not help meditating on the minute when his spirit, having quit its old familiar body, would perch, despoiled and disorientated, on a tablet in the hall of the ancestors.

That night, he could not savor the repose of sleep. In the end, fatigued by turning over on his bed, he got up and went down into the garden.

It was the eighteenth day of the fourth moon of the year Yen-Siu, and the air was blue-tinted and transparent. The stars gave the impression of being veiled and very close together. A great immobility held the trees in suspense. The ambient mildness was such that it seemed that the foliage, the trunks, and even the soil, were velveted.

Confucius perceived that daylight was about to appear and he was gripped by a mysterious desire to play the lute. He was not stopped by the idea that the hour was not appropriate for making music. He went back up to his bedroom and came back which his old instrument.

He wanted to play the tune composed by the sage Wen-Wang, which was one of the first that has master Siang had made him play when he had taught him music. He did indeed play the first few notes; but he went astray. Another tune arrived involuntarily beneath his fingers, and a slight intoxication took possession of his soul. He took a few steps, and a rubber leaf brushed his face like a plant caress. He perceived, very close to him, a bird that was looking at him fearlessly. He would have been able to touch it by extending his hand.

Something winged and magical enveloped Confucius as he was playing the lute. He was improvising now and he slid down a supernatural slope. As if a curtain were raised before his eyes, he saw things that he had never seen before. He raised his head and discovered above him the immense sky and the innumerable stars.

He had never had the knowledge of such a great miracle of colors, in a sea of blue so tender, behind a veil of mist so delicate. Never had the stars of the Dragon had that magnificent redness. He had never noticed before the harmonious clarity of the Great Bear, and the melancholy with which the star Kiao, which is opposite the sun, inclines toward the edge of the horizon when the latter is about to appear. For the first time he was struck by the eternal tenderness of Tien-Yi, unique in the sky, like a fixed gaze of which no eyelid interrupts the gleam.

How he loved the stars! He raised his arms toward them in a sign of adoration. He wanted to live while gazing at them. But they were gradually fading away. They were escaping him by paling. The daylight arrived with its inexorable regularity and Confucius began to desire with all his might a delay of the light, a rupture of the universal equilibrium, a solar extravagance that would have given him another hour of contemplation.

He went back to the house at a slow pace. Oh, let night return quickly! But the stars and their extravagance were not to appear for him again.

He climbed the stairs with difficulty. To his great surprise he crossed the path of all sorts of people, who saluted him obsequiously, although he had not seen them for years. There were important functionaries, literates, magistrates, virtuous fathers of families, all those he had loved, on whom he had leaned, all those who had adopted is doctrines and had defended them. There were quantities of them, come from who know where, who had invaded his room, and Confucius recognized many of them who had been dead for a long time, and whose burials he had witnessed. All of them had grave and grateful faces and were dressed in sumptuous costumes. They seemed to be accomplishing a ceremonial and they were saluting, saluting incessantly.

Confucius had a desire to ask them whether they had looked carefully at the sky and whether they had seen the magical blues of the constellations, the greens the color of divine jade, and the delicate blood shed by the stars Sin and Tsan, but he dared not. He could see clearly that the eyes of all the good functionaries, all the eyes rendered myopic by narrow duties, limited filial pieties, and fearful virtues, had never had sufficient power to contemplate the true sky full of the flame of the stars.

He did not say anything, and went back to bed.

And he saw new functionaries appear, new magistrates and new fathers of families, whom he did not know, and he understood that they were not yet born, that they were his future disciples in ages to come. All of them saluted him, all of them rendered homage to him, all of them had the same admiration for his doctrines, the same incapacity to see the sky, and he was the master of that virtuous and myopic population.

He turned his head away and looked upwards. The ceiling appeared to him to be lower than usual, strangely heavy, and on the ceiling there were innumerable moral sentences, which were those he had enunciated during his life. What sage truths! What good teachings! But he would have liked to be able not to see them. He would gladly have exchanged them for the smallest fragment of celestial blue. The precepts glided and grew, and multiplied, and it was his entire soul that Confucius contemplated in those rigorous, measured, reasonable texts, which were to be the instruction of humankind.

He extended his arms to chase those images away. But then the phantoms gave the impression of believing that Confucius was returning their salutation and they inclined with more ardor toward him, bent their backs ceremoniously like their conceptions of hierarchies, they shook their denuded skulls like imaginations devoid of poetry, and it was in the midst of ten thousand salutations and ten thousand ritual genuflections that Confucius entered into the lethargy from which he was only to emerge through the portal of death.

The Disappearance of Lao-Tsu

One evening, Lao-Tsu sensed a great solitude enveloping him, and he understood that his disciple Siu-Kia had died at some point in the immensity of his voyage.

He was very old and his legs scarcely supported him, but his mind was developing incessantly and becoming more clairvoyant and more active as his body became heavier and more immobile.

One evening he had a singularly clear vision of a valley of the earth, in a circle of high mountains.

In the middle snaked a placid river where lotuses flourished, so large that he had never seen their like. There were superimposed blocks of stone that had the vague appearance of houses. Cedars sheltered them and those cedars formed little woods separated from one another by terrains devoid of vegetation and strewn with white pebbles. The entire valley was enclosed by walls that were almost sheer, and could only communicate with the rest of the world by a single path that Lao-Tsu saw in the flank of one of the walls, which was so narrow that even a thin and very agile man would have difficulty passing along it.

One cedar taller than the rest was in the middle of the valley, and the sole indication that implied that the place was inhabited was a circular stone bench ornamented with sculptures, which surrounded the enormous trunk of the cedar.

An impression of serenity emanated from that mute place, and Lao-Tsu thought that it was there that the perfect men must live, the guardians of the lost wisdom and the hidden directors of humankind, of whose existence he knew by virtue of the most ancient tradition on the earth.

Into that valley my two brothers will come, Lao-Tsu said to himself, *the one from India and the one from the land where there are marble temples on the shore of the blue sea. It's there that I must go.*

Now, an ox escaped from some herd had been wandering for some time in the wild part of the garden that surrounded the Palace of the Spirits of the Earth. An amity had been born between the ox and the sage, and it was on the back of that animal that Lao-Tsu decided to undertake his journey.

He departed. He headed toward the Hang-Kou pass, by which Siu-Kia had left China. He advanced slowly, and along his path, everyone was astonished to see such a prodigiously old man going forth on the back of an ox toward the unknown regions of the earth.

His renown was great throughout the Empire, for wisdom filters by unknown paths into the souls of men and truth does not need many words in order to be heard. The governors offered Lao-Tsu hospitality in their palaces and anchorites alerted by shepherds descended from the mountains in order to see him go past. Lao-Tsu only accepted the gift of a few grains of rice and an amicable word and followed his route.

It was shortly before arriving at the Hang-Kou pass that he let himself slide down from the ox that was carrying him and lay unconscious, while the latter bellowed sadly.

The mandarin In-Hi, who commanded that region of the frontier, had learned of his passage and came to meet him with an escort. He took him to his palace and cared for him. He was a literate with a subtle mind who knew and admired the philosophy of Lao-Tsu.

When the sage had recovered, In-Hi strove to dissuade him from continuing his journey. Autumn had arrived. Beyond the Hang-Kou pass, where the Empire ended, savage and limitless solitudes extended. How could those deserts be traversed? But Lao-Tsu's resolution was made. He would go in search of the Kuen-Lun Mountains, in which the mysterious valley of the perfect men ought to be, where there was a stone bench around a great cedar, which was the goal of his journey.

To gain time and let the winter pass, In-Hi asked Lao-Tsu, as a favor, to write a summary of his doctrines for him.

And it was only in order to thank In-Hi for his hospitality that Lao-Tsu summarized in the *Book of the Way and of Love* the essential verities that he had meditated during his life.

But when the book was finished and spring had come, Lao-Tsu decided to resume his route. He refused the escort that In-Hi wanted to give him. He also refused the horses that would have allowed him to cross the desert regions more rapidly, where travelers died of thirst and hallucinations in the sands. He preferred his faithful ox, because of the amity that united them.

It was at the Hang-Kou pass that living men saw Lao-Tsu for the last time.

Ever westwards! The old sage traveled during uniform days, under an increasingly ardent sun, content with a handful of rice and a few mouthfuls of water every evening. Then the rice he was carrying ran out, and the water-skins that were suspended by his sides were empty. The air begin to burn and blinding reverberations made Lao-Tsu believe that he was marching over an immense golden mirror, enclosed beneath a lid of light. The ox started to walk very slowly, as if it were centenarian itself, until the moment when it collapsed and died.

In a westerly direction were the Kuen-Lun Mountains and the valley of the great lotuses on the placid river! In a westerly direction Lao-Tsu continued his route. After an entire day, he could still see the body of the dead ox not very far away.

Lao-Tsu sat down on the sand in order to take a little rest. The sun was setting, but it had the color of blood and disappeared in an ashen, leaden, metallic sky. From the infinity of the horizon came a bellowing wind, and that wind transported great columns of sand like mobile mountains.

Lao-Tsu thought that they were real mountains and that the Kuen-Lun Mountains must doubtless be among them. He sighed in thinking that they were so far away. But then, in the falling night, he perceived that the mountains were being transported toward him, and at the same time, he saw two other travelers who were marching in the sand and were showing him with their hands the highest summit in the moving chain.

He recognized them immediately. One came from India and the other from the shore of those distant seas of which he only knew the bright color. They were his two brothers in spirit, who had come into the world to accomplish the same mission. He wanted to call to them and he was surprised to know their names. Pythagoras, the Buddha and Lao-Tsu were together.

He stood up. He felt singularly light. Night had fallen on all sides of the horizon, and great avalanches of sand descended upon the corporeal form of the old man Lao-Tsu. But his spirit was no longer inhabiting that form. The sage of China, between the sage of India and the sage of Greece, penetrated into the secret valley where their equals were waiting for them, into the midst of the radiant clarity of the spiritual universe.

THE MYSTERY OF THE TIGER

PART ONE

The Opium-Den in Singapore

In the old quarter of Singapore there is a street with two slopes, which form a camel's hump. At the summit of that hump, among the leprous houses crushed against one another, there is a grossly-sculpted door, the upper part of which represents a feline face, and which, because of that emblem, is known as the Door of the Tiger.

One of the two slopes of the street descends toward an abandoned basin of the port, to which unusable sampans and half-dead junks are relegated, and at the spot where the hump-backed street ends on the narrow quay, a sharp stone emerges from the ground, named by the Chinese and Malay population the Shark's Tooth.

In truth, it is nowhere else but in that street, where the images of animals are everywhere, that I, the son of a dealer in stuffed beasts who had become an intrepid tamer of living ones, should have seen the first shadow of my astonishing destiny extending over my soul.

"It's at the Door of the Tiger," said Ali the Macassar, who knows the men of Singapore as perfectly as the forests of the archipelago, and who claims that the former are as savage as the latter, when I asked him to indicate the most colorful opium-den in the city to me. In the corrupt quarter that envelops the water of the old basin in decomposition like a leper's crown, there was, according to Ali the Macassar, only one unique point, one threshold to cross: the Door of the Tiger.

"The opium-den is worthy of the man who keeps it," he added. "There's a man for you."

The man was a wretched obsequious Chinaman, like all those I knew. He nearly broke himself in two in order to bow on seeing Europeans come through the Door of the Tiger.

Yes, I went through that door; I went up a sticky staircase, and I mingled with the most abject riffraff of Singapore, in order to please a fool, my cousin from Goa, who was making his fist business trip to the island and wanted, he said, to learn about everything—as if a fool by birth can ever learn anything.

Certainly, when I had penetrated into that low-ceilinged room in which the odor of opium mingled with a nauseating odor of human sweat, there was still time, and I should have obeyed my instinct. I should have rained down blows of my whip on the recumbent Malays and Chinese; I should have thrown them over the camel's hump and I should have threatened my stupid cousin with a similar correction. There would have been no risk. No one would have dared measure himself against me. They would all have fled the moment they recognized me.

Now, I had been recognized. As I went in, a voice pronounced: "That's Rafael Graaf, the famous animal-tamer." And it was the hint of admiration that I perceived in those syllables that attenuated my anger and my disgust for the fallen beings that I had just seen.

The whispers fell silent; I surprised in the heads of the extended smokers a few slight inclinations, a few fluttering eyelids marking surprise or respect, and I went meekly to lie down on a mat beside a little lamp, which the proprietor of the establishment indicated to me. For it is vanity that directs almost all of our actions. Then the events had to unfold, the characters had to appear.

Sometimes, when one reads a book, one finds the subject-matter summarized in a few lines at the beginning of the work, with an indication of the mystery that will occupy the mind throughout the reading. In the same way, hazard often places at a beginning in life a synthetic scene in which the characters come together who are to influence you subsequently, and in which the enigma is posed that will make you live and die. The fool was only an instrument, the Door of the Tiger merely the threshold of a path, for it was necessary that the goal should be attained.

"Did you know that it was Buddhist monks who first brought opium to China?"

"I didn't know that."

"A treatise on morality whose translation goes back to the Tang dynasty affirms it. The same treatise attributes to Buddha himself the invention of the pipe and the method of preparing the poppy-juice."

I burst into ostentatious laughter on hearing those stupid words murmured close at hand, and as the man who had spoken did not seem to perceive my hilarity, I guffawed again noisily and put an expression of lofty scorn on my face.

The man had only darted a single clear and profound glance at me, in which there was neither curiosity nor respect, and he resumed rolling a brown pellet with minute care, as if my presence not far away from him was of no importance.

The vague light of the lamp next to which he was stationed permitted me to see his features. He was neither Chinese nor Malay—perhaps Hindu. He expressed himself in English with a slight accent and a singsong quality in his voice. I thought on reflection, that that he was of the Mongol type, and I had a desire to pick a nasty quarrel with him, to stretch out my foot and kick him with it, or to throw my hat at the lamp and knock it over.

At that moment, however, my attention was distracted. I had the sensation that the face of a European woman sometimes loomed up at the back of the room. I thought I glimpsed large bright eyes full of a delight of curiosity and the delicate curve of an amber neck. A European woman in that dive—was it possible?

The man continued speaking, without paying any heed to me and I heard him say: "Men are all the more unhappy as they experience more hatred, and all the happier as they love more."

And, replying to someone who as facing him and whom I had not heard, he added: "Yes, develop love in oneself. But it's difficult. Opium, which is the intelligence of the vegetable kingdom, can help us in that. There are other plants and other secrets, but people don't know them. In the same way that there are several qualities of thoughts, there are juices of herbs and roots with different properties.

"In Mexico, on the moisture of stones, grows the plant peyote, which gives clairvoyance of the future. In the forests of Siam, and there alone, one finds a red graminaceous plant that procures a trance state and aids the separation of the soul and the body. By means of opium, absorbed moderately, a man is set on the path where he discovers his relationship with the animal species. And there are also the grating of certain insects, and the song of certain birds, like the rohi-rohi,[1] in which, if we know how to listen, we can find information about means of self-development."

My cousin was not smoking for the first time. I saw that by the skill with which he rolled the pellets of opium into cones, and the satisfaction that he allowed to spread over his face as he launched large puffs of smoke at the ceiling.

He held out a pipe to me. I shrugged my shoulders to signify that opium could not exert any effect on my robust temperament. But then he smiled maliciously and I thought that he was supposing internally that I feared some effect of the drug on the clarity of my ideas. I hastened to smoke the

---

[1] All references to a bird identified by this name appear to originate from an account of travels in Oceania collected by Albert Montémont and published in 1836. He does not give sufficient detail for the modern name of the species to be determined with exactitude.

pipe that he held out to me. My aspirations were awkward, and my cousin's smile remained malicious.

Now, nothing is as irritating as the smile of a fool.

I wanted to show that a man of my stripe is not modified by any absorption whatsoever, and I invited my cousin to prepare me a few successive pipes, which I aspired in a single draught, and from which I experienced neither pleasure nor displeasure.

"I prefer elephant-hunting in the forests of Borneo," I said.

I had come back from a hunting trip to Celebes and Borneo, and I was a past master in the art of approaching a elephant and firing from a few paces away.

"The more intelligent an animal is," I added, "the more pleasure there is in killing it."

It was only because my mouth was dry that I did not spit in the direction of the Mongol, whose clear gaze I had sensed posed upon me. I contented myself with scratching myself forcefully and wrapping my alpaca jacket around me to show that I was apprehensive of the vermin that might be crawling on the bodies of my neighbors.

My cousin was really only interested in the various varieties of tortoiseshell in which his father traded in Goa. In spite of that, I listed a considerable number of my cynegetic exploits or him, suddenly being gripped by a desire for stories, a desire to be heard with admiration retracing dangerous adventures.

Time passed. I deliberately spoke loudly enough to trouble the tranquility of the other smokers. Some got up and left, without, however, daring to allow their discontentment to show. The European woman that I thought I had perceived in the gloom appeared again, with the same expression of gaiety and curiosity on her face. Several times I nearly called out to her, asking her to come and lay down beside me in order to show me how she was made—but ideas were crowding my brain in abundance, and I continued talking to my cousin, who was not listening to me.

The notion of time disappeared within me and the whole night went by like an instant under the low ceiling with the thick odor of opium, the odor of human beings and I know not what of pepper, putrefaction and spring coming through the open window from the port.

From the individual whose calm features were insupportable to me, I only heard one more phrase, which seemed to me to be devoid of importance:

"The old law of Manu says: the man who has killed a cat, a blue jay, a mongoose or a lizard must retire to the heart of the forest and devote his life to the beasts until he is purified."

I did not know what the old law of Manu was, and did not care.

My soul was placid, all that was floating there, like a boat on a lake, was the necessity of offending that smoker with the Mongol face.

Now, as the air began to whiten by virtue of the approach of morning, a lizard, one of those domestic lizards that live in human houses, slid among the recumbent forms, slowly and fearlessly. It brushed me, and then drew away; and I saw it circling around the hateful smoker.

Then my early were struck by an imperceptible whistle. That whistle departed from the man's lips, and the lizard, on hearing it, without being dazzled by the light of the lamp, drew closer to him, and I even saw a thin hand, a hand with excessively long fingers, whose form was singularly repugnant to me, caress the lizard's head with a kind of amour.

The charmed beast circled another two or three times, came back to be caressed, and set forth again.

Like a spring, my foot extended. There was a slight crack. The tail of the crushed lizard made two or three spasms, and I experienced the plenitude procured by a necessary action that one has just accomplished.

I had to close my eyelids for a few seconds. When I opened them again, there was a lamp not far away, between two empty mats. The body of the lizard was no longer at the end of my foot. Someone had taken the little cadaver away.

I started to snigger.

"Perhaps that imbecile has taken it away to bury it."

I shook my cousin.

He came out behind me, shivering. I had the sensation of laughter, as bright as a string of pears, resonating in the shadows and I thought I saw once again, as I crossed the threshold, the upper body of a woman rising up. But it was too late to pay any attention to it. Above all, I desired to breathe pure air.

Outside, the freshness was exquisite. A large torn sail was flapping at the bottom of the camel's hump. The first cries of the agar-agar merchants were audible in the distance, in the side-streets. I stretched myself. I would have liked to fight someone. I lashed the air with my whip. A man should always carry a whip. The opium had definitely had no effect on me. How strong I was! What a joy I experienced in being alive!

The Cobra and the Toad

I have always been passionately fond of making animals suffer. As a child, I tore the wings off flies and made them walk across the sand of the verandah where I was playing. At ten, I made myself a bow with sharp arrows made of sandalwood, with which I targeted oxen and dogs, which fled on seeing me as if at the sight of a redoubtable monster.

In those days, the island of Singapore was not yet entirely cultivated, as it is today, and the forest struggled there with the hastily-constructed cottages and the squares of tilled ground. It was in the confines of plantations, with a few boys of my own age, that I went forth to slake my thirst for animal death. Very quickly, I became skillful at shooting the bow, but it was when my father made me a present of a Devisme rifle that my veritable exploits began.[2]

I had obtained a prize for religious instruction and the pastor, who had just dined with us, had declared that although I was ignorant of everything else, I had an innate knowledge of God, which is the essential thing. For I had had, since the earliest age, a profound scorn for books and those who read them, a scorn that I have retained while advancing in life.

Experience has taught me that there are no intelligent and useful men except those who are rebels against education and turn all their faculties toward action.

I pride myself on having thrown on the dung-heap, as well as a Bible that I never opened, the few English and Portuguese books that lingered in our house. Never read anything! What a powerful force for the character! I prevented my em-

---

[2] The reference to a rifle made by the Parisian gunsmith Jean-Louis Devisme, who was active in the mid-19th century, and subsequence references in the chapter, including the one to the Indian Mutiny of 1857, establish that this part of the memoir refers to events in the early 1860s.

ployees from going in search of the *Malacca Chronicle* when it arrived on Sunday, and for my part, I had historic events related to me orally, notably the Sepoy revolt of 1857, in order not to be influenced myself by the stupidity of those who write.

The Devisme rifle was marvelous. I shot birds in flight and shattered the heads of serpents at a hundred paces. I received instruction from the best hunters in Singapore—who, I perceived later, knew nothing about hunting—and at the age of fifteen I lay in ambush with them on my first tiger hunt.

I can say that I am one of the most courageous of all the men it has been given to me to know. A courageous man can be recognized by the capacity he has for admitting the fears he has experienced. I have been afraid, to be sure, but I have said so, I have said it aloud, if not to others, which might have harmed me, at least to myself, which is the important thing. By virtue of that knowledge of my own fear, I have become courageous, and I have accomplished the exploits that had rendered me famous from Borneo to the coasts of Coromandel, and even further.

That was the time when the number of tigers was beginning to diminish on the island of Singapore. The Resident organized hunts continually, and as he was a friend of my father I was invited to them, and even became the principal actor. I remember that when the French warship *Amazone* called in at the port, it was agreed during a dinner that each officer would shoot his tiger, and that it would be me, in spite of my youth, who would organize all the hunts.

All that is of no importance and I only say it for the record and in order to make known my extraordinary precocity for killing wild animals. I hasten to add that the French officers quit Singapore without having been able to fire a rifle-shot, and that it was only later that it was given to me to kill my first tiger. For those creature have such a prodigious ability to conceal themselves that even in places where they are abundant, like Malacca and Java, one can hunt them for a long time without ever encountering them, only to find oneself, one evening, face to face with one of them when one least expects it. But I shall talk about the mores of those mysterious creatures anyway, and the information I obtained from that acquaintance

The first tigers I saw were stuffed, in my father's warehouses. They were of all sizes and all provenances. There were black tigers from the Himalaya, which are called black although they are more yellow than the others, because they are believed to be incarnations of a Hindu goddess who is black herself and is called, I believe, Kali.

There were those from Bengal, which have exactly fifteen black rings on their tails, on a white background, and those from Mongolia, which have exactly twelve rings on a yellow background.

There were those from Siam, which have elongated mouths, those from Malacca, which are gigantic, and those from Zanzibar, which are ridiculously small because they are not tigers but simple panthers disguised as tigers.

There were also all kinds of wild animals: crocodiles, snakes, Persian lions, hyenas, sometimes an anteater, and all the varieties of Asian birds of prey. They occupied an immense glazed gallery juxtaposed with our dwelling, which overlooked the garden.

I often looked at their silhouettes while playing, and I remember that an internal force obliged me to slip into the gallery to pluck out a feather here and there, poke a muzzle with a pointed stick, or tug an ear, to insult the impotent enemy.

The proprietor of a menagerie who owed money to my father died insolvent, and the latter inherited his animals and his equipment.

While the proceedings lasted, he spent much more money on the nourishment of the wild beasts and a young elephant than the value of his debt. The desire to recover the sums advanced gave him the idea of supplementing his commerce in skins and stuffed beasts with a commerce in living animals. The commencement of his large fortune dates from that.

In his immense gardens, which extended along the border of the Chinese quarter, he had a series of cages installed, before which, twice a year, when the boats from Macao and Shanghai arrived, filed the great Chinese merchants who supplied the menageries of China. For those people, who seem at first glance purely commercial and limited in their conceptions, have an extraordinary curiosity regarding all animal species, and I believe that the most curious zoological collections in the world are found in the homes of certain rich Mandarins of Canton and Peking. I note in passing that the greatest successes I have obtained in my exhibitions of wild animals were in the latter cities, and that has contributed greatly to proving to me the intelligence of the Chinese, which I had initially misunderstood.

It was soon necessary to transform the gardens completely. In addition to the cages there were aviaries, sheds, huts, ditches, hangars, pens, stables, habitations on piles in an artificial pond, and basins surrounded by trellises for the lizards. A kind of town was instructed, with its streets and its ramparts, its perches and its dovecots, where the dwellings were adapted to the character and mores of different inhabitants: mammals, pachyderms, solidungulates, plantigrades, bimanes, ruminants, herbivores and carnivores.

It was not long after those transformations that the terrible events occurred that contributed to augmenting my hatred for the beasts whose life and death made me rich.

My mother was a saint. All mothers are saints, in principle, but I believe that my mother were more so than the others. She was also Portuguese, and had been abducted at an early age by a long-haul captain.

That captain, a certain Pinto, who gave her the marks of an ardent amour, installed her in Singapore in a delightful villa in the English quarter and went to deliver various cargoes to Batavia and Madras. He never came back, and my mother never heard any further mention of him. After a year, desperate and penniless, she was wondering what would become of her when she met my father and married him. She knew a perfect happiness with him, but she could never forbid herself a naïve admiration for that Pinto, who disappeared so mysteriously. She often told me stories full of fantasy that she made up about him, and unwittingly communicated her admiration to me.

When I was older and was better able to understand things, my admiration for the seducer who had dared to take a young woman from Lisbon and deposit her in Singapore without any further concern for her changed to anger. I would have liked to meet him and have a word with him. But my mother, in the purity of her angelic soul, did not bear any grudge against him.

The sanctity of my mother was expressed physically by an extreme facility in blushing. She had conserved an extremely fair skin tone, which became rosy if anyone spoke to her a little abruptly.

That facility in blushing contributed more than a little to augment the great filial love I had for my mother. I had always considered that sanguine particularity as the external sign of a noble elevation of sentiments, which distinguishes the true elite. That sign is, however, very inconvenient for those who bear it. I received it from my mother, and in spite of the powerful tempering of my soul and the Asiatic sun that burned my skin, an unexpected remark was often sufficient to make the blood rise to me face.

My mother, in her sanctity, suffered from not participating sufficiently in the responsibilities of her husband's profession. She wanted to play a role in the education of the animals, and that was what doomed her, for one is doomed by one's virtue as surely as by one's folly.

A Malay having brought us a toad of unusual proportions, which came from the island of Komodo, where all the monstrous species are found, my mother, in her generosity, took it into her head to domesticate it.

As one ordinarily does, she began by making it hungry, and enclosed it in a long narrow jar. I had always heard talk of a kind of hateful projection emitted by the eyes of toads in certain cases, but I had never believed it. My mother was the victim of it. After three days, she went to see what had become of the toad at the bottom of its narrow jar. Neither my father nor I was there. It was a young Malay servant girl who told us what had happened.

Scarcely had my mother leaned over the jar than her pure face reflected and expression of unspeakable horror. Her entire body began to tremble. She stared at the toad as if she could not take her eyes away from it. The young Malay came running and was obliged to pull her from behind with all her strength in order to extract her from her contemplation. She died a few minutes later without having been able to pronounce a single word.

It is notable that the gibbons that filled a neighboring cage started chattering in a frightful fashion and gazing avidly into space as if at an invisible spectacle.

It is also notable that the toad died at the same time as my mother.

Our despair was immense. Neither my father nor I believed, at first, that the toad could have had anything to do with that inexplicable death, but Mr. Muhcin, an old Buddhist merchant who frequented our house, whose honesty was legendary in Singapore, and his wisdom recognized, affirmed to us that toads, when they have attained an extreme degree of fury, can transmit death via their gaze, especially when it is a matter of a delicate and defenseless creature like my mother.

Not all toads, he added, for there are hierarchies among the animals as there are among humans. There are those which command, those which obey, those which have penetrated certain secrets of nature, and those which are ignorant of them. And he launched into a theory that I found absurd at the time, and which concluded almost by glorifying the murderous toad. I only remained convinced that there are in nature occult things that surpass the human mind, and about which it is better not to think.

My mother was Catholic and my father Protestant, with the consequence that we were equally hospitable to the pastor, the French Jesuits of the mission of Bukit Timah, and also the pious Buddhists who are the elite of Malay society.

One is generally ignorant of the situation that one really occupies in the world. The interment of my mother revealed mine to me, and the purity of my grief was adulterated by an immense satisfaction of self-esteem.

All of Singapore attended that funeral mass The Resident general was by our side, with the majority of the officers. I burst into sobs when I saw Captain MacNair,[3] the director of the penitentiary colony, file past, followed by a delegation of Malabar and Lascar convicts in new uniforms.

Thus, evil accompanies good, and I recall that in coming back from the European cemetery, behind Battery Point, I was soothed by my importance and that of my family.

My father's faculties declined with an extreme rapidity. He started reading, and that was the origin of his decadence. One is doomed by one's folly as surely as by one's virtue. Not content with seeing the pastor, he began frequenting the Jesuits and certain Catholic priests assiduously. I even believe that he had conversations on the subject of I know not what religious theories with Mohammedans and Parsees.

There was friction between us. That was the time when I took cognizance of my power as a tamer, when I began to make wild beasts crawl with the fixity of my gaze and the whistle of my whip. Thoughts of vengeance were mingled with that. The son of the woman who had succumbed to the malign influence of a toad vanquished by his will the most redoubtable animals in creation. That thought of vengeance only increased when my father died.

He read too much. Troubled by his reading, morally debilitated by it, he allowed himself to be bitten by a cobra. Fatality dictated that neither the guaco plant nor naja fat, which are the antidotes to cobra venom, could be found. In a matter

---

[3] Captain J. F. A. McNair was in charge of the penal colony in Singapore from 1858 until his retirement in 1870 (with the honorary rank of Major).

of hours, my father, who was a pure-blooded Dutchman, had taken on a leaden yellow tint what rendered him similar to a Malay of the old race. Nothing can be more painful for a son than to see his father change origin abruptly in the hour of his death.

The pomp of the funeral brought me no consolation. I knew who I was.

My character changed. When they presented themselves, I threw out the pastor, because of his citations from books, the Jesuits, because of their exaggerated politeness, and the Buddhists, because of their respect for the lives of animals. Men are few. It was at that moment that Ali the Macassar entered my household as an employee and became my companion. I no longer quit my whip. Even by night, it was within the reach of my hand.

But everything I have just said about the death of my parents is nothing. The duel had not begun. The true mystery had not yet enveloped me. It was only a year later that I was to encounter the Tiger. I am not talking about those with which the menagerie was full, but the unique one, mine, the one that was, by comparison with its peers, what I was myself with respect to men: the master.

The Young Woman on the Ladder

I was never Eva's lover. I never had the only woman that I have truly loved. Why she refused herself to me with that insensate obstinacy is what I have never been able to comprehend. Was it out of respect for the sacrament of marriage that ought to unite us? I think not. Was it out of natural virtue? Perhaps all that it was given to me to learn subsequently about her insensate caprices was only a series of calumnies invented to tarnish an immaculate life. Was it out of love for me? That is quite possible, and it is necessary to believe the most favorable hypothesis.

A short time after the evening that I had spent with my cousin from Goa in the opium-den in Singapore, I left for Batavia. Ali the Macassar went with me. We went to take delivery of a couple of panthers and purchase a collection of the blind fish that live in the subterranean lakes of Java and which volcanic eruptions cause to appear in the light on certain very rare occasions.

I consider that it is always wise not to make a show of wealth, and one of my greatest joys, when I leave Singapore, is no longer sensing around me the atmosphere of curiosity that celebrity bestows.

Instead of staying in the European quarter, in the India Hotel, where the host's table brings together the senior Dutch functionaries and important foreigners in the evening, I followed Ali the Macassar when we left the boat, after the formalities of the customs, into old Batavia, and took a room not far from the port in a boarding-house of rather paltry aspect. I contend that a man can be comfortable anywhere in the world if he carries with him a clean blanket and a mosquito-net without any holes—along with his whip, of course, in order to defend himself.

My room was on a rather elevated first floor, which overlooked a courtyard from which a fetid exhalation rose, coming from a pile of detritus decomposed by the extreme heat. A Malay coolie had scarcely deposited my suitcase in the room when, discomfited by the filthy character of the door, I went to the window in order to close it.

At that moment, a delicate, subtle, feminine perfume, an emanation of embalmed hair and silk, rose up to reach me, replacing the obscene odor. Surprised, I opened the window and leaned out.

There was a ladder set against the wall, and a young woman had just emerged from a neighboring window, and was descending the rungs lightly. She was a European, who seemed elegantly dressed. I noticed the brightly-embroidered Chinese shawl that was wrapped around her body, outlining it, a torsade of black hair negligently knotted, and an extremely small hand that was holding a rung of the ladder.

At the noise I made, she raised her head. I perceived a face of extraordinary perfection, a slightly childlike and in-genuous face with immense blazing eyes that were simultane-ously pure and terrible. There was an expression of surprise on that face, and also of delight, I believe, and then a gaiety ap-peared there. I heard a burst of laughter, launched like a bou-quet of crystal flowers into the repulsive courtyard, and the young woman disappeared.

I closed the window again and I meditated on the ex-traordinary presence of a young woman of that quality in the hovel for Chinese menials and sailors on leave in which I found myself. Why was the young woman going down a lad-der instead of taking the staircase? Was she fleeing a danger, in spite of her placid appearance? Did she know me?

The beauty of her features had made a profound impres-sion on me. With my eyes fixed on the window I remained motionless for some time. Suddenly, I perceived the sound of my door opening. I thought that it was Ali the Macassar and did not move.

I had a sensation of cold on my neck alongside the ear.

I thought immediately about the fall of one of those odi-ous house-lizards, dropped from the ceiling on to my shoulder.

I made a movement, and saw that it was not a lizard but the barrel of a revolver that had brushed me. An unknown man had come in and was holding the revolver level with my head.

The man was not young, He wore a beard and I saw by the trembling of his hand and his bulging eyes that he was completely beside himself.

The possibility of being suddenly struck by death has always given me, in danger, a singular sensation of an absolute void, of the suppression of all the surrounding matter.

"I've come for Eva," the man shouted at me, from the depths of limitless space.

And as he agitated his revolver, I noticed that he was thin and extremely hairy.

"Eva!" he shouted, again.

Abruptly, he bent down and looked under the bed.

"I don't know who you're talking about," I said, regretting not having taken advantage of that momentary inattention to leap upon him and disarm him.

"You're blushing," he said. "You know where she is, but I'll find her."

I had indeed blushed, having received that sign of superior sensibility from my mother.

I was about to protest about the insensate character of his questions and his threats, when the walls abruptly closed in around me and matter, with its compact qualities, surrounded me again. The danger had disappeared, along with the revolver and the man.

I heard the sound of a key being turned. Then my indignation burst forth. I ran to the door and shook it, in vain. The stranger had locked me in and taken the key away.

I opened the window again and shouted loudly for Ali the Macassar, who ought to be occupying a room some distance from mine. Fortunately, he was there. His taciturn silhouette was framed in the sadness of the wall, and that sight calmed me down.

Ali was a dense brute with measured actions and difficult comprehension. He had a great admiration for me, and his devotion to me was assured. He acted slowly and supported without difficulty insults addressed to him personally; but it only required me, his master, to be troubled in his presence, for him to fall into insensate fits of wrath and accomplish actions of unusual violence. That loss of reason in anger is, moreover, a curious particularity of almost all the inhabitants of the island of Macassar.[4]

I realized in a second the drama that might unfurl in the hotel if the furious Ali took it into his head to avenge his imprisoned master. I started laughing on seeing him as if it were a joke, and asked him to go downstairs and put the ladder against my window, telling him that it was by that means that I wanted to get out. He found nothing ludicrous in that, and disappeared.

At the same moment, however, there was a terrible scream in the courtyard. I saw the thin man appear, seize the ladder and break it under his foot with a single kick, with a vigor that almost made me cry: "Bravo!" Ali had to be going downstairs in the meantime, and the two men were surely about to come to blows unless I could do something.

I thought seriously about jumping, at the risk of breaking a limb. My door opened again, and the insensate individual irrupted into my room again. He still had his revolver in his hand, and as he was not aiming it at me and the situation was less dangerous, I seized the opportunity to grab him around the waist. Behind him, Ali surged forth, who, having seen the broken ladder, had come to ask for my orders.

I understood that wisdom was in the observance of a perfect calm, and that anything, even a humiliation, was better than Ali losing his reason.

"Leave us," I said to him, mildly. "This gentleman has come to visit me, and I need to talk to him."

---

[4] Macassar, or Makassar, is nowadays the name attributed to the largest city on the Indonesian island of Sulawesi, but the notional author seems to be giving the name to the entire island and its natives.

Ali closed the door again. The metallic glint of the revolver was on the floor. The man had let himself fall into a chair and he was weeping abundantly. Tears were running into his beard, which, I noticed then, ought to have been gray, but had been dyed with an excessively vivid black.

"She fled via the ladder," he stammered. "I beg your pardon, sir. But let me be, I beg you. I can't live without her."

"I did in fact, see a young woman descending a little while ago in a unusual manner," I replied, "but I give you my word of honor that I don't know her and had nothing to do with her departure."

What was most moving in the tears was that the person shedding them had a sudden desire to blow his nose, and that caused him to make a pitiful grimace. The man I had before me was a wretch who inspired nothing in me but scorn.

I put him at his ease by repeating the assurance that the individual I had perceived on the ladder was completely unknown to me.

And that's a pity! I thought, making a hypocritical gesture that signified that I attached no importance to women in general.

Then he told me that it was the matter of a young Dutch noblewoman that he had seduced. Naturally, the most elementary discretion prevented him from telling me her name.

The young woman had gone to Singapore in connection with her father's business. When she had come back, she had changed in his regard. She spoke incessantly about Rafael, an animal-tamer and the proprietor of a large animal warehouse, whom she had seen out there.

"Women," he added, fixing me with his gray eyes as if to invite me to admit the verity, "often disguise things in order to make you jealous. You spent a night near to her, in a gathering…perhaps an opium-den…"

I laughed internally at the audacity of the unfortunate man who wanted to compete with me with his gaze. To compete with the eye of an animal-tamer!

But then, from the depths of my memory, a memory abruptly surged forth. An opium-den!

I saw once again the camel's hump and the Door of the Tiger, where I had spent the night in the company of my cousin from Goa.

Through the recumbent forms lying next to little lamps, I had vaguely made out a woman's face. The young woman on the ladder had passed through the old door of sculpted wood before me, and she had seen me in that vile place, amid the clouds of the detestable smoke. She was there—in what company, and why?

I did not know. And from that moment on, the creature who was known as Eva, the delightful young woman in the Chinese shawl, was indissolubly linked in my mind with the idea of a tiger, a tiger sculpted in a door. But that was only a beginning, for it was to be forever linked with the idea of a tiger, a Javanese tiger—and what a tiger!

I was about to blush. I was about to betray myself. I turned away and I affirmed forcefully that it was some misunderstanding, or perhaps one of those inventions habitual to women to provoke jealousy—a hypothesis, moreover, that my interlocutor had just formulated himself.

He believed me. He stood up and passed his hand through his beard, which he had moistened, several times. He repeated his apologies. It was the sight of the ladder that had enlightened his mind.

On observing the disappearance of Eva, whom he had left in his room an hour earlier, he had gone downstairs precipitately in order to question the hotelier. The latter could not inform him, but had told him, glorifying himself thereby, of the arrival of Rafael, the famous animal-tamer from Singapore. The hotelier had simply said Rafael, for one often names famous men by their forename alone. He thought that that arrival, which coincided with the abrupt departure of the young woman, could not be fortuitous. He said that he had come to get her, and he assured me that he had decided to kill us both and to kill himself afterwards.

I contented myself with a smile. Pity was triumphant in me.

The poor thin man, who was Italian by origin and whose name was Giovanni, gave me a naïve summary of his life, which had no interest for me. He was the first mate of a ship, and that title seemed very important to him. It was his amour that retained him in Batavia, and he had refused several brilliant offers from ship-owners.

He added that women had always played the principal role in his life, and then he started caressing his moustache and turning it up in an utterly ridiculous manner.

He appeared to be very poor. The hotel at which he was staying was evidence of that, and the proof was completed by the appearance of his shoes, which seemed to be very old. I had a desire to offer him money, but dared not, fearing to wound him. It was agreed that I would help him to look for Eva, and we parted as good friends.

I hoped to hear no further mention of him, and occupied myself with the blind fish, inhabitants of the caves of Java, But my destiny was inscribed alongside that of Eva, and hence of his.

That Italian ship's mate was nothing but a miserable slanderer, an inventor of strange lies. He came to admit it to me himself a few days later, just as I was deploying a mosquito net in order to take a midday siesta.

He had slandered the charming Eva and he was remorseful about it. She had never been his mistress; he swore that on his honor. The young woman was absolutely pure. She had only come to see him on a business matter, for she collaborated in her father's business, and if she had left his room by means of a ladder it was on a whim and by virtue of a natural liking for sport. He, driven by an unqualifiable vanity, had wanted to create belief in a liaison with her. He begged my pardon humbly.

While he was speaking, he did not show any humility. On the contrary, he had an arrogant and satisfied expression. His voice had a deliberately monotonous intonation, like someone reciting a lesson and wanting to give the impression that he is reciting a lesson.

He curled his moustache in an utterly insupportable fashion, and the extreme heat caused drops of sweat to trickle over his face, which moistened his beard as ridiculously as his tears a few days before. I noticed that the beard had recently been dyed a vivid black.

"Anyway, I've seen Eva again," he concluded, lowering his eyes.

He did not see the glance that I cast upon my whip.

"I've told you what I had to tell you," he added, on the threshold.

"That appears entirely plausible to me," I replied, ill-humoredly.

And it was true. I was sure that the marvelous Eva had not belonged to that pitiful individual, hairy and already aging.

At that time, I could still have a certainty in that matter, being unaware that women have neither taste nor disgust, but are the servants of passing opportunity and the slaves of those who persist.

However, I did not go to sleep during the burning hour of the siesta. Separated from the world by the dreamlike fabric of the mosquito-net, I saw the blind fish with their deformed fins and iridescent phosphorescence disappear into the darkness of indifference. Neither the age, nor the striping, nor the price of panthers counted for me. The city of Batavia with its formidable avenues and equatorial gardens, that of Singapore with its villas on piles and its triple port, Malaysia with its savage islands, its volcanoes and its virgin forests, the entire earth that is said to be round and seems so flat, rotated around the visage of a young woman laughing at the foot of a ladder.

But that was to be my last peaceful reverie. I affirm that it was still an ordinary man who was taking a siesta in that poor hotel room, a man who only had moderate passions in him as yet. But the man who was to be burned by an inconceivable hatred of the animal species, the man of the Tiger, was to be born only a little later.

The Strange Indigo Plantation

I have always pleased women. Miss Whampoa, the daughter of the richest Chinese merchant in Singapore had, in a sense, asked for me in marriage via her father.

The Whampoas are a great Chinese family, for there are aristocracies in that country of a formidable antiquity, of which we Europeans have no idea, I had replied in an evasive fashion, because although the young woman was pretty, if a trifle small, she was reputed to be cultured, and I even believe that she was a poet or something like that, which rendered her entirely impossible for me.

A young English widow, enriched by speculations in land, sometimes received my visits and awaited them impatiently. It was said that she had had a few adventures, but I do not attach any importance to those trifles and I claim that a man who is a man in the elevated sense of the word ought not to care if the woman he loves has a few deviations of conduct here and there. The essential thing is to ignore them and crack one's whip if some fool attempts to provoke your jealousy by means of slanderous gossip.

I was loved passionately by a Javanese dancing-girl in the new quarter of Singapore. I firmly believe that she would have killed herself for me if I had not cleverly come to an arrangement with her mother to endow her and marry her off to some poor devil who took her way to the isle of Madura.

I was therefore not surprised by the favorable impression that I had made on Eva, and I extended my stay in Batavia in the hope of encountering her. After several weeks, however, having no news of her, I was about to re-embark for Singapore with my blind fish and my panthers.

I had just given my orders to Ali for the transportation of the animals when, just as I was about to leave my modest hotel, I found myself in the presence of a young Javanese, very carefully clad, who addressed me by name.

The young man was immediately antipathetic to me by virtue of his glacial politeness, his overly manicured hands and his effeminate appearance.

He was wearing a silk sarong and his blue kolambi[5] had orange embroidery on the sleeves. Contrary to the custom of all the inhabitants of the region, no kris was suspended from his belt. The absence of the turban or scarf around his head prescribed by the law of Islam made me think that he must be a Buddhist or profess one of those bizarre Hindu religions.

The young man was, moreover, a servant, a simple servant. He had had no difficulty, he told me, in discovering me, a Singaporean, so difficult is it for certain men to remain hidden.

He had come on behalf his master, Mynheer Varoga, the owner of a large indigo plantation situated in the district of Djokjokarta and that of Solo, whose name could not, in any case, be unknown to me.

He had crossed the great distance that separates those regions from Batavia to transmit an invitation to me. Mynheer Varoga was inviting me to an exceptional hunt. His plantations were haunted by a tiger of prodigious size and an unprecedented audacity.

The noise of gongs and the light of torches did not frighten it. Great celebrations had recently taken place in all the villages of the island in honor of the abolition of slavery in the Dutch possessions. Mynheer Varoga had had fifty shots fired that evening from a little cannon that he had imported from Europe for ceremonies of that sort. Well, the noise of the cannon had not frightened the tiger, which had carried off a woman a few hundred paces away from the place where the cannon was firing.

The three villages surrounding the indigo plantation were terrorized. A large number of traps had been dug, in vain. Mynheer Varoga was too old to hunt himself. He had heard

---

[5] I have reproduced this word as it appears in the original, but I can find no other reference to a garment of that name.

tell that a celebrated specialist in wild animals was passing through Batavia. It was on him that he was counting to rid him of the monster.

That proposition was flattering and tempting. Added to it was the attraction of the possession of the tiger if it could be captured alive. I immediately raised the objection of a journey of more than four hundred kilometers overland, but the young Javanese smiled with a irony that signified that such contingencies only existed for vulgar men like me.

Mynheer Varoga possessed one of those astonishing steam-launches that mock the absence of wind and the presence of Malay pirates on their long proas, and that launch would transport me the next day to Samarang, where horses were waiting for us. Two stages would then be sufficient to reach the indigo plantation by way of the high road to Djokjokarta.

My affairs summoned me to Singapore, where my principal employee, a myopic and limited man, was directing my business in my absence. I had just been advised by a letter from him that he was ill and awaited me impatiently.

I accepted nevertheless the proposition that had been made to me, firstly out of vanity—men are led by vanity—and secondly because of a secret and inexplicable presentiment.

It was agreed that I would take Ali, and that we would depart the following day.

I hate animals, but vegetables inspire a fervent love in me.

I find that mountains are beautiful because of their tresses of trees, and rivers only have attractions because they bathe leafy branches and fabulous roots.

When we had passed the mountainous massifs of Merbarou and Merapi; when, to the right and the left, the sky was cut out by the high lines of virgin forests barring the horizon, I ceased to be irritated by the silent irony of the effeminate Javanese, my heart began to beat faster, and I sensed descending within me the calm that disorderly nature always procures in me.

The giant areca palms, the teak woods and the centenarian banyans enveloped us on all sides and buried the road, as fragile as a silver thread, beneath their canopy.

The villages were reminiscent of dusty wisps of straw and sometimes, under a tangle of lianas, the vestiges of a temple were perceptible, a stone elephant, or a row of columns, for it appears that the island of Java, and particularly that region, sheltered the ancient civilization of a people that constructed edifices.

Then the forest, which had drawn closer to the point of overwhelming us, retreated somewhat. We traversed plantations of coffee and indigo and woods of cotton-plants. Dusk was about to fall and fireflies were beginning to furrow the air. The Javanese servant drew closer to me and showed me an accumulation of shadows that we were about to reach.

"We've arrived," he said.

There were several banyans whose trunks were so high and so enormously thick that a vast modern dwelling at their feet seemed very small.

I saw servants running in haste, but under the disproportion of the trees they gave me the impression of being children. A woman, whom I mistook at first for a dwarf, was in their midst.

As we arrived in front of the perron, everything recovered its natural size, and I perceived that the house was immense. I set foot on the ground and I recognized—without great astonishment, moreover—that the woman who had seemed minuscule to me and who advanced toward me, smiling with ease and extending her hand to welcome me, was the young woman of the ladder.

I say that I did not experience and great astonishment because my presentiment had only become more precise during the journey, especially as soon as the first shadows of the virgin forests had extended at my sides, as if there were a secret liaison between the living creature of whom I was thinking, and the ocean of benevolent vegetation.

The hospitality of Mynheer Varoga was regal. Was I not a kind of king of beasts?

A host of servants lay in wait to accomplish my slightest desires, and when I went out to visit the plantations, I perceived that the indigenes had retained the deplorable ancient habit of prostrating themselves before Europeans. I always had a desire to shout at them:

"On your feet! You're men like me!"

But I said nothing, out of respect for the old customs and in order not to make the charming Eva smile, who accompanied me and did me the honors of her domains.

I scarcely saw Mynheer Varoga. He was a desiccated and jaundiced man. He scarcely quit his bedroom, where he seemed to be mysteriously occupied. He only appeared at meals. He then dissolved in amiabilities, repeating that his entire house belonged to me, but as soon as his daughter and I were installed under the veranda he babbled a few apologetic phrases and hastened to leave us.

On the first day, I wanted to visit the traps that had been dug for the monster. I had the pointed stakes removed with which they are ordinarily fitted, and by which it is killed on falling, for I wanted to capture it alive, and I had the layer of foliage with which the traps were covered artfully modified.

I examined the places from which, by turns, oxen, a horse and two women had been carried off, and I went to all the neighboring locations where there was water and to which the tiger might go to drink.

Eva came with me, a felt hat over her eyes and a skirt slightly above the knee. She repeated to me, fixing her immense blazing eyes upon me, that there was no urgency, and that she and her father were intent on keeping me for as long as possible.

Ali and the insupportable Javanese, whose name was Djath, accompanied us in our excursions. Djath still affected to go abroad unarmed. That affectation was ridiculous, if only because the innumerable snakes that populate jungles necessitate a hunting-knife, at least. But he said, smiling, that he charmed snakes and called them by their names.

By their names! Was that possible? But when I shrugged my shoulders at those stupidities, Eva assured me that it was true, and I glimpsed her darting a tender gaze at him.

When we went out, Djath also affected to be uniquely occupied in making a large bouquet of yellow champakas and the tuberoses of a sort that the Malays call *sundal-malam*—which is to say, "nocturnal conspirator"—and are reputed to have the property of giving those who spread them over their bodies voluptuous dreams.

When we returned to the house he gave the bouquet he had collected to Eva. She immediately took it to her bedroom, not without a further exchange of glances.

I experienced a great internal anger, which I did not allow to show, and was obliged to remind myself who I was in order not to feel jealousy born within me.

Two or three times, when I was alone with Eva under the veranda, she said to me, while indicating the great forest that loomed up on the horizon like an impenetrable wall: "It's necessary to be careful, you know. The forest of Merapi isn't like other forests. It's one of the most ancient in the world and conceals great mysteries.

And I perceived that I did not understand anything about the people and things, and that everything was singular in that corner of Java, not far from Mount Merapi, on the edge of the forest of that name.

There was a tiger that roamed around the plantations and carried off sheep, oxen and even women. It did not fear the cannon, it avoided traps and the indigenes that had seen and whom I interrogated on the subject described it to me as being of supernatural dimensions.

One day, when we had penetrated into the forest and were coming back at sunset—hastily, I ought to say, because the dangers commence with the night—we heard a cry, or rather a song, a kind of strangely evocative chant, which had something religious in its tones. I distinguished words that corresponded very nearly to: "Om, Mani, Padme, Aum."

I stopped my horse and tried to go back in order to collect the unfortunate fellow, doubtless gone astray, who was wandering alone in the forest at dusk. But Eva shook her head and made me a sign to continue my route.

"It's Chumbul, the holy man. He lives far away in that direction, in the middle of the forest, and he only goes abroad by night."

"If he goes out at night," I said, "how has he not been eaten by the tiger or other wild beasts?"

At those words Eva started to laugh and Djath, who was behind her, did likewise, as if I had said something infinitely amusing and implausible.

And we set off again, while the voice resounded in the distance of the man who not only wandered alone by night in the forest but also identified himself to the wild beasts by his cries.

Mynheer Varoga's conduct in my regard, and the hidden life that he led in his room, also appeared enigmatic to me, but that was the mystery that ought to have been most easily explicable.

I was awakened several times in the night by formidable rumbles that seemed to depart from the interior of the earth. I broke out in a cold sweat in consequence, and as soon as dawn broke I ran into the house to ask for an explanation. Neither the master nor the servants had even perceived the phenomena. It arose from the volcanic nature of the terrain, I was assured, and nothing unfortunate for human beings ever resulted from that subterranean thunder.

What troubled me the most was the veritable personality of Eva, the mystery of her smile, that of the reveries into which she fell, that of her childlike gaieties, that of her coquetry in my regard.

She had explained to me, laughing, but very frankly, the incident of the ladder, and what she had told me was marked with the stamp of plausibility.

Her father wanted to change the commandant of the steam-launch that traveled between Samarang and Batavia for his business. She had gone to see the ship's mate, whom she knew to be without a job at that moment, to offer him the position. She had seen a ladder propped against the window and had thought it amusing to descend by that means.

She had learned subsequently that the mate was a strange alcoholic, a maniac who flattered himself with good fortunes that only existed in his imagination. She had divined that he had come to find me. She had seen him again and demanded that he had a further conversation with me in order to give the lie to his initial statements.

All of that was related with amusement, as something comical, because it revealed the astonishing psychology of certain conceited men. It appeared veridical to me, and made me regret not having inflicted a severe chastisement on the ship's mate.

Yes, the incident of the ladder would have had nothing compromising about it if there had not been, subsequently, a further ladder incident. The ship's mate would no longer have existed in my mind if I had not seen Djath, the Javanese with the overly manicured hands climbing up a ladder to a window: the window of Eva's bedroom.

I want to relate events in sequence, and how certain mysteries have received a plausible explanation, while others are complicated to the point of participating in the very mysteries of nature.

But the greatest of all, I have perceived subsequently, I shall never be able to resolve, because it is the one that is in my own soul, in the variety of its changes, and the unknown quality of its manifestations. The interior abyss of human thought is more profound than the mysterious forest of Merapi and the subterranean chaos from which volcanoes draw their substance.

The First Encounter with the Tiger

What is most extraordinary about a forest is the power of putrefaction.

From heaped-up vegetal detritus, decomposing foliage and the accumulation of humus, under the influence of the eternal transpiration of the soil and the trees and a native humidity charged with seeds, spring ever-renewed layers of living plants.

A forest is like a gigantic crucible of nature in which dead forms seethe incessantly and become animated, and anyone who walks there plunges his feet into a mass of disintegrations intermediate between life and death.

So the forest fills me with gravity and gives my mind a certain serene sadness.

That day, I had traversed on my own the cultivated fields and the jungle that extended for several miles around the house, and by means of a path bordered by wild pepper-trees I had reached the prodigious vault of the forest.

I had been seized abruptly by the desire to kill animals, the spirit of the hunt, which takes possession of me on certain days. I also needed to think. I had experienced a keen discontentment. I had just learned that Djath composed poems in the Javanese language and that he sometimes read them to Eva.

Now, people who devote themselves to such pastimes have always been odious to me, and it would have been painful for me to think that Eva might be interested in such stupidities.

I had slung one of Mynheer Varoga's rifles over my shoulder—a rifle with which I was unfamiliar, alas, having not brought mine with me on the journey—and I had set forth.

On the edge of the forest there was a stream that one passed over on a tree trunk. I had perceived, near the water, a marabou stork standing on one leg, with its bald head, seemingly heavy with thoughts, and its dark green foliage, which it was negligently smoothing with its beak.

I had granted it mercy without knowing why. But as soon as I had crossed the line of tall ebony-trees that loomed up at the threshold of the forest, as if they were its guardians, I started firing at all the animate beings I happened to perceive. I fired at random, without paying any attention to the result of my shots, for my personal relief and the disinterested pleasure of killing animals.

An inexperienced man walking in a forest might believe that it is depopulated. A great silence radiates around his footfalls, all the creatures in the grass and the branches immobilizing themselves as if they knew, by virtue of a reliable age-old instinct, that the thin two-legged form carrying a metal tube in its hands is the propagator of death, the eternal assassin of all species.

But the man who knows the savage world distinguishes the confused crawlings, sees the cunning figures of birds, muzzles gaping with terror because of wretched animal progeny, and he kills, rejoicing in his perspicacity and his skill.

First of all there was a parrot, which fell with a great clatter of wings, making a yellow and red patch along the black trunks. I had perceived two of them balanced innocently on a branch.

Parrots are monogamous. When they unite in a couple, they no longer quit one another, and cherish one another tenderly throughout their long life. Now, nothing can irritate me more than thinking that animals know the noble sentiment of amour, like humans, and are often more faithful than them.

I had a bitter pleasure, therefore, in hearing the second parrot chattering despairingly on its branch. Its grief was stronger than the fear of a second shot from my rifle, for it did not flee, and I heard it lamenting for a long time with almost human syllables.

Then there was a monkey that fell from a mango-tree with the fruit it was holding. It was a guenon of a small species. I had only wounded it, for I perceived it spinning on the ground without letting go of its mango, as if its wound had caused it to lose its reason. I disdained to retrace my steps in order to finish it off.

It seemed to me that a peacock was killed a little further on. I had the good fortune to crush the head of a rather large snake that was asleep, with the butt of the rifle. I fired by judgment on something stirring in the undergrowth, and almost uttered a cry of joy when I saw that it was a telagon, an enormous rat with a pig's head and a fan-like tail, which emits a noxious odor.

Then, successively, I killed a kalender,[6] a kind of fox that carries its offspring on its back, and one of those strange arboreal cuscuses that stare at you with frightened eyes.

It was a day of happy facility. I scarcely had any need to aim. All my shots struck home.

I had marched straight ahead, guided by the blind desire to kill. I had penetrated a long way into the forest by a narrow track that sometimes ended in a clearing, broadening out and narrowing in a regular fashion.

I often thought about how easy it would be to get lost in that ocean of trunks and lianas, and a kind of heaviness in the air that filtered through in spite of the opacity of the tenebrous ceiling of interlaced branches made me think that the afternoon must be in its decline.

I stopped abruptly. I suddenly felt very weary, and it required a great effort for me to reload my rifle.

I was hot. In the place where I found myself, the path was particularly restricted and the floating sea of wood was undulating at a low level, almost touching my head. I had an unaccustomed sensation of discouragement. Thousands of adversaries surrounded me. Behind every trunk I thought I could see simian faces grimacing. Forms covered in fur stirred in the foliage. Wings fluttered. Reptilian scales clicked under

---

[6] There seems to be no trace of this animal outside the present text.

the humus. How would I ever vanquish those eternal legions of animals?

I had turned back, and I made haste. Clearings succeeded one another, scarcely designed paths intersected, and I was gripped by a vague dread of going astray in the maze into which I had plunged so imprudently.

A hint of sapphire blue that spread through the atmosphere announced the impending arrival of dusk, and as if that silent signal were awaited by a population mute until then, shudderings and whisperings filled the inextricable thickets that surrounded me; a more intense winged life beat the air and singular calls of birds and monkeys responded to one another above my head.

But I no longer had any desire to make a noise by firing rifle-shots, and even avoided striking the ground too hard as I walked. I was gliding like a rapid shadow fearful of the mysterious armies of solitude.

I stopped again fifty meters from a clearing that I had to traverse. A group of gibbons of a rather large species was traversing it in the inverse direction. I thought that I was faced by humans of short stature and nearly called out to them. All the apes saw me, but they gazed at me fearlessly and continued marching, content to utter muffled growls.

I understood then that I was witnessing a rare spectacle.

In the middle of their group, four apes were holding a dead ape by the arms and legs. At the head, taller than the others, was an ape that was their guide and leader. The procession that I saw passing was a funeral cortege.

I had heard it said that gibbons had the custom of burying their dead and that they did so in secret places at nightfall. I had not believed it. I also knew that it was necessary not to disturb them during the accomplishment of that ritual, because they became redoubtable then. I stayed motionless until those strange gravediggers had disappeared into the undergrowth.

When I had resumed my route with a longer stride, however, new thoughts assailed me, and words once heard to which I had attached no importance came back to mind.

I recalled that a traveler who had accomplished a voyage in unknown regions of Burma had told me that he had been called to witness the making of a treaty of alliance with a tribe of orangutans, and that he had, by means of signs, established certain conventions with an orang who seems to exercise a certain sovereignty over his fellows.

He said that there was an unexplored mountain in northern Burma where there as an immense elephant cemetery, and that some of those animals went into that cemetery, at certain times of the year and uttered cries and made gesticulations there whose ensemble formed a kind of mortuary ceremony.

If animals were susceptible to obeying chiefs or kings, if they even had priests to invoke the powers of death, might they not have an organization, unknown to humans and vaster, permitting different species of animals to communicate with one another, to make one another party to their terrors and their misfortunes?

All the appeals with which the dusk was filled might compose a language. Via the chattering of monkeys and the stupid screeches of peacocks there had been communications from tree to tree of information that traveled a long way in the forest. And that information might say that a killer of beasts, a redoubtable enemy of animal species, had been foolish enough to allow himself to be surprised by nightfall in the forest, and was now running, hectically, in quest of the region of human beings.

To whom could that information be addressed, if not to the most redoubtable of animals, to the tiger of phenomenal size that must be a king among its own kind?

Yes, the sage Mr. Muhcin of Singapore had not been wrong when he told me that there are hierarchies in the animals and that some of them possessed secrets of nature not possessed by others, and of which humans themselves are ignorant.

It was a toad sorcerer, a toad magician, that had killed my mother by the power of its hateful gaze, and I was at risk of perishing at any moment beneath the claws of the avenging tiger, the sovereign of the forest of Merapi.

It seemed to me that I could hear muffled footfalls behind me, and a powerful breath. The coconut palms, with their uniformly straight trunks had never given me that sensation of desperate monotony before.

And suddenly, I stumbled over something soft. It was a dead parrot, the one I had killed when I had entered the forest. I darted a circular glance around me. I recognized the path on which I found myself. I was at the limit of the land of trees. I was saved.

Calm returned to me, with a certain shame. It was at a slow pace that I reached the edge of the forest.

I uttered a sigh on crossing the wall of somber ebony-trees. Before me, illuminated by the moon, the horizon of the jungle extended. Innumerable fireflies, like living sparks, were flying in all directions. In the distance I saw the great black lines, benevolent and infinite, that were avenues bordered by tall banyans planted by human hands, and I knew that there were villages there and a beautiful European dwelling where the servants ought now to be lighting the lamps.

In front of me, at the bottom of a slope, in a rather deep dip, I saw the blue-tinted water of the stream scintillating, framed by dense tamarinds.

I went down, not without looking over my shoulder several times at the forest. I went over the tree-trunk that served as a bridge and went up the other side of the slope. There was a small splash of water and I saw the bald marabou, still immobile on one leg.

Suddenly, a regret came to me. I had been favored by chance, since every shot I had fired had felled an animal. Why not take advantage of that luck again?

I knew that the river bed was encased for several kilometers, and that the animals that wanted to drink there could only reach the water with difficulty. The place where I found myself was a natural drinking-place and several trails ended there. I could not find a better ambush for lying in wait for the tiger. Then again, I had an hour's march to undertake in order to reach Mynheer Varoga's house. I decided to rest for a while and place myself on watch, facing the forest. I therefore sat down next to a small tamarind, not far from the water, with my hat and my rifle placed beside me.

Nature has granted me, since birth, one precious gift, among others, that she has never taken away from me. Whatever my preoccupations or chagrins might be, I have the faculty of going to sleep with extreme facility. Scarcely was I installed than a profound slumber took possession of me.

I do not know how long it lasted—doubtless quite a long time. My first sensation on waking up was that my Manila straw hat was no longer in the place where I had put it. The wind had dragged it into the hollow of the stream. The wind had changed direction thereafter, for the second sensation I experienced on emerging from slumber was a noxious odor of decomposing meat.

In spite of my profession, I have never been able to accustom myself to the abominable stench that beasts that devour raw flesh emit.

I felt a surge of nausea. Bit immediately, a thousand voices cried out within me: the cause, what is the cause of that frightful odor? All my faculties of attention awoke and a perfect lucidity took possession of my brain, while my hand extended mechanically and silently toward the butt of my rifle.

The tiger was facing me, on the edge of the forest. It had just emerged from the trees and it was gazing—or rather, it was sniffing, for its head was lowered toward the ground and swaying to the right and the left with an atrociously regular movement.

It was prodigious, fantastic; I had never seen one as large, and especially as long. The moon blanched its stripes, with had the appearance of being painted. Its tail was beating the air in a mechanical fashion. But what was most impressive in that demonic silhouette was its immeasurable length, disproportionate to its muzzle.

I believed for a second that I had gone back in time to the epoch of fabulous monsters. The forest loomed up higher, the little stream glowed impetuously, the marabou's leg stretched like that of a dream-bird. Mr. Muhcin's words came back to mind again. The tiger that I saw was more than an animal king, it was a torturer of the animal Hell, a sort of tiger god.

I calculated that it had not yet scented me, since the wind was blowing in my direction and it was me who what perceived its odor. Finally, my hands settled on the stock of my rifle, which I drew toward me slowly.

I remembered clearly that there was lead in the right barrel and buckshot in the left. If I only wounded it with my first shot I could still blind it at close range with the discharge of lead. The essential thing was it uncovered the weak spot in its shoulder in a favorable fashion, in order that it could be hit full in the heart. Things were, in sum, nor presenting themselves so badly.

But then something surprising happened. I perceived that my rifle had a slight movement to the right and the left, like the tiger's head. I was trembling. The shock caused by my abrupt awakening and the unexpected appearance of the enemy had shaken my nerves, and was the cause of that tremor.

And the same moment when I had that perception, the immensity of the danger was revealed to me and I experienced the sensation of space, of absolute void, that I always had on such occasions.

I knew that there was a tree nearby whose branches were not very high, and which I could easily climb. At the moment when I had sat down in order to stay on watch, I had perceived a depression in the ground in a field of sugar cane, a kind of excavation surrounded by stones that had appeared excellent to shelter me and from which I would be able to fire without being seen.

It was by virtue of idleness that I had let myself fall beside a small tamarind that could not be of any assistance to me. Where was the tree with the propitious branches? Where was the field of sugar-cane?

The landscape had retreated, had been annihilated. I could no longer see anything but a limitless extent, a void greater than that of the interplanetary spaces, where I was alone with a formidable tiger.

And in that nothingness, at a slow pace, breathing in a raucous fashion, still looking at the ground, the tiger advanced toward me.

It made no more noise than if it had been moving through space. It descended the slope of the stream while I stood up in the hope that the upright position might calm my nerves, stop my tremor, and give me the possibility of firing with certainty.

Having arrived next to the water, the tiger swayed for a few seconds, sniffed again, lifted up a little sand with its paw, and drank placidly. Then it raised its head, satisfied, and it perceived me.

It did not budge.

In three bounds it could be upon me. The wise thing to do was take advantage of its immobility to shoot, but I took account of the fact that my hands did not have sufficient surety. Calm gradually returned to me because of the professional character involved in the exchange of gazes between a tamer and a tiger, and the world, the forest, the stream and the field of sugar-cane were gradually replaced around us—but I did not stop trembling, and my hands were so cold that I was almost no longer conscious of their presence at the end of my arms.

The moon had risen above the horizon and was illuminating the scene brightly. The stripes of the tiger were mat silver, edged with black. Its tail was reminiscent of a serpent that might also have been a fan. I saw the inverted and deformed image of the beast in the stream. The sound of water running over the stones, which I had not noticed until then, seemed loud to me. I remember that, in spite of the imminence of the danger, one thought was stupidly dominant in me, which I could not succeed in chasing away.

How is it that the marabou isn't frightened by the tiger and isn't leaving its place? It wants to see how I shall be devoured.

What was going through the mind of the sanguinary creature whose bizarre phosphorescent eyes I could see, devoid of expression and devoid of flame, open immeasurably wide and fixed on me?

Did it know by means of oral tradition that an upright man holding in his hands an object gleaming in the moonlight might transmit death before he could be reached? Could it see in my eyes the mute order of a superior will? That hypothesis was the less plausible, for I did not sense my habitual power radiating from me, and even experienced a singular diminution of my being, as if I had suddenly become very small in stature, as if I were some kind of ridiculous dwarf incapable of firing a rifle-shot. But perhaps the tiger had just devoured an animal at that very moment and, although it was thirsty, it was doubtless not hungry.

Abruptly, it turned away from me. It glided rather than walked along the slope. It hesitated for another second after it had climbed it. Not a single glance backwards to look at the silhouette of the man standing there with his hands trembling and his engine of death, which lack of courage rendered useless!

It sniffed again, forcefully. A great sweep of its black and white fan, which seemed to me to displace the atmosphere all the way to the moon and the cold stars, and the solitary king with the felted paws returned to the tenebrous realm of the trees.

Only then, as if the spectacle that it had been promised had not occurred, did the marabou take off, deploying its wings, and, with a click of its beak, in which it expressed its disappointment, it rose up above the tamarinds of the stream. The flight of the philosophical bird appeared to me to be infinitely melancholy, as heavy as the ignorance of things and himself that a man bears within him.

I was sad. My hat, a few paces away from me, near the water, appeared to me to be very far away, at an insurmountable distance, for it was necessary in order to go to fetch it to draw a little closer to the forest. One is quite comfortable bareheaded, at night. I abandoned my hat.

An hour's march separated me from Mynheer Varoga's house. I scarcely took ten minutes to traverse that distance. The barking of dogs struck my ears delightfully and I held myself in check in order not to embrace all the human beings who formed an anxious group on the perron.

The Young Man on the Ladder

At this point the incident of the second ladder occurred.

I had recounted, during dinner, my excursion in the forest and my encounter with the tiger and I had done so almost without any modification, because of the force I attribute to sincerity.

According to his habit, Mynheer Varoga, always preoccupied, had left us when we got up from the table to go and sit under the veranda. He had found, as a daily pretext, a project for canals to be dug in the region, and he claimed to be drawing up hydrographic maps in his room.

I ought to say immediately that during the previous two days, Eva had been particularly flirtatious in my regard. Sometimes she fixed me with her great terrible eyes charged with sensuality, the ardor of which she immediately softened by the musicality of indifferent words; sometimes, with a familiar gesture, she placed her small hand on my arm, and I thought I felt a slight deliberate pressure. That very morning, she had given me a champaka flower, saying to me: "Keep that; it's a flower that I have held against me, and it has a strange action on the soul."

On the soul! It was not on the soul but on the body! The champaka flower awakens lust; that is well-known. I would have attributed a provocative meaning to those words if I had not preferred to believe in Eva's perfect purity. Then again, it was Djath who had picked the flower.

By the light of the stars, sitting in large wicker armchairs, we were side by side, each holding a square fan and waving it to chase away the mosquitoes. In the distance, the last lights in the villages were going out. All the servants must have gone to bed, for a great silence enveloped the environs of the house.

Eva fell silent. The conversation had suddenly died between us, giving way to the more eloquent speech that has no need of syllables to express itself.

I looked at Eva. She was inclined in her armchair beside me and her head was tilted toward me, quite close to mine.

The moon had fallen behind the line of trees, with the consequence that there was not enough light to distinguish the young woman's features precisely, but I thought I recognized an expression of expectation. I thought that the moment had come. I took a hand, which she did not draw away, and kneeling down, I told her that I loved her. Then, tenderly, but with the reserve due to a young woman, I put her hand to my lips and brushed it.

That did not produce in her the effect of confusion and tenderness that I hoped,

I heard youthful, sonorous, sincere laughter falling like a cascade. I had the sensation of little pearls rolling across the whole veranda. It was very brief, and she put her fan over her face immediately.

"Why are you laughing?" I said, believing that there was some exterior cause that I could not perceive.

Eva lowered her fan. There was an expression of gaiety on her face, and also slight disappointment.

"I'm laughing because you're not a very modern man. But that's of no account. I love you dearly. It's very late. The story of your dangers during the day has exhausted me. We'll talk about this again tomorrow, if you like."

She had stood up. I did not know what to say. I had a confused dread of having let an opportunity pass. I told myself that perhaps...but no, that was not possible. I kissed the hand that Eva held out to me again, and she disappeared into the house. She ran up the stairs that led to the upper floor, and it seemed to me that the musical pearls were still being strung out behind her.

I could not sleep. I marched back and forth for a long time on the veranda. I would have liked to have accomplished an astonishing exploit, to see the tiger appear in front of the house and to battle with it bodily. I was discontented. I was perplexed. Then the impressive silence of excessively serene nights weighed upon me.

That silence was disturbed by a bizarre whistle. I did not pay any attention to it at first and went back to my room. It was situated on the first floor and formed the corner of the house at the front. Although quite distant from Eva's, the balcony of wrought wood was perceptible.

Once in my room I checked to see whether some mosquito had not slipped under the net and might be in the process of reaching me. Then, as the heat was suffocating, I went to my window once again in order to breathe.

Instinctively, I looked to see if the there was still a lamp illuminated in Eva's bedroom. No lamp was lit, but there was a ladder placed against the wood of her balcony, and someone was climbing that ladder that I immediately recognized by his costume as the Javanese Djath.

He was going up without any precaution. He was not looking fearfully to the right and left. Having arrived at the top of the ladder the movement he made to enter the room obliged him to turn around, and for a moment his eyes were fixed in my direction. I do not know whether he saw me, for I immediately threw myself backwards.

I could not believe that he was expected by Eva, that Eva had given him a rendezvous in her own room in the middle of the night. I was internally convinced that Eva loved me and it appeared to me to be impossible that a young woman who bore so much ingenuousness in her face was capable, after having heard a declaration of love from a man she loved, of whistling mysteriously in order to summon a young Javanese poet to her side.

What, then, could be the meaning of that nocturnal visit? Did Djath perhaps have a criminal intention? Was a drama about to unfold? I listened to see whether any scream rang out. There was nothing but a silence, heavier than before.

I dared not rush into Eva's bedroom. I thought that Djath might have seen me, that he had gone back down while I was deliberating, and that I would find myself in the presence of Eva alone.

Whatever the pretext might be, after the confession of my amour, my coming into her bedroom was unworthy of a gallant man. People are only too ready to assume that an animal-tamer is an ignorant brute, a being habituated to ferocious beasts, inapt in the delicacies of procedure that women like.

Time was passing, and it was necessary to do something.

My father had always told me that when one hesitates uncertainly between several courses of action, it is always necessary to take the one most in conformity with current morality, to behave as the majority of men would behave. The guest of a house who had discovered an event of that order ought to inform the master of the house, the father of the family.

I did not reflect any further, and ran into the large circular gallery that overlooked the interior courtyard. That gallery was only illuminated by the declining moon and it was very dark. I reached a door and knocked on it without being absolutely certain that it gave access to Mynheer Varoga's bedroom.

At first I got no response. Perhaps Mynheer Varoga was asleep? I knocked harder, waited, and knocked again. After quite a long time I heard dragging footsteps that I recognized as those of Mynheer Varoga. The noise of footsteps was accompanied by the sort of murmur to which people irritated at being disturbed give voice.

"Who's there?" said a voice behind the door: a voice that could not be that of a man in the process of placidly drawing up hydrographic maps.

"It's me," I replied. "I have something to tell you."

There were a few seconds of silence, and then, clearly and imperatively, Mynheer Varoga's voice resounded behind the still-closed door.

"Excuse me. I can't let you in. We'll talk tomorrow." And he added, in a peremptory tone as if he were responding to my mute insistence: "There will be plenty of time tomorrow. I'm finishing a very important map."

Again there was the sound of his dragging footfalls, which were drawing away. He had not waited for my response. Doubtless he had found my nocturnal visit untimely. I dared not persist.

As I was about to go away, I was struck simultaneously by the bitter perfume of opium, which seemed to be emerging from Mynheer Varoga's room, and by the sound of a door closing on the other side of the gallery.

A little cascade of light pearls resonated in the distance, strung out over the indecisive shadows of the low palm-trees of the courtyard: Eva's laughter, slightly ironic, but which assured me that she was not in any danger.

As soon as I had returned to my room I leaned outside. The ladder had disappeared.

I had a confused sentiment of being ridiculous, and was only able to console myself by telling myself that my actions throughout the evening had been those of a delicate and honest man. I only went to sleep thanks to my exceptional faculty of slumber, which I had already experienced a few hours earlier.

My anxieties disappeared the next day and gave way to the most foolish tranquility.

Eva explained herself to me in the most honest, the mot cheerful and the most delightful fashion. It appears that I am not a modern man that that I do not understand anything of the soul of a young woman who lives in Java, but who has spent two years of her life in Paris and London.

It is necessary that I have to get it into my head that there are women who are cultured, who read books, who like poetry.

I was cowardly and dared not admit my profound horror of such things.

Eva is one of those cultured women. It happens that one of her Javanese servants is a descendant of the ancient kings of Java, a young man extraordinarily versed in the history of the literature of his native land. Eva takes advantage of his great knowledge. In the evening he deposits on her window certain poems that he has copied, and which she reads before going to sleep. As the window is high he uses the aid of a ladder. What harm is there in that?

Eva does not hide it from me that I was very indiscreet in going to knock on her father's door at night. Her father smokes opium and fears more than anything else that someone might discover that. No one is unaware of it among the servants of the house and even their relatives in Batavia, but everyone puts on a semblance of not knowing it and of believing in his canal project, of which they ask for news and of which he makes chimerical designs. The best thing for me, therefore, if I am tactful, is not to make any allusion to my nocturnal visit.

I pride myself on having tact. I have not said anything to Mynheer Varoga. It would, in any case, be difficult to tell him anything, for I only see him during meals and he always disappears rapidly as soon as they are over. I have put off until later the care of turning him away from the deadly habit that renders him so thin and jaundiced.

My father was right. It is always necessary to behave in accordance with the rules of current morality. I am recompensed for the manner in which I have acted by Eva's love, a love that she has not declared to me, but which I divine in all her gestures.

Princess Sekartaji's Robe

My father might have been wrong, and new rules are necessary for new beings. Perhaps there was a profound and innate perversity in me, which caused the series of misfortunes that I am going to relate. Perhaps what happened was written in advance and I was only an actor in a play already determined in the mind of a god.

The point of departure of everything was the costume of Princess Sekartaji.[7] Who was that princess and when did she live? It does not matter. I even believe that she was only a favorite and that if King Ami Louhour had her murdered, he had good reasons for that. But that Sekartaji had worn, doubtless at some celebration or ceremony of ancient times, a costume of which painters celebrated in Java had immortalized the memory.

"I want you to see me today in the costume of Princess Sekartaji," Eva said to me after breakfast.

It was the day after the day when I had attempted to speak to Mynheer Varoga about my love for his daughter and my intention of asking for her hand in marriage.

In a hurry to get back to his room he had replied to me evasively, and laughing. He had tapped me on the shoulder and said to me: "I'll wager that that's what you wanted to talk to me about the other night. There'll be plenty of time to discuss that matter tomorrow. At the moment I'm completing my great canal project."

And he rubbed his hands together with the satisfaction of a man who is about to exhausting but agreeable labor.

---

[7] The name Sekartaji features in numerous items of Javanese folklore, but the one featured here, the wife of King Ami Louhour who was killed by him because he wanted to marry someone else, was also known as Angrene. She was the mother of Prince Panji, the hero of many such folktales.

159

He had climbed the stairs lightly, leaving me confounded by astonishment at the scant seriousness that some families accord to matters of amour, which are so grave.

So, I was sitting under the veranda, trying by way of distraction to chew the frightful Javan siri,[8] when a maidservant came to inform me that Eva had put on Princess Sekartaji's costume and was waiting for me in her room in order to show it to me.

I went up the stairs and along the gallery, and I knocked on Eva's door.

"Come in, come in then, since I'm expecting you," a joyful voice shouted to me.

The gilded gauze muslins of the window were drawn and a secret twilight bathed the room. I could not distinguish anything at first, and then a little laugh informed me that Eva was extended on the Indian carpet in the corner to the right, amid thick cushions.

I considered her, open-mouthed with surprise, emotion and admiration.

Princess Sekartaji must have lived in times when the sentiment of modesty had not yet developed. Perhaps King Ami Louhour had only had her put to death because she gave a bad example to his people by the astonishing lightness of her costume.

Eva was before me, almost naked to the waist. Only a network of fine crimson silk covered her breasts. Her hair was entirely thrown backwards and retained by a massive golden comb whose weight seemed to oblige her to hold her head very high, and which gave her profile an unaccustomed authority.

---

[8] A plant by this name is mentioned in a history of Java published in 1817 by Thomas Stamford Raffles, the great pioneer of Singapore, from which the author might well have borrowed numerous details deployed in his story; Raffles also summarizes the story of Ami Louhour and Sekartaji.

An azure Javan *chelama-chindi*[9] was wrapped around her loins, but it was so supple and so transparent that it only rendered the contours of her body more distinct. The legs were naked, like the torso, with rings in serpentine form that made an imperceptible metallic music when she moved.

Eva had painted her teeth with golden plaques, by means of a procedure still used by certain bayaderes of the isle of Madura. Sumpings were hanging from her ears. She had rubbed her shoulders, her breasts and her arms with a blue-tinted odorous powder that gave her flesh an extraterrestrial coloration. She was enveloped by spirals emitted by an incense-burner containing a hot aromatic oil. Something supernatural, more voluptuous than the odors, more secret than the filtered golden light, escaped from that precious body.

"The costume is rigorously exact," Eva said, without irony. "It's Djath who designed and reconstituted it."

Then an intoxication took possession of me. I would have liked to press that delicate form between my arms, to respire the breath or her painted teeth, wrench the heavy comb from the hair braided over the narrow blue neck.

I reached out my arms, but she evaded me.

"I even have the areca nuts you see," she said, making an allusion to some unknown event in the distant life of Princess Sekartaji.

She was holding the nuts in her hand. Doubtless I ought to have taken them in order to obey a ritual of which I was ignorant. And as I did not, she started to laugh and threw them in my face.

I pursued her around the room. It seemed to me that I was a hunter who wanted to seize a butterfly. She spun around me with laughter that had become bizarre, and her perfume, a perfume of flesh mingled with subtle vegetal essences, intoxicated me.

---

[9] This garment, too, appears to have no recorded existence outside the present text.

And it was then that in my inner depths the terrible thought was born, obscure at first, but rising, becoming precise amid the tenebrous ooze of instinct.

No, I was not the eternal hunter that I had always been. I was a wild beast in quest of a prey. I was the tiger of the forest of Merapi, the tiger itself, and I sensed my jaw elongating immeasurably and the lengthening of claws at my fingertips. I had become, in the chamber perfumed by aromatic oil, the tiger that only thinks of slaking its fury by crushing flesh.

Perhaps, like the beast I had encountered, I emitted an insupportable odor of flesh, for Eva suddenly ran to the door and opened it. It seemed to me that she was no longer laughing, and she said: "I'm going to show my costume to my father."

I followed her into the gallery and I went downstairs slowly.

O Lord, if you exist somewhere, protect man from the irresistible force that drives him to the possession of his feminine counterpart. Protect him from the perfume emitted by hair and the movement of arms, which are more intoxicating than any alcohol.

Deliver him from the desire to seize bodies to squeeze them and to sink his teeth into them as wild beasts do, for that desire is more prevalent in the soul than the sage counsel of a father and the duty of acting with delicacy that is imposed by reason.

O Lord, protect man from the blue tint of skin, a source of suffering, from the delicate curve of the neck, a road to misfortune, and from the fugitive line of the lips, a cause of calamities.

The Human Tiger

Everything that happened thereafter was vertiginous. I believe I remember that I sat down in a rocking chair and that I lit a cigar. Then I extinguished it, and Eva immediately appeared before me.

She had an authoritarian and decisive air. She was no longer wearing the costume of the princes but a sort of man's jacket with a very short skirt, which she donned in order to ride a horse. I noticed that her blue-tinted powder, hastily removed, left on her skin an azure tonality that made me think of the vestiges of dreams of which one retains a confused memory after awakening. One of her teeth, at the side, had conserved a fragment of golden plaque.

She wanted to make a long journey on horseback, she said, to show me the lamasery of Kobou Dalem.

We departed. There had not been any mention of Djath. Only Ali accompanied us.

Chance is favoring me, said an interior voice within me, where bestial desire was already nascent and growling.

First we took a poorly-traced route along the edge of the forest. It was there that we saw, sitting on a stone at the foot of a mango-tree, a hideous being, a kind of living skeleton perfectly designed beneath parchment-like skin, with hair so long and so thick that I immediately wondered from whenever it could obtain its substance. Like the monkey that I had killed the previous day, he was holding a mango in his hand.

By way of a joke, I was about to make him a sign that it was necessary for him to eat a great many in order to grow a little fatter, when he rose to his feet on seeing me and pointing at me, pronounced maledictions that I did not understand.

"That's the ascetic Chumbul," said Eva. "He must have heard your rifle-shots yesterday and he's bearing a grudge against you for having killed his friends the animals."

I shrugged my shoulders and we went on.

The path became almost impracticable so much did it go up and down among the lianas and vegetation of all kinds.

We suddenly found ourselves confronted by two colossal statues representing individuals—priest or gods, how would I know?—kneeling beneath rovers of verdure, with interlaced serpents around their arms.

"They're the Rechas of the temple that is on the right."

A little further on, there was a stone elephant, entirely caparisoned, whose trunk was lying on the ground in an utterly ridiculous manner.

I thought about the absurdity of that supposedly civilized ancient people, who had found nothing better, as a sign of civilization, than reproducing images of animals in stone, in the corner of the world that is the most infested with living beasts.

"There's the lamasery," said Eva, admiringly, "designating a few wretched stone buildings that could be distinguished in the trees at a place where avenues ended that were so encumbered by vegetation that it would have been possible to go along them on horseback.

I nearly uttered a cry of surprise. We came across a small group of silent individuals. They were clad in dirty red cotton robes and wore bonnets of the same color. They were surrounding a man dressed in the European style, but very simply, whose face I thought I recognized. I noticed that the man had a brightly colored straw hat, spattered with mud, the form of which recalled the one I had lost.

Eva had bowed respectfully; I saw that she had turned in my direction and was urging her horse forward. Naturally, I pressed my own, and it was only afterwards that I remembered the man I had just encountered among the lamas. It was the individual that had been so antipathetic to me in the opium-den in Singapore.

"I regret," I said to Eva, "not having been able to tell that Hindu or Mongol in European dress how disagreeable I find his face, and how sickened I am by his manner of caressing lizards."

Eva raised her eyes to the heavens.

"He's also a lama, but a traveling lama," she replied, with a hint of veneration in her voice. "There are those among them who sacrifice themselves, tearing themselves away from the happiness of solitary meditation to aid other men, those who have need of it, barbarians like you and me."

I did not attach any importance to those words, for the tenebrous desire was inhabiting me, pouring forth treasures of cunning and putting a hypocritical serenity into my features.

"Isn't it necessary to let the horses rest a little?" I said, mildly, instead of declaiming about the stupidity of lamas who condemn themselves uselessly to live in deserted places in order to worship imaginary gods there.

"We aren't going back by the same route," Eva replied. "We're going to go around the forest mass that we have on the right and stop for a while in a wood of ebony-trees that I know. We won't be very far from the house then."

Eva gave the impression of knowing the country perfectly, and that dispelled any worry on my part of going astray in the uniform forests.

We soon reached a place that one could only call an ebony wood with difficulty, since there were, as well as ebony trees, bamboos, areca palms, nibong palms and all kinds of huge, hairy, bristling trees whose names were unknown to me.

But Eva knew perfectly well where we were; that was the main thing.

We dismounted. A few vague trails terminated at the place where we had stopped.

Then my heart began to beat faster, and I said, without looking at Eva, in the most indifferent manner possible: "Ali could guard the horses while we walked along one of these paths to stretch our legs. Would you like that?"

I raised my head imprudently. Our eyes met while she said yes. Doubtless the reflection of the beast was in my face, for she suddenly hesitated and nearly changed her mind. Then she made a little insouciant and superior gesture, which made me think of my own gesture when I cracked my whip in the midst of my animals.

We walked for quite a long time. I looked for a place sufficiently devoid of long grass for me to be able to invite her to sit down without her being afraid of snakes.

Nothing conscious subsisted within me but the determination to realize my desire. By virtue of an inexplicable split, I was ashamed of myself, but when that shame surfaced I saw the face of Djath, his sensual mouth and his manicured hands with painted fingernails. Then a phrase I had once heard returned to my memory.

A man ought never to permit a woman to toy with his desire.

Then a surge of self-respect rose to my cheeks and I felt myself blushing as I walked

"In what epoch, exactly, did Princess Sekartaji live?" I asked.

That date left me profoundly indifferent, and I only asked the question to break the silence.

Eva must have understood the vanity of the precision, for she replied: "What an exciting profession yours is! I would have love to tame animals!"

She did not know that she was in the process of exercising that métier, and that it was a human tiger who was walking placidly beside her.

The path had broadened suddenly and we had arrived in a clearing. A great suffocating immobility weighed upon the forest, and I perceived at my feet the slow, seething of germinations, fecund and sexual, like the mystery of life.

We had stopped. I reflected on the most favorable fashion of seizing Eva from behind, in order to place my lips on hers before she had taken account of my embrace. I envisaged as improbable the hypothesis that she would be thrown by that kiss into an absolute intoxication and that any struggle would be unnecessary. I let the rifle that was slung over my shoulder, which was inconveniencing me, slide to the ground, saying: "Would you like to sit down here?"

But my voice, which emotion rendered similar to a growl, betrayed me.

Eva turned round, saw me with my bestial mask, flushed with blood, uttered a slight nervous laugh and, either as a joke or out of veritable dread, started running along a path that was neither facing us nor to the right, as she was later to claim, but to the left.

Surprised, I hesitated for a few seconds. Then I wanted to catch up with her, and I launched myself after her.

This flight, I thought, *is perhaps one more coquetry. But she has no doubt as to the manner in which she will be seized when I reach her.*

Eva's coquetry carried her a long way. I had no idea that a woman could run so fast. She galloped, no doubt intoxicated by her own speed and the air charged with vegetal miasmas, and while she ran I glimpsed the perfection of her slender legs, and my desire increased. I identified myself once again with a tiger pursuing its prey, snuffled in the same fashion, and the identification was so complete that I sometimes surprised myself making bounds in that example, which slowed down my progress.

Eva went at hazard. She took a path, and then another, and I have no idea how long that would have lasted and whether I would succeeded in overtaking her, when I tripped over a tree-root and fell. The muffled exclamation that I uttered then made her stop and retraced her steps.

"You've hurt yourself," she said to me, in a curious voice that did not reveal any commiseration.

No, I had not hurt myself. I was vexed. Eva was no longer afraid. A tiger should not fall.

"It seems to me that we've come a long way. I'd like to recover my rifle."

And then we looked at one another, seized by the same apprehension. Among these clearings and paths, so similar to one another, would we be able to find our way back?

I emitted that doubt aloud, while Eva kept her anxiety to herself. She even shrugged her shoulders.

I could be tranquil. She had an admirable sense of direction.

I recalled then that my compass was still in the small leather bag attached to my saddle-bow.

After half an hour of walking we had not found the clearing where I had so foolishly deposited my rifle, and I expressed to Eva my assurance that we ought to turn round.

A long argument followed as to whether the path that we had taken when we had started running was to the right or the left, relative to the path by which we had come on leaving Ali and the horses.

Eva claimed that she had turned right. I said that it was left. We convinced one another reciprocally, and ended up both rallying to the hypothesis that the path we had followed at the moment of abandoning the rifle was directly ahead of us.

When we had marched for quite a long time in the direction chosen by Eva, which was not the one we had just judged appropriate, it appeared to us that we were in error. Eva reproached me for having driven her by my foolish insistence to take a path that led nowhere, and wanted to head along a new path of her choice.

That path ended in a mass of enormous rocks that we had not previously encountered.

Suddenly, a sapphire coloration slid furtively and sadly through the branches and announced the advent of the abrupt night.

We were irrevocably lost, and the absence of a firearm prevented us from signaling to Ali the direction in which found ourselves. I believe, in addition, that we had covered a great enough distance for us to be unable to hear any shots that he might fire. We lent our ears in vain. Only the odious voices of a thousand animals, hateful whistlings, ironic chatter and satisfied yelps resounded under the foliage.

Then Eva affected a cheerfulness that she did not feel deep down. All this was not very serious. We would dine on a few mangoes and content ourselves with their juice to slake our thirst.

Ali would doubtless not go back without us. Her father would not experience any great anxiety, since he knew that his daughter was with me and Ali to protect her. He would think that we had stayed overnight at the lamasery. In the morning, I would climb a tree in order to see the direction of the sun, and thanks to her innate sense of orientation, we could not fail to find our way.

In the worst case, supposing that we could not rejoin Ali in the morning, the latter would return to Mynheer Varoga's house and a search would be organized, with rifle shots and the sound of gongs, like ones that had already been carried out in similar cases. The unique danger consisted of spending a night in the forest, at the mercy of wild beasts. But I had· matches; it was sufficient to profit from the last glimmers of twilight to find an open space. There we would make a big fire, and we could repose without fear, and even chat agreeably before going to sleep.

Everything that Eva said was true, in sum, but she was not taking account of the wild beast that does not fear flames, the interior beast of the soul.

The Temple of Ganesha

"I know exactly where I am," said Eva, on seeing the debris of columns and sections of collapsed walls emerging under the verdure. "We've doubtless returned to the temple of Kobou Dalem. The Rechas ought to be here."

The Rechas! There were no Rechas. Eva was obliged to agree that we were not in the presence of the temple of Kobou Dalem, but an entirely unknown temple of immense proportions.

I thought that we might discover a room there, or even the niche of some idol that might serve as a shelter, but everything was too large and too ruined. We found a sort of stone gallery, which we followed. The moon had just risen and permitted us not to stumble over the roots that sometimes cleaved the flagstones, or fall into pits that suddenly opened up at our feet.

Eva ran on ahead and I shouted to her incessantly to be careful. Sometimes an enormous Buddha loomed up, or a dragon of singular form. It seemed to me that I was hallucinating. And suddenly, we found ourselves confronted by a broad, curving, prodigious stone stairway framed with bas-reliefs. We went down the high steps, full of emotion, and Eva grasped my hand, so impressive was the central area in which we arrived.

It was a courtyard, a great circular space surrounded by the mass of the edifice, which was reached via two monumental staircases, one of which we had descended. The courtyard was strewn with toppled columns and the debris of statues. Eva and I advanced into it slowly, shoulder to shoulder, and did not weary of looking around at the monument, which had become higher, more redoubtable and more mysteriously mute as we drew closer to that interior center.

Heaps of cornices, pyramids and sacred animals loomed up on all sides, intermingled here and there with the fan of a palm-tree or a jet of bamboos that nature had sown at hazard in order to mock the symmetrical effort of humans. And in the accumulated architectural fragments there were innumerable reproductions of giant beasts: granite buffaloes, coiled marble serpents and fabulous birds with deployed wings, with the consequence that, in the solitude of the moonlit night, our refuge was populated by the terrifying images of the beasts we wanted to flee.

That place was, however, the safest of those we might find. At the foot of a column I cleared a sizeable space, cut brushwood, made a heap of it, and set fire to it.

The flame delivered us from our apprehensions. It permitted me to distinguish that the base of the edifice formed a series of regular niches and that in each niche there was a seated human individual, a stout and short individual with a broad belly and the head of an elephant covered with a pointed bonnet. Hundreds of stone men with elephantine heads were sitting in hundreds of niches, considering us silently.

"That's Ganesha, the god of wisdom," Eva told me. "I've never come into this temple, which has been abandoned for hundreds of years, but I've heard mention of its existence. We're much further away than I would have supposed, but I know where I am now."

Eva did not want to renounce the privilege of knowing the places where she had led us astray.

She had lain down some distance from the fire on a heap of ferns and dry leaves. We had eaten mangoes collected in the forest and drunk coconut milk. We were invaded by the wellbeing of physical repose and the intoxication of immobility.

We began by darting frequent glances at the two stairways, of which we saw the somber steps disappearing into the heights of the monument. I sensed that Eva was imagining, like me, a slow descent by the monstrous tiger, imagining its phosphorescent eyes fixed upon us. Then she took a handful of branches and threw them on the fire in order that the rising flames would cast their floating conflagration over the entire tenebrous circus.

Gradually, however, that obsession vanished and gave way to a bizarre attraction, an inexplicable magnetism of obscure stone forms, an attraction that I felt materially and which gave me more than once a desire to run to the stairways and climb them. Naturally, I resisted that desire.

Instead of going to sleep, Eva sat up several times, as if she had heard a mysterious call—not an appeal coming from far away, which might have been the cries of Ali or people searching for us, but a nearby appeal, perhaps that of a voice coming from the very mystery of the ancient stones.

"Didn't you hear it?" she said to me in a low voice, alert and anxious.

It was that movement, which she made two or three times, that inexplicable movement, to listen to something that was not resonating, that was the cause of everything that happened.

I swear that if she had gone to sleep peacefully, full of confidence, I would have watched over her slumber until dawn. But she sat up, attentively, while looking at me from the corner of her eye with half-closed eyelids. Her taut breasts appeared beneath her light jacket. The shoulders and the neck, leaning forward in the movement that she made in order to listen, revealed an animal character that I saw for the first time. In the entire silhouette of her body there was something moving, troubling and voluptuous.

The more I recall that hour, the more I am convinced that coming toward us from the profound forest was the haunting of the multiform bestiality of which it is the ancestral lair.

The cries of jackals and the calls of night-birds responding to one another formed an insensate language that almost communicated a desire to walk on four feet, to crawl like serpents, to howl like wolves, to utter prolonged guttural cries like nocturnal owls.

The perfect equilibrium of my faculties prevented me from yielding to those follies. But I surprised myself by dancing to the right and the left like a bear, and Eva, sitting up in front of me, suddenly had a different aspect.

I saw, in the firelight, her nostrils quivering, her breasts rising and falling. Her mouth was redder, and had the effect on me of a little blood that I ought to drink. A human bodily warmth came to me from her, more intoxicating than all the terrestrial perfumes emerging from the innumerable cassolettes of plants and flowers.

There was, in her manner of extending her upper body, a secret desire to be tipped back, an offering of her blue-tinted skin. Her face suddenly changed expression, her eyes losing their gleam, the blood of her lips palpitating. Intelligence seemed to quit her at the same time as I sensed it disappearing from my own face. We were nothing more, at that moment, than two animals sniffing one another, rejecting one another and desiring one another.

It was then that I hurled myself upon her. Did that attack render her reason or did it, on the contrary, cause her to lose it? I cannot know; I shall never know.

I must have been hideous. She repelled me forcefully. I tried to seize her again, but I only grasped her jacket, which ripped, at the same time as her chemise, in the backward movement that she made. That uncovered her shoulder and one of her breasts.

What happened then in Eva's soul? Did the man she loved—for I am convinced that she loved me, even though I never had any proof of it—appear to her to be more redoubtable than the forest, with all its dangers? Had her reason been corrupted by dread? Did she hear an occult voice calling to her? Was there a magical influence in that abandoned temple?

I do not know. Suddenly possessed by an inconceivable lightness, Eva launched herself across the courtyard, climbed one of the two monumental stairways and disappeared from my view.

I was convinced that she had sat down at the top of the steps. Already, confused by my action, I had called to her several times, begging her pardon.

As I did not obtain any response I climbed the stairway, while reminding her that it was dangerous to draw away from the fire and swearing to her on the head of my beloved mother that I would not recommence my unworthy attempt.

My surprise and perplexity were great on not finding her. I shouted with all my might to make her come back. There was no response. Then, frightened, I started running along the round path that dominated the temple. I fell into holes, I scaled statues. I was still shouting.

That lasted a long time. The moon disappeared. My voice broke because of the effort I was making and I ceased to be able to make Eva's name resonate. I believed that she was still hiding and refusing to respond to me in order to punish me. Several times, I thought that she had gone back to the fire, and I returned there, only to set forth again immediately and resume my search.

Finally, after an eternity of waiting, during which I stirred the ashes of the dead fire mechanically, I perceived the silhouettes of coconut-palms cut out against a livid azure. Abruptly, a red light inundated the temple and I distinguished around me all the Ganeshas with the elephantine heads, in their derisory immobility, their abject indifference and their limitless sadness.

Eva was not there. I could not imagine what had become of her, and the thought of her occupied my soul entirely. No sound any longer emerged from my exhausted throat.

A large flock of birds, of a species I did not recognize, rose up to my right and striped the sky slowly. I had a great sensation of physical cold, and the entire earth appeared repugnant to me, like an extent of marshland, stagnant waters populated with crocodiles.

Suddenly, I started circling several times, with increasing rapidity, like a horse in a circus, between the walls of the temple, along the mute figures that extended their trunks toward me inexorably.

Then I climbed one of the stairways, traversed the round path, stumbled through the collapsed walls, the fragments of porticoes, the formless idols, the half-buried galleries and hurled myself straight ahead into the forest.

Eva's Disappearance

I must have run for a long time.

The more I try to resurrect in memory the end of that night in the temple of Ganesha, the more convinced I am that anxiety and the absence of sleep are insufficient to explain the demented thought that forced me to run, and the more convinced I am, too, that there was in Eva's flight another cause than offended modesty or the dread of an amorous man throwing himself upon her.

I must have run into a tree trunk, fallen and lost consciousness. When I woke up, I was lying on the ground, and I was immediately struck by the sensation of a heavy head-dress circling my skull. I made the gesture of removing my hat, but I was bare-headed. I merely had an enormous bump on my forehead, almost resembling a horn. I was in the middle of a clearing, in rather bright light, and I calculated that the day was already well advanced.

The events that had unfolded since the previous day came back to me with horror, but appeared to me to be remote, in a distant past.

There were two parrots on a branch, which uttered a few grotesque sounds from time to time. A kind of small antelope showed its quivering muzzle amid the foliage. In spite of my preoccupations, my hunter's instinct caused me to regret not having my rifle.

I made a great effort to reach my watch. It had stopped.

I perceived that, along with my watch, I had taken a handful of ants out of my pocket. I had them all over me, on my garments, and I watched them running in long files over my legs and my chest for some time. I was ravaged by a sensation of thirst, but I stayed there nevertheless, almost without moving, near the parrots and the antelope, in the middle of the ants, putting off the moment of action until later.

Suddenly, the muzzle disappeared and there was a rapid glide among the leaves. At the same time, the parrots flew away. I immediately assumed that the senses of those animals, more subtle than mine, had perceived a danger. What? Immediately, I thought of the tiger.

What had frightened an antelope and parrots also ought to frighten an exhausted man who had a horn on his forehead, but a singular apathy took possession of me. I remained where I was, without moving.

And then, very distantly, through the depths of the forest, very sad and heart-rending, I heard a growing noise. It was something analogous to one I had heard in my childhood during certain popular festivals in Singapore. There were tom-toms, gongs, and sometimes a salvo of rifle-fire, and then a long cry that was prolonged like a chant, with desperate notes.

I understood immediately what it was. People were searching for us. Men were coming in my direction with the arms and voices that are their blessed privilege. But certain sad memories of childhood are so nostalgic that everything that recalls them constructs the heart dolorously. The greeting came to me with a fairground song, an evocation of fireworks and the port decked with a thousand lanterns. I got to my feet without enthusiasm.

I fell down again immediately, perceiving that I had a sprained ankle.

Then an interminable hour went by, perhaps several hours.

Birds pass above my head, animals flee. The cortege of saviors advances slowly. They are not far away now, but I cannot call out to them; my voice is still broken and I am incapable of uttering a sound.

Sometimes there is a silence. The chant dies away. They must be reloading the rifles. Perhaps the hour of return has sounded, and the people coming toward me are changing direction and going back.

The wait is so long that I am almost resigned to that.

177

Let them go back! I shall lie down under that tree and go back to sleep.

And suddenly, I launch myself forward on one foot, seized by a frenzied desire to recover my fellows, and hop from tree to tree, leaning on the trunks many making futile efforts to articulate cries for help.

A great noise of gongs resonates in my ears, and I am suddenly gripped around the midriff by Ali the Macassar. Twenty Javanese surround me and I see their eyes fixed upon the bump on my forehead.

"Eva?" I say, immediately. No sound escapes my lips, but everyone understands, and seems to be asking me the same question.

Eva, it is explained to me, has not yet been found, but perhaps the other search-party, directed by Mynheer Varoga on the other side of the forest, has been able to find her and bring her back safe and sound.

If one thinks about the prodigious agglomeration of life in movement that an equatorial forest contains, it does not appear astonishing that a human being can disappear there without leaving any trace. One is even surprised that a human being can traverse it and emerge again without being dis-aggregated and assimilated, consumed by tentacles, by mandibles, by suckers, by the thousands of animal or vegetable organs with which that multiform body is covered.

If one falls there and loses consciousness, it requires a miracle to wake up alive—a miracle that was produced for me. I attribute it to my magnetism as an animal-tamer, which must, in that circumstance, have driven away the wild beasts.

There are ants and termites that, in a matter of hours, can reduce a body to the state of a skeleton of perfect cleanliness. There are jackals that are alerted not merely to the death of a creature, which might be explained by the odor, but of its state of ill-health, even its weakness or discouragement.

They do not follow the hunter who is returning home tranquilly by a familiar path, whereas they arrive from all over the forest behind a man who has gone astray, as if they had been informed by some occult message of his anxiety.

There are vultures full of patience that lie in wait for the definitive immobility. There are panthers, and above all tigers, which provoke that immobility with the formidable club of their paw. Those throw their prey lightly over their shoulders and carry it away, to break it and butcher it at their ease, in inextricable thickets, places inaccessible to human feet, where it is never found.

There are tigers, and in the forest of Merapi, there is, above all, the Tiger.

No one mentioned it during the feverish searches of those ten terrible days, and those ten nights, sleepless even for a temperament like mine, which has received the reparative gift of going to sleep with facility.

Everyone thought about it incessantly, and formulated the horrible hypothesis internally, only to reject it as soon as it was formulated. But I ought to say that no material indication, no trace of any struggle, no fragment of torn clothing ever gave substance to that hypothesis.

The workers of the indigo plantation, the inhabitants of the villages dependent on Mynheer Varoga and those of the neighboring villages, worked in relays with a perfect devotion.

The cannon never ceased to resound. The resident in Djokjokarta sent an officer and a detachment of soldiers from the Dutch garrison to multiply the search-parties. He came himself, on the fourth day, and for the hundredth time I told the story of the fateful night, naturally omitting from the story the surge of animality that had thrown me toward Eva, my struggle with her, her torn jacket and her uncovered breast.

I was devoured by remorse. But everyone likes to be per-suaded of what is most convenient for him. I had entrenched deeply in my mind the idea that I had nothing to do with Eva's insensate flight. She had listened several times to appeals coming from who knows where, which I had not heard. That was the mysterious cause of the disaster.

I gave myself reason by recalling Eva's coquetries. A young woman who deliberately displays herself semi-naked in the costume of a princess, who goes to see a ship's mate in his hotel and leaves his room by means of a ladder, who receives a young Javanese by night in her own bedroom, cannot be frightened by the desire of an amorous man and a breast bared before him.

In any case, I had immediately called her back and begged her pardon. The cause of her flight could not be the fear of being taken next to the fire, on fern-leaves, by a man she loved. There was an occult cause, a mystery in which some magic was mingled, and I attributed, without being able to explain it, the evil influence that had acted on Eva to the stone animal figures, the men with elephantine heads, in the temple of Ganesha.

Mynheer Varoga's grief was of a silent order. He had grown old abruptly. He repeated several times, when I formulated my hypotheses before him: "My daughter was so bizarre!"

Then he shrugged his shoulders, as if he had just heard the discourse of a limited man.

He spent his time in the forest. I suppose that the lack of opium contributed to giving him an astonishing feverishness. I saw that he was incessantly holding himself back from running to his room in order to smoke. Two or three planters, friends of his who knew his habits and knew how dangerous the abrupt privation of opium can be, exhorted him on several occasions, in my presence to go up to his room. Tracing a hydrographical map, they said to him benevolently, would be an excellent distraction from his dolor.

He did not want to. He replied that he had been far too busy with maps and canals and had neglected his daughter. He meant by that that he had smoked too much.

The loss of a cherished individual always commences by being a source of remorse.

I saw very little of Djath. In his ardor to search, he only came back late in order to sleep. I supposed that he was going to look at me in a hateful fashion. He did not look at me. Several times he passed beside me without seeing me. I believe that he had effaced me from the world. I had the sensation of only being a void in his presence, and I was irritated by it, but I did not judge the moment propitious to chastise him. I was obliged, because of the same reason of propriety, also to postpone another chastisement.

Broken by the fatigues of a day of searching the forest and by the suffering that my injured foot was still causing me to endure, I had gone up to my room after dinner and was sitting there, very melancholy, by the window.

The house was full of Mynheer Varoga's friends, from the surrounding area, and Dutch officers from Djokjokarta and even Samarang, who had come on learning of Eva's disappearance to lend us the support of their futile activity. That caused a great agitation in the old dwelling, and there were even tents set up under the branches of the age-old banyans.

Almost all the noise was extinct. In the far distance, salvos of rifle fire could be heard at regular intervals, which were fired all night long from posts organized on the heights. The indigo plantation's cannon had fallen silent for the first time, for lack of ammunition. There was no moon. The darkness was compact.

A little further away, a large cast-iron lantern suspended from a palm-tree made a ruddy circle. I distinguished under the veranda the flame of a single cigar. With the smoker, whose voice I recognized as that of the owner of coffee plantations, there was another man who was not smoking.

Involuntarily, I heard some of their phrases, and thought that they were talking about me, in connection with Eva's disappearance, but their conversation only reached me in a few fragments, the while remaining quite unintelligible.

"I believe he's a man completely devoid of intelligence... Such a profession... The most delightful of young women... What imprudence on Mynheer Varoga's part... The responsibility incumbent on the man who..."

The coffee-planter was launching puffs of smoke toward the sky and seemed to be questioning his interlocutor, as if the other might have a special insight into the tragic case of Eva.

I leaned forward and I saw that the man who was not smoking had a straw hat on his head similar to the one that I had lost a few days earlier while lying in wait for the tiger. He was now talking about the temple of Ganesha, I heard this:

"Ganesha, or Paleyar, or Inahika, is the god of intelligence, of numbers, of truth, and of chastity, for all those thinks are linked. Yes, a seated man, to whom immobility and meditation have given a broad belly, a man who has the head of an elephant, such is the image of wisdom. From the animal kingdom of which we are the issue, we draw the essential truths that permit us to surpass the human realm.

"That is the meaning of the symbol, Wisdom has an animal base. Fidelity, obstinate labor, enthusiasm in the love of that which is superior—what noble sentiments the animals teach us!"

I remember those remarks because of their complete absurdity, which would have made me burst out laughing in other circumstances. The man with the cigar was asking questions and the other was replying slowly, with a distant indifference.

"Perhaps, perhaps!" he said. "The secret of everything is love. By love one elevates the animals within oneself, by hatred one transforms oneself in their image. In the ancient stone reproductions of the temple of Ganesha there might be a force encapsulated by the sorcerer sculptors two thousand years ago. That force might have acted in accordance with laws unknown to us."

I was trembling with emotion. Unfortunately, what followed was spoken in a low voice and only scraps of sentences reached me.

"No, not Eva, assuredly. But an animal-tamer, a man who steals their liberty from beasts, who torments them, who makes them suffer. There are certain base natures that act upon the most delicate beings in their entourage. Those powerful natures are protected by their own depravity. They do not suffer from the evil that they emit and which forms an armor for them. They debase others without even knowing it."

I almost fell out of the window, in order to see the face of the man who was speaking and who was accusing me without proof of having caused Eva's death by the baseness of my nature. I sensed that, in spite of its unreasonable character, the accusation had some truth in it, and that augmented my fury.

The two men had stood up and I recognized the man in the straw hat. He made the gesture of refusing a cigar that the other offered him as he left.

"No, never cigars," he said.

I nearly intervened and shouted that it was a wretched hypocrisy, a false affectation of sobriety.

The man who seemed to have such extensive knowledge of the temple of Ganesha did not smoke cigars, but he smoked opium. He was a wretched deviant, a frequenter of opium dens, an habitué of hovels; it was the man who had caressed a lizard so tenderly in Singapore, in the Street of the Camel, beyond the Door of the Tiger. That was what I nearly shouted in the silence of the night.

And I nearly shouted something else.

That so-called traveling lama was wearing my Manila straw hat on his head, which he had found, God knows where: my hat, which I recognized very well when he passed under the lantern suspended a little further away, from a palm-tree.

That man accused me of having a base nature, and he was wearing my hat on his head!

I made myself a promise to get it back some day.

The Tiger Captured

The days went by. Discouragement took possession of souls. Good will wore away. The number of consolations diminished. The tents in front of the house were rolled up. The abandoned labor was resumed in the indigo plantation.

Before leaving, I wanted to see the temple of Ganesha again, and I went there with Ali and half a dozen Javanese, for it had been agreed that no one would go abroad in the forest any longer except in numerous company.

Every corner of the temple had been explored. There were a thousand traces of the passage of men, and there was no point in searching there for traces of Eva. That had been done on the first day, with no result.

In the middle of the day the temple did not have the same mystery as at night. I found it terrible, however, with its pitilessly circular form, the regularity of its staircases and it mute figures. Ancient wisdom had an appearance so diversely strange that it resembled madness.

Just as we were about to draw way definitively, I retraced my steps and examined one of the individuals with an elephant's head at close range I saw that it had four hands. One held a conch, another a disk, a third a club and the last a lotus flower.

Then, I have no idea why, perhaps for vengeance, I broke off the end of the trunk and some of the petals of the lotus with the hilt of my knife, which fell miserably to the ground.

Thus, the man was not absolutely vanquished by the stone, since he had the power to mutilate it.

I only informed Mynheer Varoga of my departure at the last minute. I wanted to avoid long emotional farewells. He was not unaware that I loved his daughter and that I was as unhappy as he was. To my great surprise, he quit me very coolly. I supposed that the individual who was wearing my hat must have done me harm in his mind, and my chagrin was very sharp.

I no longer know the reason for which Ali the Macassar stayed one day longer than me. I was to wait for him in Samarang, where we were to take the boat together.

I was invited to lunch by an officer of the garrison and it was in his house that I learned the sensational news that immediately excited the town,

In the confines of the forest of Merapi, in one of the traps that I had prepared personally with the admirable artistry permitted by my knowledge of beasts, the monstrous tiger had been found that was the terror of the region: the one that had carried off two women before my arrival, the one that everyone suspected, without expressing the suspicion, of having devoured Eva.

There could be no doubt about it, it appeared, it really was that one. No other tiger of such enormous proportions had ever been seen, and the first people who had seen it in the depths of the trap had fled at the sight of it.

I was weary. I was no longer hoping for anything but to get back to Singapore. There was a boat departing for that city. As Ali had not joined me by the evening of the appointed day, I embarked without him.

It was Ali who did everything. There is no doubt about it; if I had been present, I would immediately have put the tiger to death with a bullet. But Ali, finding himself alone, was intoxicated by the pride of representing me. He believed that he had a duty to defend his master's interests. In principle, Mynheer Varoga had promised me ownership of the tiger if it were captured alive. Such a tiger represented a value of three hundred rupees. Ali did not allow that value to be destroyed by a few rifle shots. He redeemed the promise made and presented those who wanted to kill the wild beast with a very clever argument.

It was necessary to make the monster suffer that had terrified the region for so long. His master would take charge of that—did he not have good reasons for doing so? And he winked in a significant fashion, he told me later, which everyone understood.

To get a tiger out of a deep trap and enclose it in a cage seems a complex problem to ordinary people. It is, reality, child's play. There were cages in Djokjokarta of which the rajah made use for combats of ferocious animals, of which he was a celebrated enthusiast. Ali obtained one easily. Then he did everything himself, aided by a few Javanese whom he was obliged to pay very dearly, so great was the terror the tiger inspired in them.

He nourished the animal, while waiting for the arrival of the cage, with meat containing pellets of opium, dosed in order that it was neither excited nor poisoned by the opium, but cast into a sort of lethargy. Then he put lassos around the feet and neck of the animal and hoisted it up.

The taciturn Ali became cheerful in recounting that he had had all the difficulty in the world preventing them from bringing the cannon and aiming it at the beast, solidly bound and almost asleep.

He also described with pride his triumphant departure from the indigo plantation, and with modesty his arrival in Samarang, where his fidelity in my regard had been put to the proof. The Rajah of Djokjokarta had sent a messenger to him who had offered him three hundred rupees as a personal gift for him if he had consented to sell the beast; the price for the latter would have been paid to me in addition.

Ali's merit had been all the greater because he no longer had any money on him and did not know how he was going to spend the entire week in Samarang that would elapse before the departure of a boat for Singapore.

Fortunately, he had remembered the name of my Batavian banker and had been wise enough to go and see his correspondent in Samarang, who had immediately made him the necessary advances.

There had been even more difficulty at the moment of departure.

An old commandant of the Dutch infantry who lived in Samarang, and who had crises of alcoholism, had taken it into his head to kill the tiger with revolver shots, claiming that it was shameful to let it live after the drama that had just unfolded. Ali had been obliged to spend the last three days and three nights beside the tiger's cage and not to quit it for an instant.

I remember the singular impression that I experienced when Ali, who had just supervised the disembarkation of the cargo in the port, brought it to the door of the house.

Dusk was about to fall. There was a Chinese festival in honor of some Chinese sage or other, and as my gardens were on the edge of the Chinese quarter, the air was resounding with the noise of petards, detonations and raga music. Children were screaming and singing, and the ensemble resembled what I had heard in the forest of Merapi when I had woken up alone with a bump on my forehead and a fistful of ants in my hand.

The carriage that brought the tiger stopped outside the gate. It was drawn by horses accustomed to wild beasts and had no fear of them. The tiger was silent. The cage was covered with a canvas sheets, in order that the sight of the beast, of which there had been talk in Singapore, did not arouse the whole population.

In spite of that, a crowd of Chinese in a festive mood came running and formed a vast semicircle. They were laughing, as they had a habit of doing for everything. Ali, who was conscious of the importance of his role, wanted to please the crowd, and just as I appeared on the threshold, attracted by the noise of the vehicle, he removed the canvas.

The tiger was lying down and did not get up. The vast rumor that rose from the Chinese, amazed by the sight of it, did not seem to interest it. In the semi-darkness, it fixed its strange, immense phosphorescent eyes on me alone—eyes that I recognized by virtue of having contemplated them in a similar twilight.

Nothing could deflect its gaze, neither the children who tried to poke it with sticks not the jolts of the cage went it went through the gate. It had also recognized me.

It seemed to me that it experienced the same sadness that I did, that in the sway of its neck there was a fatigue analogous to mine. We both felt the same miserable anguish, of beings about to enter into an unforgiving struggle, who are bearing the burden of their own ferocity.

In spite of the cage, the whips and the pikes, I did not feel that I was the stronger in that contest. There was an element that escaped me, an unknowable weapon that I sensed in my adversary's possession, and, while the cage rolled past the other cages and the Chinese shouted with joy, I was sad, horribly saddened by all my hatred against beasts, which I was about to concentrate so justly against that beast, more ferocious than all the rest.

PART TWO

The Tiger's Eyes

I have always considered myself to be very intelligent because I have refrained from books and culture, and my mind has developed under the direct influence of life, but I have never been able to say with certainty whether my fundamental nature is veritably good.

It is difficult to establish in the soul of a man the difference between goodness and wickedness. One is good with certain beings, bad with others. Generous sentiments are relative to the manner in which one has slept or digested one's meal.

I do not know whether I am good, but I know that, possessed by the passion of vengeance, I abandoned myself to that passion with the same ardor as if it had been a duty.

Ali the Macassar had not deceived Mynheer Varoga's indigo growers, the unfortunate inhabitants of the valley of Merapi. His master, the animal-tamer, had good reasons for making the captive tiger—the giant tiger, the tiger unique in Java—suffer.

I began by enclosing it in the most solid and sturdiest cage I possessed, for savage animals find unexpected reserves of strength in certain fits of fury.

With its astonishing jaw resting on its forepaws, the tiger was obstinate in remaining motionless and silent, plunging its gaze into mine as soon as I appeared before it. To force it to move and make it turn in its cage, I first deprived it of nourishment, for the first effect of hunger on wild beasts is the ancestral pursuit of prey.

When I had made it hungry, I made it thirsty for days. But, as if it understood my desire and had resolved no longer to satisfy it, it lay down again after thousands of rotations, and started snuffling in a sinister fashion, without losing sight of me.

I was seized by an imperious need to hear it roar. I woke it up as soon as it fell asleep by hitting it with an iron bar, but it contented itself with growling, and I was the one who experienced the rage I wanted to communicate to it.

Then I had a Malay spear brought to me, and I pierced one of its paws all the way through. It finally roared. That roar drowned out all the voices of the beasts, filled my vast gardens, converted into a menagerie, and resounded in the neighboring streets. But that terrible roar, that cry of pain and impotent fury, did not have the effect of engendering fear in the other animals that the voices of lions or tigers usually have.

On the evening of the pierced foot, as if they were responding to an order, all the beasts woke up in their cages, a communication was established, and a breath of revolt passed over.

The monkeys leapt, suspending themselves by their tails, throwing fragments of coconuts through the bars, chattering furiously and showing their teeth. The Andean condors opened their wings as if they were about to fly away to their distant lands. The eagles stretched out immeasurable talons. The tapir began to sniff stupidly; the peccaries bumped into one another; the bear danced with its arms crossed; an opossum, forgetting all maternal sentiment, through its offspring against the wall of its cabin; the gavials made their jaws snap outside the mud of barred ponds; the anteaters cleaved the air with their projecting tongues; the hyenas sniggered; the tortoises ran around the garden sticking thin heads out of their carapaces in an unaccustomed fashion; the sleeping snakes reared up and made their skin crackle; the panthers responded to the jaguars; a giraffe capered at random, launching kicks; two domesticated elephants started to trumpet desperately, as in the days of rut; and even the educated fleas who were being trained by one of

190

Ali's nieces made jumps so prodigious that they disappeared into the grass forever.

All the wardens were on their feet instantly. Whips cracked. A few revolver shots were fired. The elephants' mahouts came running. Order was reestablished before nightfall, and only the fleas were lost.

But I could not comprehend what had happened, and my fury increased at the complicity of sorts that I sensed around me between the beasts.

After a time, I ended up being, as it were, hypnotized by the tiger. I thought about its phosphorescent eyes when I woke up, I thought I saw them in front of me and got dressed in haste in order to run into the garden, wake the tiger with the spear or a red hot iron and stare into its eyes, stare into them untiringly.

That desire to gaze at the tiger became an obsession, a daily torture so great that I suffered from it physically. My features became taut and I became thinner under its empire.

In order to rid myself of it, I conceived, in accord with Ali, the project of putting out the accursed eyes, the enormous magnetic eyes. I had two steel points forged separated by a breadth almost equal to the tiger's head and I fitted them to the end of a pikestaff, in such a fashion as to be able to destroy both the green-tinted eyes, the emerald irises the color of absinthe stirred with water, with a single thrust.

The cruelty of that action did not appear to me too great, in the same way that it appeared normal to Ali. For we both thought about our anguish of previous days, when we were searching the forest of Merapi to the sound of tom-toms, thinking about Eva gone astray, and her body doubtless torn apart by the monster in some inaccessible lair.

A single thrust! I wanted its two eyes to be punctured by a single thrust. When the double-pointed spear was ready, I took advantage of a moment when the tiger had its muzzle strength out on its paws, facing me, and when it was staring at me with its immense pupils, with irises the color of the underside of the leaves of the nibong palm and certain stars on clear autumn nights.

Instead of trusting myself I had the absurdity of listening to Ali, who claimed to have learned in early childhood to throw a spear and was sure that he would not miss. I entrusted the care of puncturing the eyes to him.

The tiger must have understood. In spite of the rapidity of Ali's movement, it made a movement of the head and stood up with only one point profoundly embedded in one of its eyes, the left eye.

The roars that it uttered were frightful. But the desperate dolor was confined to those sounds, and the menagerie around the tiger, henceforth one-eyed, remained silent.

It had reared up on its hind feet, dragging the lance, and in the movement that it made, it fell back on the shaft of the weapon and snapped it cleanly.

Ali wanted to start again, but I prevented him from doing so. The spectacle of that open eye was too atrocious. Then again, I immediately felt that the magnetism emitted by two staring eyes had disappeared, and it could no longer be emitted by one alone.

I was free, and I wanted the tiger to retain the faculty of recognizing, through the bars of its cage, its master and torturer.

The Suffering of Beasts

My hatred for the beasts was augmented all the more because I had consolidated it with all my love for Eva and my sentiments of filial piety.

I brought an old Malay woman from Malacca who was celebrated for her knowledge of poisons, and I bought some of her secrets from her. With her collaboration, I extracted venomous substances from certain plants and the oil of certain fish that had the property of provoking suffering without causing death.

With a bitter and profound joy, I fabricated subtle mixtures, composed of ingredients capable of devouring the intestines of animals, and I slipped them into carefully cooked pellets of flour.

I poisoned all my snakes. I had an incomparable collection of them.

I possessed delicate blindworms, metallic in color, with reflections of tin and copper; typhlops like needles, so small that they might have been mistaken for worms if it had not been for the noise of their minuscule fangs; pythons similar to tree-trunks; eryx boas of the Thébaïd with regular yellow and black patches that made them reminiscent of a chessboard rolled around a stick; amphisbaenas with cylindrical bodies and obtuse heads; cobras of every sort; hooded najas; horned vipers; spectacled snakes; dancing snakes, and a phenomenal tortrix with an immeasurable tongue in a sheep's head.

Very few died. The science of my old Malaccan woman was great. I could not, unfortunately, contemplate as I desired the suffering of my ophidian enemies. The pain provoked leaps and redoubtable somersaults. It was necessary to attach the lids of the buckets in which the snakes lives with cords, and I had to content myself with the sound of hissing and the desperation of thrashing tails.

The children of Singapore obtained a silver coin for every toad's head they brought me. I had collected a large number. I had just bought from the crew-master of a vessel that had arrived from America a family of Surinam toads, which are curious toads with a triangular head and a long neck endowed with a certain slenderness.

I subjected them to the same fate as my snakes.

Ali having chanced to enclose one those Surinam toads in a cage with a large grass-snake, I was witness to the terror of the Surinam toad, which stretched its tremulous neck to breaking point and died of fright before being swallowed by the snake.

That gave me the idea for a new torture: that of fear.

I enclosed the weak with the strong, I brought victims and executioners face to face. Then I delivered my snakes to long-beaked jabirus, to my boat-billed herons with broad and short beaks, to my marabous with knife-like beaks, to my agami herons with beaks like sword-blades. I delighted in the cracking of dorsal spines, the friction of scales, the crushing of flat heads.

My mind underwent a singular evolution.

The bloody eye of the tiger, the death of the snakes and the toads, after the dolor of the poison, did not appear sufficient to me. I wanted to make all the beasts suffer, for L sensed that there was a bond of narrow kinship between the most various species.

Once, I set fire to the plumage of a heron that had displeased me and made it run like an avian torch in a courtyard in which I had enclosed it.

I was irritated, to the extent of being woken up at night, by the intelligence of a couple of baboons from Siam and their offspring.

They were of large size. They lived in a hut at the bottom of the garden, drank and ate in the human fashion, carried out petty tasks on the indications of my employees, and were always friendly and mild. Every evening, at the moment when the sun disappeared over the rocks of the Carimon isles, and every morning, when it rose above the leafy shores of Battam and the China Sea, they uttered cries, standing upright, and there was something sacred in their gesticulations reminiscent of the rites of a primitive religion.

I had denied for a long time that animals might worship the sun. I had made fun of travelers who had told me that in upper Siam they had witnessed, on the edges of great forests, veritable religious ceremonies accomplished by the ape population at sunrise.

I saw with my own eyes a scene that left me in no doubt in that regard.

I had got up earlier than usual one morning, and I had the idea of going to watch my family of baboons. I perceived them in the auroral twilight emerging from their hut and arranging themselves silently in a semicircle. When the first ray of sunlight reached the summit of the tallest palm tree in the garden, the father of the family, whose eyes were turned toward the palm tree, raised his two arms, and at that signal, they all uttered a simultaneous cry in which there was an unaccustomed gravity.

But then, either by virtue of forgetfulness of the ritual or by natural puerility, the smallest of the apes, which as a child, quitting the place designated to him, set about performing two or three capers and rubbing the top of his head comically. A great consternation took possession of the entire family, and the father, seizing his son by the neck, administered a severe correction with the back of his hand, and then threw him into the hut, where his moans told me that he had been imprisoned by paternal order until dusk.

I never thought about God and did not practice the Protestant religion in which I had been brought up, but I attributed to religions in general a superiority toward which I refused to elevate myself. I could not bear the idea that those creatures of the forest participated in an ideal that was prohibited to me.

That same evening, I deposited a bowl full of wine and rice alcohol on the threshold of the baboons' hut, and I did it again the next day and the following days.

The effects made themselves felt rapidly. The apes lived in drunkenness and lost the qualities that made them loved. Instead of provoking admiration by their lively intelligence and whimsy, they became ridiculous buffoons that amused all my personnel. They ceased to sweep and run errands. They started to steal, and their mildness changed into malevolence.

I came to watch them again, at sunrise. They no longer stood up straight. They no longer uttered rhythmic cries. They ran round the empty trough where the wine had been, licking its walls and giving one another reciprocal slaps. The God that had commenced being born in their souls was dead.

I also suffered because of the amity of a frightful yellow dog and a lion.

One of my employees had put the dog in the wild beast's cage to see how it would be devoured. To his great surprise, the dog had not manifested any terror, nor the lion any desire to devour that prey. They had played together and had finally gone to sleep with the one between the other's paws. There was talk about that amity in Singapore, and many people came to see the two animals in the same cage.

As the dog obtained its nourishment from the lion's allotment without provoking the slightest anger on the part of its companion, it had an excess of meat and contracted a sort of mange. I simulated a profound disgust for that malady and used it as a pretext for having the dog killed.

Desirous of proving to myself that animals are not capable of a true sentiment of amity, the next day I procured a yellow dog the same size as the first and very similar, and had it put in the lion's cage. But the latter flew into a terrible rage. It killed that caricature of its friend with a single stroke of its claw and roared despairingly for a long time because of the memory of the mangy animal that had been extracted from its affection.

A domesticated beaver had constructed a habitation in earth of an extraordinary comfort. It had transported two kittens there, found who knows where, and was raising them with solicitude.

Miss Whampoa, having come to see some new animals that I had received from Africa, noticed the kittens, which were covered in splendid fur. I hastened to offer them to her, not to give her pleasure, for I thought that the rich young Chinese woman was ridiculous by virtue of the affectation of her literary expertise, but with the objective of separating the beaver from its adoptive children.

The Whampoa house was on the other side of the river, behind the Chinese quarter. A high wall separated it from that district. The following morning, there was a desperate beaver at the foot of that wall, which had traversed Singapore, moaning, and being stoned by children.

I also tortured beos.[10]

Beos are little birds, very rare, which have all the colors of the prism in their plumage. They possess nerves of such an incredible delicacy that the sight of a little spilled blood is enough to make them die. They have received the gift of musical knowledge, and they suffer and faint if they head a false note.

I had half a dozen of them for which I had paid very dear. As they were originally from northern China, I thought that Chinese music was that to which they would be most sensitive.

I hired a raga player with orders to play the beos tunes that were frightfully false, and to scrape his instrument in a discordant fashion. The avian musicians immediately screeched as if they were being stabbed with needles. One of

---

[10] The name beo, in connection with birds, is usually attributed to the common hill myna, and the author's reattribution seems to be entirely fanciful, as are many of his subsequent improvisations, which have the overall effect of transforming his natural history into a deliberately "unnatural history"

them lost its reason and drowned itself deliberately in the bowl from which it was drinking. The others expired by virtue of the shredding of their nerves and I watched with satisfaction death running through those little plumed rainbows.

My hatred of beasts drove me to augment my menagerie with a collection of monsters, as if I found a satisfaction of that hatred in the deformation of species.

I procured an Icelandic dwarf horse and one of the rare donkeys, also dwarfs, that are only found in the Andaman Islands, where they live in a wild state. They were both as big as a medium-sized dog. The horse had a very long tail, the donkey extraordinary ears that almost hung down to its feet.

I bought, for its weight in gold, an Eastern Australian fox whose tail forms a large hairy parasol under which it sleeps; a vampire bat with a head reminiscent of that of a Chinese philosopher and which had long drooping moustaches; and a platysternon turtle from the River Tachygla that had a cranium as hard as a stone and a soft carapace on which Tibetan characters were very clearly engraved.

Ali the Macassar made a voyage to the Celebes and Komodo Island, where representatives of vanished species still live. He had the good fortune to capture a zanglodon,[11] a kind

---

[11] The zanglodon, never accommodated to the official jargon of biology, was a species reported to French readers by Camille Flammarion's pioneering popularization of paleontological science *Le Monde avant la création de l'homme, ou le berceau de l'univers* [The World Before the Creation of Man; or, The Cradle of the World] (1857), where it was described as a gigantic but relatively slender Triassic dinosaur. The original "specimen" was sold in the U.S.A. by Albert C. Koch, a showman who had exhibited a supposed sea serpent in New York in 1845 and subsequently attempted to cash in on the fashionability of dinosaur bones by faking various other finds of that nature. Such was the popularity of Flammarion's work that the fictitious creature continued to enjoy a fugitive existence in the cryptozoology of Henri Coupin's oft-reprinted

of fish-lizard that can run on two small hind feet almost as quickly as a man; a stegosaur, a kind of fish-porcupine with a hooked beak; and a moa, a ridiculous ostrich with bulging eyes like bubbles of milk.

I accommodated in vast aquaria all the curious species of the submarine world: white and horned hogfish, filamentous scorpion fish, Japanese puffer fish, remoras with suckers, hammerhead sharks, narwhals and manatees with feminize teats and sketches of human arms.

But I brought into my collector's passion a desire for deformation. I cut one of the dwarf donkey's ears off, but only one; I shaved one side of the vampire bat's moustache, but only one; I distorted the Tibetan characters of the platysternon turtle; I sawed off horns, dyed skin and invented apparatus for deforming the shapes of monsters and rendering them more monstrous.

I believe that in that epoch of my life, the grief caused by Eva's death and my thirst for vengeance disturbed my mind slightly. I committed a thousand imprudences. I went into the cages of the most ferocious animals armed only with my whip. I wrestled with a polar bear. I made a band of a dozen hyenas labor, which are the most profoundly stupid and evil beasts in creation. I separated two male jaguars that were fighting one another. There was only the cage of the tiger of Merapi that I did not penetrate, for I knew with certainty that my power of mastery stopped there, and that as soon as I had crossed the threshold, I would be torn apart in a matter of seconds.

And yet, I became a Panikia. A Panikia is, as everyone knows, the possessor of a secret formula that acts upon the mind of an elephant and which, when its syllables are pro-

---

Les Animaux excentriques (1906). The species plays an important role in Odette Dulac's Dulac's novel *...Tel qu'il est!* (1926; tr. as *The War of the Sexes*, Black Coat Press, ISBN 9781612274058, which is also replete with Buddhist mysticism, and which Magre probable read.

nounced, nails the animal in place, even if it is wild, and renders it docile and faithful.

One is a Panikia by virtue of a secret that is transmitted from father to son under the guarantee of the most sacred of oaths. As the number of Panikias in Malaysia must not diminish, by virtue of a mystery that it is vain to attempt to explain, a Panikia who has no children must choose a man he esteems in order to confide his marvelous power to him.

An old Malay from Timor, finding himself very ill, made the journey to Singapore in order to transmit the magic formula to me in exchange for an oath and fifteen rupees to pay for his funeral.

I have never believed in the nonsense that constitutes superstitions. I nevertheless gave the Panikia from Timor the fifteen rupees and engraved in my memory the four words and their intonations. It is said that anyone who reveals them is enchained to the will of the first elephant he sees, so I shall not reproduce them, for one never knows what might happen in the domain of hidden things, but I refrained internally from a stupid credulity.

Some time after that, I was offered for purchase an elephant named Jehovah, which was reputed to have a rather rebellious nature and was the color of ash, which gave it a considerable value. It was brought to me and, mechanically, I pronounced the Panikia's formula. To my great surprise, it immediately bent its knees before me, and trumpeted amicably.

The mahout, who must have been jealous by nature, hastened to tell me that that flexing of the knee was the only thing he had been able the animal. I attributed that reverence on Jehovah's part to the fact that it had recognized a master in my person, and I bought it.

The rebellious ashen Jehovah became attached to me in a singular fashion. He uttered plaints when I quit him, and when I appeared on the threshold of the hangar that was his habitation he displayed manifestations of extraordinary joy that almost resembled dances. I acquired the habit of only going out in Singapore on his back, and as he obeyed my slightest words and understood me marvelously, I did not take a mahout with me.

The love that Jehovah had for me and the astonishing intelligence he showed in obeying me orders quickly became celebrated, and flattered me to begin with. But a time came when, going down the great avenue of palm trees leading to the resident's house, at about six o'clock, among the horsemen and the canopied carriages, I heard from my red silk howdah the name of Jehovah linked with mine in the mouths of the common people.

That kind of equality in celebrity displeased me, and I acquired the habit of pricking my elephant with the spur every time his name resonated in my ears along with mine. That treatment did not irritate him because it came from his beloved master and he bore it patiently.

On day, when I was going through the Chinese district in order to reach he heights of Bukit Timah via the road alongside the river, which is the part of Singapore as yet uncultivated, children who were playing scattered on seeing me, shouting: "There's Jehovah, the elephant the color of ash."

I, the master, no longer counted. I was no longer anything. I passed by in my red howdah and people only saw an ash-gray elephant, and shouted: "There's an elephant going by!"

I had departed in the hope of shooting a few lynx, and I had brought my carbine. As soon as the road plunged into the woods, I urged Jehovah on, who began to trot, trumpeting joyfully and sometimes making the efforts to turn his head in the hope of perceiving me with his little amicable eye.

I placed the extremity of my carbine under his ear. I knew at exactly which point I had to aim in order to strike the animal dead instantaneously. I also knew that I was risking my life, for I could have been crushed by the fall of the enormous body. But my life counted for little for me, and I took pleasure in the risk.

No, the children would no longer name the celebrated Jehovah as he passed by. Celebrity was made for men, not for beasts.

I fired. Did the elephant know that it was his master who was striking him, or did he think, confusedly, that death came to him by an incomprehensible fatality?

He was not preoccupied by that problem in the final second of which he disposed, and his solicitude was for me alone. Scarcely had the shot been fired than Jehovah, as he collapsed, projected his trunk backwards, enlaced me and deposited me gently on the ground on the side opposite to the fall of his body.

A single second, in which there was an infinity of devotion.

O Lord, if you exist somewhere, protect man from the belief that he has the right to kill animals as he pleases, from the strength that drives him to cause wings to tumble from the trees, from staining the thickets of the forest with blood; deliver him from the folly of the hunt, from the tyranny that he exercises over four-footed people and people clad in feathers; deliver him from the pride that makes him think that he is the king of creation; deliver him from the evil that is within him.

Mr. Muhcin's Visit

Mr. Muhcin came to see me.

He had been a friend of my father and I had honored the little fan-merchant since my childhood for his probity, his mildness and his modesty. I found only one ridiculous thing in him: that of being a Buddhist; but I excused him for it, thinking that it came from his Hindu origin.

He was a thin, pale man with eyes devoid of brightness but filled with benevolence, with a long yellow-tinted beard. He had aged a great deal since I had last seen him. That was because, he explained, his health was not excellent.

I had taken him into the large reception room, and, under the immense panoplies that covered the walls and the Chinese and Sinhalese suits of armor, with his back stooped and his head projected forward, he seemed even smaller, even more insignificant. I thought on seeing my large stature beside his in a mirror that we represented entirely different species of humankind, and I smiled internally.

I understood that he had something to say to me, but did not dare. He had always been extraordinarily timid. Then again, I am imposing. Several times he took pinches of tobacco from his snuff-box and made the gesture of taking it, but as he was trembling, the tobacco spilled on his jacket, the decrepitude of which I remarked.

I knew that his modest commerce in paper fans in Choulia was far from being prosperous and I had recently been told that his business was going badly. The idea suddenly occurred to me that he wanted to borrow money.

That idea was quite agreeable to me, for my fortune was very large; I had never cared much about money and it would have been a veritable pleasure for me to oblige Mr. Muhcin. I almost tapped his fragile shoulder and said: "How much do you need, Mr. Muhcin? I'm here."

But no, that was not what had brought him.

Mr. Muhcin was very interested in me. He had learned that I had had great misfortunes. He wanted to know about them, to share them, perhaps to lighten them.

I nearly shrugged my shoulders. Was a man of his age, shut up for years in a shop selling cheap fans capable of understanding anything of the amour that I had experienced?

However, I gave him a detailed account of my voyage to Java, my encounter with Eva, her disappearance and the capture of the tiger.

"I understand," he said, softly, "that it's perhaps…"

And he touched his forehead with his finger as if making allusion to some madness, but I did not grasp the meaning of the gesture.

"Have you not heard," he asked me, after a momentary silence, "that there is in the region of Merapi a lamasery of women?"

I did not see what connection that could have with my story, but I suddenly remembered that Eva had, in fact, mentioned a lamasery of Buddhist nuns that was in the mountains, a little further on than the lamasery of Kobou Dalem. I also remembered the respectful intonation that her voice had had when she talked to me about it.

"Yes," I replied. "I've heard that there was a lamasery of women in a very wild region of the Merapi mountains."

"In that case," said Mr. Muhcin, excitedly, "it must be the one that depends on the abbey of Palte in Tibet. Their abbess is a Khoutouktou and that sect of female lamas renders a particular worship to the goddess Dorje Pagmo, who is represented with the head of a sow."[12]

---

[12] Dorje Pagmo (or Pakmo or Phagmo), the most important female incarnation in Buddhism, translates literally as "Diamond Sow" and is supposedly a reincarnation of a goddess, but the idea that the goddess in question is represented with a sow's head in a fashion analogous to the Hindu god Ganesha appears to be a invention of the author. The confusion of Buddhist ideas and Sanskrit scriptures, common in French Oriental

As he pronounced the word Khoutouktou, Mr. Muhcin had lowered his eyes with a sort of veneration,

"A Khoutouktou," he went on, "is the incarnation of a Tibetan saint. At this moment there are very few incarnations on earth. We are in the Kali Yuga, by which I mean the age of iron."

I started to laugh wholeheartedly. "I won't hide from you that I have no sympathy for Buddhist lamas. There is, in particular one among them who inspires a keen aversion in me."

I was thinking about my Manila straw hat.

"I'm a Buddhist myself," said Mr. Muhcin, softly. "There is in the teachings of my religion...that's the reason, in any case, that I've come to see you...the purpose of my visit..."

Mr. Muhcin started to stammer. He attempted to take a pinch of snuff and spilled it again. He finally articulated: "There is this in the laws of Manu: The man who has killed a cat, a blue jay, a mongoose or a lizard must retire to the heart of the forest and devote his life to the beasts until he is purified."

I had heard that phrase before, but I could not recall where or when. It enabled me to understand why poor old Muhcin had come to find me. He wanted to make me remonstrations regarding my manner of treating animals. I took pity on him and I listened to him in silence, for it is necessary to have respect for old age, even when it is senile.

There was talk about me in Singapore. There had been a matter of a heron set alight, a beaver deprived of its adopted children, an elephant that I had killed. Mr. Muhcin had loved my father a great deal. He loved me too. He was saddened by seeing me mistreat my brothers, the animals.

I was gripped by laughter again at the idea that I might be considered as the brother of the Javanese tiger.

---

fiction, basic to the present novel in the citation of Manu, continues with M. Muhcin's reference to Kali Yuga (of which his translation is idiosyncratic).

"I don't know," I said, "who this Manu is about whom you're speaking to me, and more than this Khoutouktou of Tibet, and I believe that it's not very interesting for me."

Without seeming to do so, I had orientated the annoying sermonizer toward the exit door.

"It is, in the contrary, very interesting for you," he told me, raising his trembling finger and lowering his voice as if it were a secret matter. "I promise you to seek information about this lamasery of Javanese women. I promise you that. Naturally, it will be necessary for you to promise me to do nothing if..."

He did not finish. I was scarcely listening. I told myself that he had been right to touch his forehead with his finger, and I was astonished that he was able to be conscious of his senility. It was only later that his words came back to me.

I watched him draw away in the street. He stepped aside discreetly when he crossed someone's path. He appeared not to want to inconvenience the passers-by. How small and timid he was! I thought of his wretched business that was collapsing, and the low-ceilinged sunless room behind his shop where he spent his days.

A Buddhist! How pitiful!

Inès

I had seen Eva for the first time as she was descending a ladder. I saw Inès for the first time as she was climbing a staircase: the great stone staircase of the resident's house.

She was wearing a black dress fringed with gold, so extraordinarily low cut that I wondered by what miracle she was able to keep it on her shoulders, and I thought immediately of the robe of Princess Sekartaji.

Heavy tresses in which a rose was pinned made a somber fame for Inès' face, which expressed a joyful impishness as well as a sovereign authority. She advanced with a perfect ease in her semi-nudity, launching smiles right and left, seemingly searching for someone with her gaze.

I learned subsequently that Inès had arranged to meet someone at the resident's soirée, but that it was her eternal habit, wherever she was, to be in quest of a Frenchman, for the French realized for her the arbitrary ideal of amour that she had formed. I did not know of that particularity at the time.

I had sometimes encountered Inès under the palm trees of the royal avenue, in a caleche with two white horses, and she had always put on a semblance of being unaware off my existence.

I knew that she was Portuguese by origin, that she belonged to the illustrious Almeida family, and that she was the widow of an English general who had lived in Batavia, and then Singapore. Although ruined, she lived in a lavish style. It was said she had contributed to her husband's death by foolish expenses and her irregular conduct, but I was accustomed not to lend credence to gossip circulated about women.

No one ever mentioned her without adding, respectfully: "She's an Almeida!"

I was leaning on the stone balustrade of the staircase as she came upstairs, darting the gleaming gaze of her dark eyes to the right and left. She was visibly looking for someone.

Does one ever know with women, even the Almeidas? I could not help taking a step forward.

We found ourselves face to face. She darted an icy glance at me, surveying me from head to toe. I felt a formidable influx of blood to my face, and became ridiculously crimson. At that moment, the breath of one of the great straw punkas that was being agitated close to us by a uniformed negro detached a petal from the rose that Inès had in her hair, and that petal came to rest between my eyes.

I closed them momentarily. When I opened them again the resident was extending his hand to Inès, who disappeared with him into the crowd, smiling.

The soirée was being held in honor of Admiral Rowley,[13] who was going to Japan on the *Batailleuse*, and the elite of Singapore had been invited. I only appear habitually at those kinds of celebrations in order to show myself, to affirm to everyone and to myself that I was a member of the elegant and rich elite. I make haste to leave as soon as I have been seen any my presence has been noted.

That evening I stayed. I spent my time following the marvelous Inès from group to group. Contrary to my habit, I was not lethargic. The swish of her black dress with golden fringes possessed a virtue that overexcited my nerves.

Inès affected not to notice me, but I was sure that she had, for she sometimes darted a glance at me in which there was an irony that I could not explain. I experienced a chagrin because of it, and abruptly decided to leave. It was very late. The reception rooms of the residency were empty. The negroes in the cloakroom were drowsy.

---

[13] Captain Charles John Rowley (1832-1919) was briefly in service in the China Sea and Japan during the early 1860s, aboard the *Renard*, but was not promoted to Vice-Admiral until much later in his career. None of the other members of his illustrious naval family seem to have been in the region at the time when the story is set.

Having arrived on the threshold I perceived that it was raining. My house was some distance away and I was only wearing a thin new suit, which I did not want to see spoiled. I stood still for two minutes, listening to the noise that the large raindrops made on the leaves of the palm-trees in the square.

"Why, it's raining," said a voice behind me.

I turned round. I was face to face with Inès again, as I had been at the beginning of the soirée when she was climbing the stairs. I felt myself blushing with the same intensity and I stared at her, searching for a phrase that I could not find and trying to dissimulate my embarrassment with an attitude full of carelessness.

"You're making me blush by looking at me so intently," she said, benevolently.

She was not blushing in the slightest, and I thought that the action of assuming my redness was evidence of great tact.

At the same time as the two white horses of her carriage stopped outside the door, and abrupt downpour descended in a squall over the square, and a tempestuous gust made shutters rattle in the distance, agitated the branches and threw rain in the face. A Chinaman in a white costume had bounded forward and was holding the door open.

"It would be unchristian not to take you home in this weather," said Inès. "Follow me."

The last phrase was spoken like an order. Before I was able to respond, she had wrapped a large shawl of snowy silk over her shoulders and had run to the carriage, where I joined her."

Inès had not asked me for my address. I was unable to doubt that she knew me by reputation. The confirmation of my celebrity was very agreeable to me. I do not know what phrase I stammered to thank her, but Inès attached no importance to it, and as her shawl had been soaked by the rain she took it off.

That contributed to blurring my ideas.

"I don't believe there was a single Frenchman at the resident's soirée," said Inès, making allusion to her constant preoccupation. "The French travel so little! Are you not from a French family?"

I told her that I was not, striving to formulate a eulogy to the Dutch people, but that did not appear to interest her. I rapidly observed that she was only lending a distracted ear to what I was saying.

Suddenly, she started talking to me about Eva. She had known her well, she told me, two years before, when the Varogas had spent a winter in Batavia.

That poor Eva had such a passionate appetite for life. Oh, he was not afraid of compromising herself! Society is so malicious! But was it not the fault of her father, who smoked opium incessantly and paid no heed to her? The story of the son of the American consul had wronged her greatly. And that of the Javanese prince, which everyone knew. How had Mynheer Varoga been naïve enough not to perceive that the descendant of the ancient emperors of Java had disguised himself as a domestic servant out of amour? Nevertheless, one was obliged to recognize that the French did not interest Eva. What a bizarre nature! What a bizarre double nature! With all that thirst for sensations, had she not spoken several times to Inès herself about her desire to convert to Buddhism? How could such a duality be explained?

And Inès insisted ardently on hearing my personal explanation.

I could not furnish any. I did not understand very well. I was suffering from memories returning to my mind. I was intoxicated by a delicate perfume of a slightly weary woman and a faded rose. I was overtaken by a languid feeling, a desire for voluptuous tenderness, and it seemed to me that the white horses were carrying us away, to the clatter of the rain, into a solitude of dreams.

Mechanically, I repeated: "A Buddhist! How pitiful!"

It was the Javanese prince who had pushed her in that direction. Besides which, there were two lamaseries in the vicinity of Mynheer Varoga's indigo plantation and Eva liked to converse with the female lamas who wore red robes and must be extraordinarily dirty. For a time, Eva had made confidences to Inès. Well, Eva loved pleasure above all. She preferred physical beauty in a man to great intelligence. She had often shown it, too!

And with that, Inès glanced sideways, in a way that meant: *you know something about that!* which I thought inappropriate. But I was hearing everything as if in a dream.

It was a very curious problem that a woman endowed—here Inès stopped and resumed, after a pause, emphasizing every syllable—with as much temperament as Eva might have desires for a religious life, to be a mystic, and not a Christian mystic but a Hindu mystic.

For a long time, Eva had no longer practiced her religion. She had Tibetan talismans and sachets blessed by saints, inhabitants of the Himalaya. Follies, pure follies! Inès was almost annoyed with her, for one can do anything—can one not?—but it is necessary not to touch the sacred.

If I, personally, a witness to the entire drama, had not been sure of Eva's death, if I had not had formal proof of it, Inès considered it as possible that she was, at the present moment, voluntarily enclosed in a convent of Buddhist nuns.

I know how necessary it is to take little account of the divagations of women when they talk about one another. Inès must have taken Eva's jests for realities. I had had enough conversations with Eva and I was perspicacious enough to have taken account of such a ludicrous religious penchant if it had existed in her soul.

The coachman must have made a detour, for we ought to have arrived at my house a long time ago.

With an extreme skill and opportunism in which I excel, I had taken Inès' hand, and she had not withdrawn it. The rain was making mysterious designs on the window-panes. I sensed that we were traversing dead quarters. Something fluid and ungraspable enabled an anticipation of the imminent advent of dawn. I respired Inès' warm breath, and her love of life was communicated to me by the hand I was holding. She had

211

stopped talking, and it seemed to me that she was about to faint.

All of a sudden, she said: "We've arrived."

The carriage had stopped. I saw the gate of a garden, an unknown villa.

Lightly, Inès leapt out of the carriage and ran the few steps that separated her from the entrance door.

I nearly said: *This isn't my house!*

But I stopped myself.

My dominant preoccupation was to conduct myself as a gallant man and not to yield to some gross temptation. The night in the temple of Ganesha had taught me a terrible lesson.

"Well, come on!" said the voice of Inès, with a hint of impatience.

I joined her. We were in a room whose floor was covered in mats and cushions, illuminated, in a confused manner, by an oil lamp. Lacquer gleamed on the wall. A large orange and green parasol was suspended from the ceiling.

I heard the carriage outside, drawing away.

"I'll go home on foot, walking, as soon as the rain has eased."

I thought I was showing delicacy by those words. Inès closed the door abruptly, and then, slowly, removed the shawl that she had put on again in order to reach the house.

"My shawl is soaked," she said.

She took two or three steps and I noticed that there was something feline in the movement of her shoulders that made her resemble a panther.

She came back toward me, smiling slightly ironically. "Do you have a cigarette?" she asked.

I searched feverishly for my cigarette-case.

"Here's a light," She struck a match and held it out to me.

She was very close to me, and it seemed to me that she was also offering me her lips.

I blew out the match. I was about to take Inès in my arms, but at the moment when the flicker of the flame was

212

extinguished, I saw a man with a fat belly and the head of an elephant looking at me. I sensed that Inès' lips were moist and warm. But I refused to think about that.

We smoked in silence.

By virtue of one of the abrupt caprices familiar to it, the rain suddenly stopped.

"I'll go home walking, very slowly," I said again.

A faint wan light tinted things outside. In the garden I saw large red champakas rendered heavy by the water, and leaning over. Inès accompanied me to the gate, walking on tiptoe in order not to dampen her small shoes.

I seized her abruptly, and she allowed herself to come toward me without resistance. For a second, I had her mouth moving under mine. But voices rang out. A group of coolies was advancing with a lantern.

We separated, and I bore Inès hand to my lips.

"And I asked you whether you were French!" she said, laughing, as I drew away. "No, you're not at all."

The Straw Hat

I am arriving at the most important event in my life, which was an evil action, consciously accomplished.

I shall not recount in detail how I was brought to marry Inès, what singular detours she took in order to arrive at that result, the enormous figure of her debts, which I paid, and the certainty that I acquired of her total absence of love for me. All that is of no importance. The most considerable events of existence are neither deaths not marriages, nor the catastrophes that occur, but certain small facts that have a secret influence on the evolution of the mind.

The day after my marriage coincided with some Chinese festival or other, which was not merely celebrated in the Chinese campong but also in the Arab and Hindu quarters.

I had the habit on such occasions of following the customs practiced by my father. I opened the ground floor of my house and the gates of my garden, and the crowds came all day long to admire my collections and my animals.

In the middle of the afternoon I was leaning on my elbows at a window on the first floor distractedly gazing at the Sinhalese with effeminate faces, the bronzed Hindus with floating hair, the Malabar women with noses ornamented with pendants and ankles garnished with silver rings, and the familial Chinese in black lustrine with corteges of children. They were all filing in front of the cages under the surveillance of my wardens and a few Sikh policemen in white uniforms and red turbans sent by the resident, and I was listening with satisfaction to their admiring cries and their fearful murmur when they contemplated the one-eyed Javanese tiger.

Inès, who was in the next room, suddenly came into the one where I was. She was holding a letter in her hand, and she said to me, smiling negligently and without looking at me: "I forgot to tell you that I received a letter a few days ago from one of my friends in Java."

She had the same expression of bitter satisfaction on her face that she had had several times during our engagement, in order to tell me disagreeable things, such as indications of enormous sums to pay or accounts of encounters with extremely seductive Frenchmen.

I took the letter and I scanned it. It contained nothing interesting for me. It gave news of many people in Batavian society that were unknown to me, and seemed merely to be a sequel to a previous letter.

I was about to return it to Inès when I read the postscript.

We know nothing more about the lovely friend of the prince, the so-called fiancée of the animal-tamer. Her father, it appears, is smoking more and more and is hardly visible. Someone entirely worthy of faith who has been to see him claims to have heard him say to someone with whom he was having a very animated conversation: "My daughter is dead to me henceforth."

I dropped the letter. Inès was shifting objects around the room and watching me from the corner of her eye.

If Eva's father had declared that his daughter was dead to him, did that not imply that she was alive for others?

At that precise moment, my gaze, which I had been parading at hazard over the multicolored crowd garden, was stuck by the silhouette of a poorly-dressed European. He was gliding modestly along the cages and he stopped in front of the Javan tiger. I noticed his ridiculously narrow and short trousers, his cheap cotton shirt and the absence of a tie, but above all, I noticed his hat, a superb Manila straw hat with a broad supple brim, a hat that I knew: my hat.

The man I could see, who was in my home, was the charmer of lizards in an opium-den on the camel's hump, the so-called traveling lama, the priest of a grotesque cult in which Ganesha was worshiped, the individual who was so antipathetic to me and whom I suspected of denigrating me to Mynheer Varoga and perhaps to Eva. And he was wearing my hat!

I straightened up. I went downstairs at a run and launched myself into the garden.

As the noise I made he turned round, I saw his large bright eyes, the calm expression of his face, his perfect ease in his ridiculous garments. It even seemed to me that he took a step toward me with the movement that one has when one perceives someone to whom one has something to say.

But I had already seized him by the collar of his tie-less shirt. I was acting at hazard, without a preconceived plan, driven by the heat of anger, the mysterious force of hatred that suppresses all reflection.

"You stole the hat that you're wearing from me!" I cried, with a sincerity that I extracted from the profound ignominy of my lie.

Malabars, Sinhalese, Chinese and Bouguis formed an amused circle, immediately insulting the hat-wearer who, shaken by my vigorous hand, appeared by far the weaker of the two of us.

All my employees came running, but my physical superiority was so obvious that they did not even think of lending me a hand. I relaxed my grip slightly.

The man did not resist. I discovered in his features the expression of repulsion and saddened surprise that perfect purity can have in sudden contact with cynical bad faith, brutality and the most atrocious ugliness of life.

That only augmented my wrath.

The English police are very well trained. More than any other police in the world, if two men are having an argument, they immediately take the side of the better dressed, the one who belongs to the higher social class.

The policemen who intervened did not ask for any explanation. They threw themselves upon the man accused of theft as on a professional thief and brutally dragged away the inoffensive creature that I had just thrown into the circle of evil, and who did not make any gesture of protest.

The law in Singapore had not yet been subjected to the repercussions of the reorganization of the law in India. It was rapid and harsh on the poor, as all law is that has more concern for order than justice.

In matters of theft or armed attack, an English judge pronounces without appeal, and there is no futile procedure or advocate's eloquence. The judge is solely assisted by an indigenous adviser, Hindu, Chinese or Malay, charged with enlightening him as to the habits and customs of those peoples, and also serving as an interpreter.

I was summoned to the tribunal the following day. I had reaped so much approval from everyone for having a thief arrested that I had ended up convincing myself that I had accomplished a laudable action and I went there with a tranquil conscience.

The courtroom was an old colonial monument dating from the foundation of Singapore, and justice was rendered there from the height of a small platform on which the judge was seated, in a room with bare walls, constructed in cyclopean stone blocks, the immensity of which was meant to impress the indigenes. There was a post of sepoys outside the door, whose sergeant gave me a military salute when I went past.

Everything happened very rapidly and from beginning to end my self-esteem was caressed by the external sighs of consideration that everyone manifested for my person.

In addition to the salute by the sepoy sergeant I note the obsequiousness of the English hatter who had sold me the straw hat and whom I had cited as a witness, the movement of curiosity that passed through the audience when I appeared, and the slight inclination of the judge's head, which meant: *I am an impartial judge; I give neither approval not disapproval to those who appear before me, but I can see at a glance what kind of person I am dealing with.*

The judge was an old man, fat and bald, with very small and very bright eyes.

The man with the hat emerged abruptly between two Sikh policemen from a low door behind the judge's platform. He was bare-headed and handcuffed. He had the drawn features of someone who has slept badly but his face had an extraordinary calmness that might easily have passed for the cynicism of a criminal habituated to thefts, the arrests that follow thefts and the sentences that follow arrests.

I avoided looking at his eyes. I encountered them momentarily and I saw, to my great surprise, that they were even brighter than the day before, but deprived of their dolorous astonishment and entirely exempt from reproach. That was insupportable to me, and my irritation increased when I perceived, in responding to an insignificant question from an assistant, that my voice was ill-assured.

The indigenous counselor ordinarily tempers the severity of the judge, and pleads the cause of the accused, but it was not possible in this case to summon any counselor, the accused having declared himself to be Tibetan and speaking English perfectly.

From the start, the case seemed to be settled in advance.

The clerk asked me my name and qualities with a nuance in his voice that meant: *this is purely a formality, we know them well.*

A little laughter departed from the crowd when the Tibetan, asked for his name and place of origin, replied that his name was Djohal and that he belonged to a lamasery situated in the Himalaya in a location not mentioned on any map. An old man from the suburb of Choulia in whose home he stayed in Singapore was his only guarantor.

The old man had been summoned. He was called. A faint exclamation resounded in the audience when a very old Hindu clad in rags advanced tremulously. He as extraordinarily timid and he only spoke Hindi in a northern dialect that no one understood. Suddenly, impressed by the majesty of the tribunal, he began to weep.

The judge begged him, impatiently, to withdraw.

There was further laughter when the accused, responding to a question from the judge, declared that he had found my hat floating in a stream in Java and that he had fished it out with his staff. He had thought that there was no harm in putting on his head a hat adrift on a watercourse. He sensed the implausibility of that explanation, but he was obliged to give it because it was true.

The mildness with which he expressed himself seemed to everyone to be hypocrisy. In the lassitude of his shoulders there was a sentiment that all struggle was futile, that he was caught in the trap of human malevolence and that he could not escape therefrom.

The judge shrugged his shoulders. He knew what was what. He asked me to take the oath. I read in his little eyes and his broad and wrinkled face: *Simple formality! I know you as a perfect gentleman of renowned honorability.*

It was impossible for me to retreat, although I would have liked to, at that moment, with all my heart.

I held out my hand, but I did not recognize the sound of my atonal voice. And suddenly, I experienced that sensation of a void around me that I only felt when I was in mortal danger.

I found myself alone in a limitless space, a profound abyss from the depths which I summoned up, in a blank voice, the false oath, the eternal testimony of the injustice of the strong against the weak. Around me there were high stone walls, not those of the courtroom but a succession of peaks, all the Himalayas with their inviolate snows, their secret lamaseries, and their legendary mysteries. The man with the hat was in the distance on a ridge, with a serene visage, rigorously exempt from evil. And behind him, through him, in a vertiginous panorama, all the events of my unjust and stupid existence unfurled. Bloody parrots fell from trees, stags belled desperately, monkeys wept over their dead, herds of buffaloes fled, owls flapped their wings, blue jays fluttered, a great tiger's eye bled. And I, the killer of beasts, my hand extended, in the midst of those extravagant images, pronounced the formula of the iniquitous oath.

That only lasted—that surely only lasted—for a few seconds. But during that rapid interval, that eternal time, my duplicated mind was fixed, with an extraordinary lucidity, on the face of the judge and following the changes in his physiognomy.

219

His little eyes were fixed at first, randomly and indifferently, on a corner of the tale in front of him, which he was tapping with his hand, like someone awaiting the end of something unimportant. The absence of timbre in my voice made him look me in the face, and at the same time, his hand was immobilized. And while I pronounced the formula, a great attention crystallized his features, his minuscule eyes lit up, and I saw, without a doubt, the clarity of the truth appear in his broad face and transform it.

I was so sure of that, that I experienced a sensation of infinite relief and I was tempted to speak to him to affirm to him that what he was thinking was true and that I was in the process of making a false oath.

Oh, if he had attempted to confound me, to undertake the defense of the classless man unjustly accused, I believe that I would have clasped him to my bosom for the light of integrity that I had perceived in his gaze.

But he was a coward, like all the rest, and like me. Has anyone ever heard mention of a judge accusing a rich and well-known European of making a false oath, in order to defend a vagabond?

The light of justice was effaced from the judge's face. Behind him the beasts disappeared, the snowy Himalayas became the walls of the courtroom again. The social order that had nearly been troubled by the lie of an honorable gentleman and a flash of perspicacity on the part of a judge was reconstituted around me with its pitiless power.

I heard an indifferent voice pronouncing the minimum penalty that English law prescribed for recognized theft.

In the hubbub that followed I rediscovered my self-confidence. The hatter was indignant that the thief had only been sentenced to fifteen days in prison, without the corporal punishment of the whip that is usual in similar cases. I saw the old man from Choulia run forward as the accused was about to disappear thought the low door. He fell rather than prostrating himself and, seizing a flap of the man's grimy coat, kissed it religiously.

I do not know whether the sepoy sergeant saluted me as I went out. I was crossing the square at a rapid pace when I heard someone running behind me. I turned round and saw Mr. Muhcin. He must have witnessed the court session. I extended my hand to him but he did not take it. He remained silent for a few seconds and then, making an effort, in a low but resolute voice, he said to me:

"It often happened, with your father, whom I loved, and even now, it sometimes happens that you stop in my shop, as in the house of a friend. I beg you, henceforth, not to do that again. You might encounter, when he comes out of prison, the thief of your hat, and I would not want to expose you to that encounter."

Mr. Muhcin spoke with a firmness that I had never known in him. I kept silent.

"Men who are too different from one another," he went on, "ought to remain apart. I would be grateful if you would consider henceforth that we do not know one another. I shall even avoid saying good day to you if I encounter you, and I beg you to do the same."

I continued to remain silent. Then Mr. Muhcin turned round abruptly and went away slowly.

The Sam-Sings

There is no mystery that is exterior to us. Everything is within us, and when a light flares up, it is in an abrupt fashion. Perhaps the oil in the lamp has been poured for a long time, the wick moistened unknown to us, but the brightness is sudden.

My cousin, the fool from Goa, was passing through Singapore.

He was not as stupid as I had thought. He was only occupied with tortoiseshells, in which he traded. He only liked to talk about tortoiseshells, to touch nothing but tortoiseshells; he compared them, he evaluated them and bought them amorously. But it is a solution appropriate to life to specialize in the study of one form of matter and to cherish its infinite variety.

He was my guest, and it was to oblige him, to keep him company, to know the difficulty he had in procuring mottled shells and shells from the isle of Réunion, that I went with him that evening through the putrid quarter of the old port, on to the camel's hump, into the opium-den which one penetrated by going through the Door of the Tiger.

Inès had smiled strangely, her smile charged with contained satisfaction, when we had expressed our intention of going out without her.

"Doubtless I'll go out too," she had said, "and I might be late back."

The Chinaman bowed, the stairway was as sticky as when I had gone in the first time, the atmosphere was opaque and stifling, the same forms were lying next to little lamps; nothing had changed in the opium-den. I noticed, however, in the obsequiousness of the Chinaman as he indicated a mat near the window to us, something hateful and terrified, a fashion of avoiding making contact with my garments, that he had not had during my first visit.

Our entrance had provoked whispers, and when we were installed to the right and left of the lamp, our immediate neighbors—Malays or Hindus, what do I know?—got up silently and went to lie down a little further away, in the smoke through which we distinguished flashes of hostile gazes.

My cousin pointed that out to me with a certain dread and asked me whether it might not be opportune to leave again. But I smiled and showed him my whip, which I had set down beside me.

In any case, he had commenced the description of certain incrustations that the artists of Delhi make on perfectly white shells, from which high-priced boxes are fabricated. He was burning to continue. He continued, while grilling opium over his lamp with agility, smoking and making me smoke.

And it was in that darkness, in the midst of evocations of white boxes garnished with enamels in Delhi, fans whose fabrics come from Persia and combs of which the working has incomparable specialists in Benares, among the mats and hard leather cushions, that a lamp lit up among the little lamps that strewed the floor: a lamp that my cousin did not see, and of which the wretched men in the opium-den were unaware; an invisible lamp, a dazzling interior lamp.

Time had passed; how many hours, I have no idea. It began with the strange, monstrous, unexpected desire to caress a lizard. I felt in my fingertips the imperious appetency of a light caress on the small icy head.

My cousin of the shells was facing me, but his back was turned to the window, while I, on the contrary was facing it, with the consequence that I could not see what was happening inside the room, the recumbent smokers, those who were coming in and those who were leaving.

I saw my cousin raise himself up slightly on one elbow and parade a circular gaze full of anxiety over the smoky region behind me.

"We aren't safe here," he told me, in a low voice, leaning toward me.

I responded with a light musical whistle.

"Why are you whistling?" he asked me, surprised.

"In the hope of domesticating a lizard. Aren't there a few around us?"

"There are a lot of lizards," my cousin replied. "I believe we've strayed into the midst of a band of Sam-Sings."

Singapore was terrorized, in that epoch, by a Chinese secret society that was known as the society of the Sam-Sings. All the thefts and all the crimes that were committed, not only on the island but throughout Malaysia, were attributed to it.

"Near the door," my cousin went on, "there's a gathering of men of evil appearance whom I recognize as Sam-Sings, and the Chinaman who is the tenant of the house has just designated us to them with a frightful sign of the head,"

I had smoked a good deal and I was experiencing, under the influence of the opium, a delightful physical bliss and a perfect optimism at the same time as a desire for immobility. Everything around me appeared to be harmonious, and nothing was lacking but the presence of one of those little lizards so frequent in Malaysian houses.

I did my best to reassure my cousin. We were surrounded by excellent people. I knew the Chinese tenant of the Door of the Tiger. In any case, no one in Singapore would dare to attack a man like me. Then again, I was determined not to make any movement.

I had not even turned my head. A little lizard had just appeared within the radius of my gaze. It was on the sill of the window and I saw it gliding obliquely along the wall.

But my cousin put down the pipe that he was holding in his hand and I saw his eyes staring anxiously over me into the darkness of the opium-den.

"Some time ago," he said to me, "you had a thief condemned to prison. He must be linked, like al thieves, with the association of the Sam-Sings, a few members of which must be habitués of this shady house. It's probable that they're meditating a vengeance against you, and, in consequence, against me, your companion."

I made a negative gesture. I recommended him not to move, in order not to frighten the lizard, which was now very close to him, and I began whistling again.

But my cousin, who, contrary to what I had thought momentarily, was not a fool and a timorous fool, sat up, begging me, still in a low voice, to put myself on the defensive, for he had just seen the glint of a naked blade.

His movement caused the lizard to disappear into some crack in the planking.

"It's true," I said, "that the Malays excel in throwing the kris. They do so with disconcerting rapidity. I've seen more than one kris embedded in teak wood, which is very hard, so profoundly that it was difficult to pull it out.

And I continued to remain motionless.

I had pronounced those scarcely reassuring words in order to punish my cousin for causing the lizard to flee by the abruptness of his movement. I was not thinking in the least of turning round in order to see the redoubtable conspirators. I was very comfortable in the position I was in. I did not shift my head by a fraction of an inch but I pronounced, mechanically, as if someone were dictating the words to me, the sentence overheard in the same place during my first visit, the sentence that returned mysteriously to my memory:

"Men are all the more unhappy as they experience more hatred, and all the happier as they love more."

I was astonished myself to be pronouncing such words and I saw that my cousin shared my surprise, for those words did not correspond at all to my personality and he ideas I habitually expressed. But he had a graver subject of interest and he did not question what I had just said.

He was still looking at the other extremity of the room, while, prey to a total indifference as to security or danger, life or death. I was breathing deeply and placidly. My tranquility was so complete that I cocked my ear in order to hear whether a kris was going to whistle over our heads. I even designated mentally a point in the planking where the blade, having missed me, would be embedded, vibrating. There would be time then to get up and take a look.

No blade of any kris vibrated. My cousin's face gradually became calmer and the expression of terror he had on his features ended up disappearing.

"We've had a narrow escape," he told me. "I believe we owe our salvation to the unexpected arrival of a man of indefinable type, wretchedly dressed in the European style with trousers that are too short, who calmed that band of fanatics with a glance."

I saw by the fashion in which he was looking at me that my cousin considered that, among the dangers suspended over his head, there was his companion's loss of reason. So he exhorted me to a prompt departure, and he added: "They've all gone now."

An immense need for sincerity was within me, and drove me irresistibly to tell him that I had always considered him to be stupid, that I had then judged him less stupid, but that at present, I had returned to my original opinion.

He contented himself with shaking his head, attributing those words to the effects of the opium, and, in a suppliant voice, he asked me to accompany him in order to leave, He was convinced that if he went downstairs and crossed the threshold of the Door of the Tiger alone, without the aegis of his companion, he would surely be murdered.

He added, but as something of lesser importance, that there was also mortal peril for me in remaining in that place.

He invoked to vanquish my desire for immobility the name of his mother, who was waiting for him in Goa, and as I was not touched by the image of my virtuous aunt, whom I had always judged to me even more stupid than her son, he named my own mother, the saint from Portugal, whose name has never been pronounced before me in vain,

I got up immediately. The opium-den was deserted. I went down first. We emerged without encumbrance.

The Song of the Rohi-Rohi

I perceived, with surprise, as we went along the harbor, that for the first time in my life, I had forgotten my whip.

"I'll go to look for it tomorrow," I said.

My desire for immobility had been replaced by a desire for movement, for an indefinite stroll through the transparent night air.

As my cousin, now reassured, was beginning explain the utility of a turtle's feet in the fabrication of molten tortoise-shell, I took advantage of the attention he was devoting to his subject and a street corner to start running abruptly in a direction opposite to his. I had no difficulty losing him.

As if in a dream I crossed the series of bridges over the pools that surround the port. I went along Mr. Whampoa's gardens, and, taking the road along the riverbank, I plunged into the interior of the island.

I was possessed by a singular lightness. By the pale light of the stars I saw the bungalows suspended on the hillsides, gardens surrounded by hedges of wild sunflowers and aloes, and avenues hastily carved through the forest.

There was a sound of wings as I passed by, in the tree-branches, of flocks of nocturnal birds that I was scaring away. The sentiment that the light creatures might have in rising up into the delicious night air, traversing floating vapors, rising higher than the treetops, gave me a curious sentiment of envy, a desire to fly like them into space, and I surprised myself by opening my arms while running and waving them as if I were a winged man.

Now I climbed the point of Bukit Timah in order to discover from its summit the harbor, the strait, and the horizon of the seas. I had passed the establishment of the Jesuits when the presentiment of the dawn spread a mysterious confused whiteness around me.

The road terminated at the summit of the point in a vast clearing, and in the middle of that clearing, towering over the mass of nopals, areca palms, bamboos and banyans, like a dominating broom, was a prodigious coconut-palm.

And at the moment when I reached the clearing, a rohi-rohi, a minuscule bird perched on the highest branch of that coconut palm, commenced its regular song, the annunciation of the rising sun.

My first thought, an inexplicable thought, like none I had ever had before, was to climb the coconut-palm and sing with the rohi-rohi. But that attempt would have been vain, in view of the height of the tree. In any case, the bird would have flown away.

I listened to the song of the rohi-rohi, and found an unknown beauty in it that filled me with emotion. It seemed that I understood the profound meaning of that matinal harmony. The rohi-rohi was celebrating the transformation of darkness into light. It was perched at the summit of the astonishing coconut-palm in order to contemplate from that vertiginous post the appearance of the sun in the China Sea and to glorify that apparition.

But what troubled me profoundly was the correspondence that I established between the song of the bird and my own interior desire to see the light. I too felt that the rising sun was imminent, that the shadows of evil were about to dissipate in the forest of my thoughts, and I would have liked to be able to watch, from the height of a coconut-palm in the open sky of the soul, the birth of my sun.

And there was also something in the song of the rohi-rohi that I had never heard, and whose meaning remains full of mystery for me. I distinctly heard something like this:

We are born of one another, we are all brothers. From the bosom of the beasts ma has taken his form. With my plumage and my beak, I am the son of the coconut-palm that shelters me, and the sunlit coconut-palm takes its own substance from the original earth. Glory to the sun, which rises to illu-

minate the family of living beings! For we are born of one
another, we are all brothers.

I stood on tiptoe and stretched my neck in order to distinguish the shape of the bird.

Very high, in the whitening sky, I believed I could see the minuscule rohi-rohi, like an animated dot, the miraculous singer to which I would have liked to be similar. It must live under a leaf of that azurean tree and recommence its song of delight every morning.

And suddenly, I was struck, as if by an arrow, by a frightful idea. The Jesuits who lived a little further away, and whose chapel I could make out from the place where I was, prided themselves on being skillful hunters. They ate birds for their meals, and one old father, particularly venerated for his charity, whom I had encountered a few days earlier, had said to me:

"Come to see us at Bukit Timah one morning, and we'll give you a rohi-rohi ragout to eat."

The marvelous bird was at risk of falling under the lead of the pious Jesuits, charitable fathers who ate animals. I was tempted at first to run to the entrance door of the establishment, to hammer on it with my fist, to launch myself into the chapel where certain matinal offices were being celebrated, and to intimate to the Jesuits the order no longer to kill rohi-rohis, under penalty of having to deal with me. I had tamed wild beasts, I would certainly be able to tame Jesuits.

I had already taken a few steps when I reflected and stopped. Who was I to act thus? Was I not the animal-killer *par excellence*, the great hunter of the forests of Malaysia, the buyer and collector of beasts as well as their executioner. If it had known of my presence, the inoffensive rohi-rohi would have preferred to traverse the immense Sea of China with its little wings rather than sing by my side.

It had not seen me, but it might see me and recognize me by virtue of those strange identifications of humans that the beasts, even those belonging to the less intelligent species, transmit in their language. The best thing for me to do, in order not to trouble the aerial musician, was to go away quietly.

Slowly, I went back down the path that I had climbed. My former joy had disappeared. I walked with my head bowed, without haste, and because of that I noticed an ant on the ground, which was dragging, with great difficulty, an enormous wooden twig toward an anthill where other ants were already occupied with their astonishing subterranean labors. I took the twig and placed it at the entrance to the anthill. The laborious ant showed neither gratitude nor astonishment at the benevolent intervention of a giant, but resumed its task as if nothing had happened.

At the same moment there was a noise amid the foliage. I perceived the head of a rusa, a deer with curved horns and a long beard. I saw its grave eyes for a second, and then I heard its precipitate gallop. But I did not have the regret that I would have felt the day before of not having a rifle in order to kill it. I would, on the contrary, have loved to caress its fearful head, to tug its beard in a friendly fashion.

I was astonished myself by such a sentiment. It was a new man who was descending from the heights of Bukit Timah.

That new man suddenly went up again at a run. He turned right without pausing, and made an immense detour in order to return toward Singapore, looking behind him frequently and fearfully to see whether anyone was pursuing him.

In order to go down again I had taken the road along the river, which I had followed with Jehovah, and had just recognized the place where I had put him to death. At the foot of a copal tree covered with white flowers, trunk lowered, looking at me sideways with his eyes full of faithful sadness, I thought I had seen the elephant the color of ash, which had given itself to me entirely, and which I had killed.

"What a mystery our soul is," I said to myself, as I walked through the streets of Singapore.

It was only in front of my door that I thought about Inès, who must be anxious about my absence. And I said to myself

in a low voice something else I had once heard in the opium-
den: "By means of opium, a man is set on the path on which
he discovers his relationship with the animal species."

The Departure of Inès

I never went back to look for my whip. I went so far as to forget its existence. I would not be astonished if it were in a natural history museum in Shanghai or Canton at this moment with my name written in golden letters on a red streamer.

Inès did not show any anxiety at my nocturnal absence. Having come back late, as she had said, she had gone to bed placidly, had woken up in a delightful humor and had gone out, singing a French refrain to take a stroll among my animals. It was then, without anyone being able to explain why, that she received a slap from one of the wine-drinking baboons.

She uttered loud screams and gave Ali the Macassar an order to kill the beast with revolver shots. The latter, who knew the price of the animals, refused to do it. An argument followed, and I arrived in the meantime.

Scarcely had the reasons been explained to me in very ardent terms than I declared that the only guilty parties were those who were wicked enough to give wine to monkeys, and I promised to punish them in an exemplary fashion.

I was not unaware, in speaking thus, that I was the only one to have made that offering of wine, but I was sincere nevertheless, for I promised to punish myself. I supported Ali for not having wanted to kill an inoffensive beast.

Inès never forgave me for leaving left her unavenged and it was from that day on that she strove on a daily basis to humiliate me by reminding me what a difference there was between the noble family of the Almeidas and a simple Dutch animal-tamer. It was from that day on that she went out with increasing frequency, that her speech became increasingly bitter, and her demands for money more numerous.

My character changed. I did not plunge into the profound meditations that were habitual to me. I ceased taming wild beasts. I sealed up the door to the gallery of stuffed animals, the sight of which had become insupportable to me.

The baboons no longer had anything to drink but water, but to my great surprise, they did not recover their intelligence and continued to show signs of drunkenness, staggering and accomplishing a thousand unreasonable actions.

It was only on looking back on myself, observing the change brought to my soul by the song of the rohi-rohi on the point of Bukit Timah that I understood the secret range of certain internal modifications and that, among humans as among apes, there are intoxications that do not pass.

My cousin from Goa had a deal in tortoiseshells to make in Batavia. He was to pass through Singapore in order to return to Goa. He consented, on my urgent insistence, to lose the five or six days necessary to go from Batavia to Samarang and from there to Mynheer Varoga's indigo plantation. I awaited his return with a feverish impatience. But the man who charges a fool with a delicate enquiry is quite insensate!

My cousin was younger than me, but he was one of those men who are born important and believe themselves to be invested with the mission of being the spokesmen for what is reasonable, and to spread good advice as banana trees spread bananas.

I walked for long hours back and forth in the harbor when the three-master docked that made the service between Java and Singapore. My cousin was the last to disembark. Immediately he tapped me on the shoulder in a protective manner, and when I had made him climb into the carriage and I interrogated him anxiously, he commenced by summarizing the deal in shells that he had just concluded. He gave the impression of remembering thereafter the mission of scant importance that I had entrusted to him.

I had a beautiful and charming wife, who was moreover, an Almeida, an honorific title that made itself felt as far as good society in Goa, which looked favorably on him personally for being the cousin of the husband of an Almeida. I ought to be content with that and no longer think about chimeras. Those chimeras had caused him to make a very tiring journey. The hotel in Samarang was uninhabitable. The price of hiring horses was exorbitant. He considered that he had risked his life in going along the mountain range from Merbarou to Merapi, but he did not regret it since he was able, thanks to that voyage, to bring his cousin back to reason.

"What have you learned on the subject of Eva?" I asked him, while my heart was beating forcefully in my chest.

"Absolutely nothing," he replied. "And I deployed, in order to come back with that absence of news, a skill of which you have no idea. I do not believe that I will give you overmuch pain by announcing the death of Mynheer Varoga to you. You were, in sum, only slightly acquainted with him. He has been buried, to the surprise of all his European neighbors, according to the Buddhist rite. He had requested that, it appears, before dying.

"The lamas of Kobou Dalem all came to his burial. Men only. In any case, the existence of the lamasery of women is uncertain. The people in the villages that I interrogated in that regard were all mute. They were also very reserved with regard to the disappearance of Eva. They seem to consider her as dead. I say *seems* because the hypothesis you have envisaged has been envisaged by others.

"But what a singular mentality the Javanese have and how mysterious they are! I was only able to understand them thanks to my profound knowledge of Hindi, and above all the Malabari dialect, which has many words in common with Jawo."

My cousin rubbed his hands together proudly and added: "You could have sent any other European messenger and he would not have been able to learn anything positive."

"You learned something positive, then?" I said.

He shook his head and, after a rather long calculated pause, he said: "I've learned, on reflection, that mysteries are dangerous and bad, because they're mysteries, and only tangible reality is good. For you, the tangible reality is Inès.

"You can still imagine that Eva, having lost her reason, either because of the redoubtable character of a temple or a forest or because of your attitude"—here my cousin darted sideways at me, creasing his eyes, a gaze imprinted with the bourgeois libertinage that is more odious than the basest debauchery—"that Eva fetched up in a lamasery of women and that she is still there. You can imagine that by one of those eccentricities to which woman are subject, she is happy with ascetic creatures, that she has converted to their religion, Buddhist or otherwise, and that she is walking at this moment, clad in a red robe, between walls of beaten earth, in one of the most remote places on earth.

"She might, in that case, have let her father know that she was alive and that she no longer wanted to leave the lamasery, and that might have permitted him to say to someone that his daughter was dead 'to him.'

"We might have been able to learn the truth through the mouth of Mynheer Varoga, but he has now died for everyone. He must, in any case, have been a singular eccentric, since, raised in the Catholic religion, he had himself buried as a Buddhist. And that might be an indication of the extravagant decision that his daughter might have made. There is a singular folly of Oriental religion in the Varoga family.

"But those are only hypotheses, and in any case, what's the point of examining them? It's much more plausible and scarcely any sadder to think that the young woman died under the teeth of wild beasts. The probability has great force. She is dead, but Inès is alive. She holds a grudge against you, I believe, because she was struck by a monkey, but that's of no importance. She's rather sensible to the homages of the French, but there aren't many Frenchmen in Singapore. Believe me, the best thing for you is not to think about Eva any longer."

The carriage stopped at my house, and I could not get any more out of my cousin.

I shall not extend myself on the various particularities of Inès' character and the manner of her conduct in my regard, for they have no connection with the motive that has impelled me to write these lines. I shall only say that the affection I had for her changed into a hostile indifference from the moment that I saw her, one rainy day, crushing with the tip of her umbrella the inoffensive snails that emerged innocently on to the ground of the garden in order to wander there slowly, leaving behind them a wake of silvery slime.

She had become more cheerful. She often spoke to me with a kind of bravado about a delightful Frenchman of noble family who she saw in the home of one of her friends and called himself de Bourbon. In order not to be accused of jealousy, I never pointed out to her that the name was too French, and had too historic a character, to be real.

It was then that I felt that she was totally detached from me. And it was in the same epoch that curious disappearances of objects began.

The box in which she put her jewels was the first to go. It was a pretty Persian box with a miniature on the lid. I noticed thereafter that Inès no longer threw over her shoulders the shawl of Indian silk from Calcutta that she loved so much. I found a drawer empty in which they were usually fans and a collection of multicolored scarves.

I crossed the path one day in the doorway of a sailor laden with an enormous package, carefully wrapped up. As Inès seemed to be supervising the departure of the package I asked her what it contained. She replied with a feigned negligence that she was having a few chemises altered and that her seamstress had sent her husband, who was a sailor, to collect them.

"Those," she added, "are petty things that do not concern men."

I contented myself with relying that, considering the enormity of the package under which the back of the robust husband of the seamstress was curbed: "What a quantity of chemises!"

I do not know how Inès found a valid pretext for pronouncing the name of the *Étoile d'Argent*, a superb three-master that was in the harbor of Singapore at that moment and which was to set sail the next day for Zanzibar. Among all ships, that was the only one on the subject of which her lips ought to have remained mute, but Inès belonged to the category of women who have an interior spirit that obliges them to say everything that their reason forbids them to say and which they have an interest in not saying,

I learned, therefore that the captain of the *Étoile d'Argent* was a noble Frenchman named de Bourbon, whom Inès had had the opportunity to meet in the house of one of her friends.

And immediately afterwards, as Inès had gone to take her habitual excursion at six o'clock on the royal avenue, a domestic came to tell me that there was a visitor in the drawing room who had not given his name.

I sometimes have singular intuitions. I knew immediately by intuition that the visitor who wanted to speak to me was the delightful Frenchman of a very ancient family, the captain of the *Étoile d'Argent*.

I went to the drawing room and as soon as I opened the door I perceived that I was mistaken. I had before me the Italian, the ship's mate, that I had met in Batavia and whose room I had seen Eva leaving by means of a ladder.

He had not aged. His moustache was turned up and recently blackened by dye. He seemed hairier than before and he had the animated and satisfied air that success gives certain men.

He started the conversation with a spontaneous gaiety that I had not known in him. He had never had anything against me. Life is a succession of events without logical sequence. One loses, one recovers. The world, vast in appearance, is actually rather small.

He was glad to announce to me the prosperity of his affairs. A considerable group of ship owners had finally recognized his nautical capacities. He had command of the *Étoile d'Argent* and was setting sail the next day for Zanzibar. It was on that subject that he had come to see me. His owners were in Pondicherry and he did not know anyone in Singapore, or hardly anyone.

Now, he needed a liquid sum of five thousand rupees for certain personal expenses that he would have on arrival in Zanzibar. He had come to ask me for them. He knew my fortune and how little I cared about money. He counted on paying my back in quarterly installments. The name of his owners and the situation he had just obtained would answer for him.

I had experienced, on opening the door of the drawing room, a disagreeable sensation when I had observed that my intuition was false. That disagreeable sensation had been followed by an agreeable sensation when I had perceived that the intuition was accurate and that the Italian I had known was none other than the so-called Frenchman named de Bourbon—for I have always been proud of that intuitive gift. And I had a further intuition.

The man in whose presence I was, the commandant of the *Étoile d'Argent* had only thought of me to lend him that sum of five thousand rupees because Inès, my wife had advised him to come to find me. She alone had been able to tell him about the incapacity I had to resist making loans. She had often reproached me for my facility in giving money, except in the cases when she asked for it herself. There had been a kind of conspiracy between them. And my intuition grew.

That seducer with tinted moustaches, that lady-killer, had conceived the project of abducting Inès, my legitimate wife, and he was about to carry it out, in accord with her. The five thousand rupees were only being asked from me to serve for the purchase of a house and an installation in Zanzibar or elsewhere,

Jewels, dresses and underwear were already aboard the *Étoile d'Argent*. I was being reduced by that graying adventurer to the most ridiculous role one can imagine, since, not content with taking my wife, he was counting on me to give him the money necessary to live with her.

A great calm took possession of me. I seemed to reflect on the possibilities of that loan and considered the panoplies of weapons that ornamented the walls of my drawing room. I settled on a group of krises that had, according to my father, belonged to the former Sultan of Borneo, a bloodthirsty man who had the custom of putting his wives to death when he was weary of them. The krises were sharp and perhaps poisoned. I took a step toward the panoply in order to unhook two. My resolution was made. I would fight the man who wanted to steal my wife.

And I opened the window in order to summon Ali the Macassar in order that he could witness the combat.

I can say that at that instant, I heard the song of the rohi-rohi. It was not singing its hymn of fraternity on the branch of the coconut-palm. It was singing internally, within my soul, and in that second, everything appeared to me that I ought to do, everything that it was indispensable for me to do, by virtue of a profound law that I had determined myself by my actions.

I closed the window again.

Events were enchained harmoniously. Beings were being moved like pawns on a chessboard. The cynical Italian adventurer had arrived at his time in order to permit me to realize, thanks to his intervention, the sovereign idea of my life.

I smiled benevolently, and that smile delivered the man from a great weight. So be it! I consented to lend the sum. I had it exactly in my strong-box, in Indian rupees, in consequence of the sale, made that day, of a family of elephants. No contract. A simple receipt.

He signed with his real name, which was Giovanni, and when everything was settled he was belatedly ashamed. The rupees were in a rather heavy leather bag, and he passed it awkwardly from one hand to the other, so awkwardly that I thought he was going to drop them...

But no, he tried to put them away in a pocket that was too narrow. However, he was suffering. He must have thought, in order to reaffirm his soul, about Inès' body in his arms, and the languorous abandon that she so rarely had with me be-

239

cause she must have it often with him. Amour has its terrible
necessities.

At their door he commenced a phrase that he could not
bring out and which had no exact meaning. I thought I understood that he was seeking to prove to me the spontaneous
character of his visit. He had come of his own accord; no one
had advised him. He attempted thus to disengage the responsibility of Inès on the question of money. She was only an amorous woman, he alone was a wretch.

I almost forgave him because of that.

One wonders whether certain events are very fortunate or
very unfortunate. I never knew in which category to place the
departure of Inès.

She had manifested the day before the desire for a morning excursion, and she had given the coachman an order to be
outside the door with the carriage at eight o'clock.

The facility with which a woman detaches herself from a
place where she has lived has always been a cause of astonishment for me. No, I had no chagrin when I heard, for the last
time, the familiar little noises that one hears through the com-
municating door between two bedrooms, the closing of the
catch of a traveling bag, the rustle of a mantle thrown over the
arm, and the glide of a light but resolute step; no chagrin, because of the project that was born in me, which rose from the
depths of my being toward the surface of my consciousness
and which blossomed like a lotus in the sun; no chagrin, but a
little disgust when I saw, a few hours later, from the window
where I was leaning, the face of the coachman running into the
garden in search of someone to whom he could tell what he
knew.

He found the Malay who looked after the monkeys. I understood his gestures as he explained his wait on the harbor,
how he had seen his mistress going on a launch to a ship and
departing on that ship for Zanzibar.

I heard him repeat: "Zanzibar!" His face reflected a sentiment of joyful and satisfied baseness. The Malay whom he

240

was addressing also repeated: "Zanzibar!" laughing stupidly, and behind them, a large monkey that was nibbling the shell of a coconut, occasionally stopped to grimace, and whistle, as if he too were saying: "Zanzibar!"

No chagrin, but the sentiment that the rooms of my house had vaster dimensions, containing fewer items of furniture and having the unexpected resonance of empty rooms.

But it was then, that same day, by virtue of the astonishing law of compensation that presides over everything, that the letter from the Rajah of Djokjokarta reached me.

The Menagerie Delivered

The Rajah of Djokjokarta had no need to offer me an enormous sum. I would have responded to his appeal for nothing. He was needlessly anxious about having made me his offer too late, and that I would not have time to arrive on the day when his father's birth was to be commemorated. I had time. I was ready to devote my entire fortune to the purchase of vehicles and the hiring of ships. He asked me to come with the most curious elements of my menagerie, not forgetting a certain tiger from Merapi of formidable proportions, of which he had heard mention. I intended to satisfy the old animal-lover and organizer of combats between wild beasts fully, and take him all of my beasts, the entire menagerie.

In any case, I possessed almost all the equipment necessary for the voyage. It was that which had served for my triumphant tours of China. People sawed, forged and labored in my garden for days in order to be ready for the appointed day. It required no less than seventy mobile cages to contain my animals. I only had to hire the horses necessary to pull them. I did not leave any animal at home, not a single tortoise or hummingbird.

I had charted from the owner the three largest junks in the port, because of the convenience offered to my vehicles by the vast hold of a junk, where there are neither staircases, partitions nor a division into floors.

All of Singapore watched the embarkation of the most magnificent menagerie in the world. Ali the Macassar had preceded me in order to organize our arrival in Samarang and procure the supplementary horses that would permit us to reach Djokjokarta with the minimum possible delay.

The sea was favorable. No incident troubled the voyage. We arrived in the port of Samarang on a resplendent afternoon and the seventy vehicles quit the junks before nightfall and were installed in the location chosen by Ali from which they would set forth the following morning.

I observed with annoyance that the Rajah had sent me, firstly out of courtesy and secondly to hasten my coming, an important functionary from his palace. He was an aged Javanese, obsequious and covered in jewels, who was proud of bearing the honorific title of Widana. That individual was capable of hindering the realization of my project, but as that realization drew closer, I sensed within me extraordinary resources of skill and treasures of cunning as well as the optimistic cheerfulness that is the essential factor in triumphing over all difficulties.

As I was about to go to the residence in order to obtain the safe conduct necessary for the transportation of my menagerie across the island, I met an officer in the harbor whom I had met in Mynheer Varoga's house, and with whom I had sympathized. He put himself at my disposal to accompany me and abridge the formalities. It was appropriate to hurry, he said, because it would soon be the time when the offices closed, and a delay of a few minutes might oblige me to wait until tomorrow.

We leapt into the carriage of the rajah's envoy and departed at a gallop.

As we turned into an avenue on arriving at the residence another vehicle that was turning passed us. It was not the individual occupying it that I noticed, it was his hands: delicate hands, strangely manicured, which he carried in front of him like precious objects. I recognized them. They were Djath's hands.

It seemed to me that the owner of the hands leaned forward slightly and that he stared at me, but without seeing me. His gaze passed through me as if I did not exist. He had already disappeared when I got up in order to tell the coachman to turn around and follow his carriage. But the rajah's envoy, seizing me by the arm, gave him a contrary order with a wink, and reminded me with a form politeness how necessary it was to conclude the formality of the safe conduct before the offices closed.

"The Prince of Matarem," said the Dutch officer. "He's only just recovered from the illness from which he nearly died. But he's happy now. What a romantic story!"

We were getting down from the carriage. The officer stopped abruptly, like someone who has pronounced one word too many and has perceived it. "It's true," he added, "that you know that story better than me."

I wanted to say no and to beg him to tell me what he knew about Djath, but the Widana had taken me by the arm and drew me along a long corridor to an office, which he almost made me enter by force. The formalities took a long time, and the officer left us without my being able to interrogate him further.

"The Rajah of Djokjokarta has such a curiosity for ferocious beasts and he is waiting for you so impatiently!" the Widana said to me to excuse his haste when we emerged from the resident's palace. "Do you think that we can arrive tomorrow evening?"

I replied that if my calculations were correct, we would stop overnight the following evening in the vicinity of Mynheer Varoga's indigo plantation, and that we would reach Djokjokarta the following morning.

"The rajah will be satisfied," I added, smiling with a tranquil serenity.

Thousands of rohi-rohis were singing in the Javanese forests, but they were not singing as high as the one I heard singing within me, and whose marvelous harmony gave me a kind of permanent intoxication.

The seventy vehicles jolted and rolled over the roads with barkings, grunts, chatterings, yappings, cracks of whips and the calls of the conductors.

The Widana marched at the head with his servants. He was mounted on a white mule. To his right, a Malay on horseback held a parasol; to his left, another agitated a punka. Behind the mobile cages and the vehicles containing the tents, the pikes, the nets and the provisions the deputy handlers, the wardens and the servants responsible for the nourishment of the animals formed a long file of horsemen, and on the heels of that singular and unusual cavalcade the villagers came running, and followed us with their eyes, wide with astonishment.

In the evening, the tents were deployed, fires were lit and people went in search of water, and it was not until very late, in the middle of the night, that the cries of the animals and men died down.

I was obliged, on the morning of our final stage, to slow down our progress slightly, for it would almost have been possible to arrive in Djokjokarta before nightfall. The Widana represented to me all the advantages of that, and I made a semblance of having the greatest desire to do so, but I caused the midday rest to be prolonged considerably, with the result that when the sun set we were only in view of Mynheer Varoga's indigo plantation, as I had promised.

On a blast of the whistle that I gave, all the vehicles stopped and I galloped as far as the Widana who was in the van, with his escort. I gave Ali a sign to go with me. I then represented to the rajah's envoy how wise it would be if he left us there and went on to Djokjokarta that same evening, which would be possible with his excellent mule and his servants' good horses. Thus, he could calm his mater's impatience, announce our arrival and make preparations for it. Before my insistence, the Widana fell in with that opinion.

I added in a peremptory tone that I intended that Ali accompany him.

There was no reason for that. There was even every reason for him to remain, given the surveillance that he maintained and the services that he rendered. But I declared that I would replace him during the evening, desiring expressly that such an excellent second could repose until the following day.

They departed. They had only taken a few paces when I called Ali back. I wanted to shake his hand again, to shake the hand of that faithful and taciturn companion, nothing else.

Perhaps he read a part of my resolution in my eyes, for he asked to stay with me, and a contained emotion that he did not manifest by any sign radiated from his entire person.

After dinner, the wardens would want to spread out into the villages from which they would heard the clamors of festival arriving from afar. It was necessary that someone spent the night on watch. Then again, he alone was informed of the nourishment to give a wild babirusa recently acquired, which was not habituated to captivity and had been giving signs of desperation since the departure.

I made a gesture that brooked no reply. I would take charge of the babirusa. A handshake and that was all, Ali the Macassar followed the Widana on horseback. I observed on following him with my eyes what a profound sadness there is in the backs of men that one will never see again.

I had learned at Samarang that the indigo plantation had been closed down and abandoned since the death of Mynheer Varoga. It was not in that direction that I took the caravan of vehicles. I left the three villages to my right and, by a path bordered with pepper-trees that I knew, I reached the edge of the stream at the point where there was a wooden bridge, a little upstream of the slope where the tiger had appeared to me for the first time and where the wind had carried away my hat.

On the other side of the bridge, between fields of sugar cane and wild pineapples, there was a vast extent of uncultivated ground. It was there that I had the tents erected and arranged the vehicles, not in the usual circle but in a long line parallel to the forest.

We began by giving food and water to the animals. Then my employees came together for the meal around several fires, in accordance with their sympathies, or rather, their races and religions. There was the Chinese group, the Malay group and the negro group. A Parsee from northern India, who had an unsociable character and a rudimentary intelligence, was considered as a pariah by everyone, and kept apart.

That evening, I exhibited the most amicable gaiety. I had wine distributed and I noticed that everyone drank it, including the Muslims. I even addressed a few words to the solitary Parsee, who did not reply.

I thought at first of giving my entire troop a collective authorization to go to the villages, which were not for away. We had seen the light of fires and heard clamors in their direction. They must be celebrating the same festival as in Djokjokarta. But I thought it better to have the appearance of conserving a part of wardens around the vehicles in order not to awaken the suspicion of the others.

I therefore sat down familiarly by the Chinese fire and confided to them that they were authorized, the Chinese alone, for their good services, to go to amuse themselves in the villages that I described to them as particularly joyful, and the direction of which I indicated to them. I did the same for the Malays and the negroes, so cleverly that the camp was soon deserted, each group being convinced that it was leaving the vehicles under the guard of the other groups. Only the unsociable Parsee did not take advantage of the liberty that I offered him and remained lying down with his head under his blanket.

All that had taken time. The night advanced. The moon rose. The immense forest seemed to loom up suddenly, more mysteriously menacing.

It was then that I began opening the cages. Some had locks, others hooks, other catches, others had sections that slid on grooves. Those were the most numerous because they were the most convenient for transferring the animals from one cage to another. I knew the manipulation perfectly, and it was not there that I could be hindered.

The difficulty consisted in making the animals believe, in the presence of a sudden liberty, in the reality of their good fortune. Did they suspect some trap? Or was the terror that I inspired in them stronger than any other sentiment? At the sight of me, when I opened the doors to them, they remained fixed in a fearful immobility.

I was obliged to seize armfuls of night-birds and throw them into the air. They began by falling as if they had no wings. I saw the stupefied roundness of their eyes, and something vexed in the movement of their necks, as if they were the victims of some new joke on the part of their torturer. Then, suddenly, almost all together, they flew away, and rose up very high, and very far, above the mass of the forest, as if they wanted to reach the distant region of the stars.

The monkeys gave the impression of having received an order, and all ran together, gamboling, into the middle of the camp, seeking to pick up the vestiges of the meal. Several followed me, one holding a walnut, another a banana-skin, grimacing behind me, and it was only when I approached the cage of a savage animal that they ran away.

Apart from the babirusa, which launched itself like a bolide with a mighty grunt of joy and disappeared into the forest in a second, the animals remained taciturn before their open cages or continued sleeping. I was obliged to go and fetch a long whip and a pike in order to oblige them to emerge from their dream of slavery and take advantage of their liberty.

Then I experienced a frenzy to finish with it. I opened all the cages in succession; I whipped, I poked, I struck, I ran from one place to another with an extravagant activity. In a few minutes the camp was covered by all the species of animal in creation.

The dominant noise was the whinnying of the horses. They were all attached together, near the bridge. I heard them bucking and pulling at their tethers. Those that had made a pact with humans and served to transport their captive brothers must have feared the vengeances reserved for traitors. But the liberated beasts had no such thoughts. They were struggling against a profound bewilderment, an infinite sadness.

An opossum went to great trouble gathering its offspring, which had dispersed. A peacock displayed its tail, but that was to put on a brave face. A spiny echidna rolled up into a ball in order to deliberate silently on the course of action to take. A boa made a perfect circle, from which its head emerged, full of anxiety and timidity. A korbi-kalao[14] attempted to perch on my shoulder to ward off the evils that it foresaw. The bear swayed, dreaming. The helmeted cassowaries agitated the protuberance on their skull and seemed to be saying: "Who knows?" A giraffe lowered its head modestly. A panther crawled. A family of Persian lions accustomed to jumping through hoops marched sadly behind the male, and sometimes a lion cub made a nonchalant little bound through an imaginary hoop. Hyenas laughed skeptically. The son of the heron that I had burned clicked its beak in a sinister manner. The Australian fox fanned itself with the plume of its tail. The dwarf donkey shook its only ear. All the beasts awaited the orders of the whip-bearing tyrant. None believed in the generosity of man.

All of a sudden, there came from the profound forest, the realm of vegetation and humus, an aromatic breath, an odor of herbs, putrescence and life, slightly humid and slightly peppery, an essence of decomposition and seeds transported by the wind.

The boa uncoiled. The platysternon tortoise started running with an incredible speed. The panther's body undulated. A cuscus launched itself along a tree-branch and was lost in the foliage. All the lions started bounding regularly and filed after one another as if they were passing through hundreds of hoops. The tapir raised its mobile nose toward the heavens, like a votive offering. The crocodiles slithered. The wolves ran. I heard the wall of the forest creaking, the water of the stream resonating, splashed by the dives of aquatic creatures.

And then the great Javan tiger, which had not yet been freed, started to roar. That roaring hastened the dispersal of the frightened animals in all directions. I darted a glance around me. Even the monkeys had regained the trees, but they were

---

[14] This bird is mentioned in the same early nineteenth-century sources as the rohi-rohi, again without sufficient detail for the modern name of the species to be identified.

249

leaning down and seemed to be waiting curiously for what was about to happen.

I perceived the solitary Parsee in the same place, his head outside his blanket, gazing at me with an indifferent and stupid expression. I wanted to preserve him from the risk that I was about to run. Then again, if I were to be torn apart, I preferred to be in the heart of the forest.

I traversed the camp. I chose two horses habituated to wild beasts and I harnessed them to the cage of the one-eyed tiger and headed toward the somber line of trees.

The moonlight permitted me to distinguish a path broader than the others, in which I engaged. I went some distance, all the way to a clearing where I stopped, and where I unhitched the horses. A crack of the whip, and those faithful servants of humans went back the way they had come.

We were alone, the tiger and I, in the middle of the forest, separated by the bars of its cage. I considered it for a moment, and it seemed to me that the single eye that gleamed in its mask, its great green phosphorescent eye, was a lamp that illuminated not only the clearing before it and the trees surrounding it, but also the infinite depths of my soul.

No, I did not have the slightest hesitation. I wanted to go on to the end.

What happened was much simpler than I had been able, confusedly, to imagine.

Once the bolts that were maintaining it had been removed, it was only necessary to pull one side of the cage toward oneself. The cage was very heavy and it was necessary for me to seize the bars with both hands in order to slide them. They slid with a metallic screech, and I then found myself beside the open cage. It would have been necessary for me to lean forward to see what the tiger was doing inside, and I thought about the rapidity of a thrust of a paw that might have fractured my skull. I heard the redoubtable being respiring, and those few seconds seemed infinitely long to me.

Suddenly, I had the sensation that it was beginning to walk. Slowly, it emerged. Its head was lowered and it was sniffing. It turned lightly in my direction, and then there was nothing more, except for a frisson of ease that was prolonged in the tangle of lianas into which it had launched itself with a vertiginous velocity.

A sentiment of solitude such as I had never had before weighed upon me. It was not yet the hour when the rohi-rohis commenced singing in the coconut-palms. I looked anxiously to the right and the left. Had I not done what I intended? Everything would thus be well.

I began to weep.

PART THREE

The Hermit of the Forest

It is raining. The rain is making a loud noise in the foliage high above. I do not see it falling. It oozes, it penetrates, it bathes everything. I am taking advantage of it to write these last lines regarding my way of life. I regret having left in Singapore the notebook to which I consigned the principal events of my life. How I would laugh now at its complete stupidity, if it could reread it! How different I am from what I was! But why be astonished by that? Trees lose their bark and animals their fur. A man is also stripped of his old ideas and he acquires new ones that are younger and more solid.

I am living in the cabin of the ascetic Chumbul. For how long? I have no idea. Perhaps a few days, perhaps weeks. By marching at random, straight ahead, I encountered that cabin, made of branches crudely embedded in the soil and joined together by lianas, in the middle of the dense stand of nipas, pandanus and parasitic orchids. The ascetic Chumbul was sitting beside the cabin, his legs crossed, in the process of meditating. I waited until he had finished, and then I coughed loudly to attract his attention. I approached him and I understood, by the forward movement of his upper body, that his head had acquired the weight that death gives the human cranium. I dug a grave at the foot of a flowering copal with a bizarre implement that I found in the cabin and I buried the ascetic there. At first I had fabricated a cross with two pieces of wood and I was about to stick it in the ground when I remembered that the ascetic was a Buddhist and that the emblem might have offended him if he had been able to see it.

Now I live in his house alongside his tomb and, desirous of rendering honor to him in some manner, in exchange for his hospitality, I repeat morning and evening, before the copal that shelters him, the kind of prayer or invocation that I heard him sing in the evening, and which has returned to my memory:

"Om, Mani, Padme, Aum."

I did not imagine that one could be so contented, alone, in the middle of an immense, profound, amicable and maternal forest. How wise that ascetic was beneath his deplorable thinness! He had found the best way of living. I have just thought, suddenly, about the thousands of fools whose are going along the royal avenue in Singapore, exchanging greetings or contemplating the Chinese shops, and I uttered a burst of laughter so loud that it almost drowned out the noise of the rain in the foliage.

What characterizes life in the forest is the large number of occupations that absorb all your time. It is necessary to find mango trees and coconut palms for one's nourishment; it is necessary to go to the stream, at a place where it is profoundly enclosed by a hermetic lid of foliage, and draw water there with Chumbul's pitcher. It is necessary to collect leaves in order to have a healthy bed and young branches in order to rest one's head on an agreeable pillow.

Then too, I have taken it into my head to accomplish various tasks. There are several anthills near the cabin to which the rain has caused terrible damage. I saw subterranean galleries exposed to the light and a host of workers with narrow bodies transporting small objects with great precaution, which are larvae, sacks of provisions or perhaps idols. I have commenced wooden constructions above those ant-hills in order that the rain will fall to the right and the left of their openings and no longer cause upheavals in the dwellings so carefully built.

In the branches of a nearby banyan there are several families of white-handed gibbons. I observed that the nests that they had constructed with woven fern-leaves were only mediocre shelters against the rain, either because the apes are not naturally ingenious or because they had received an insufficient ancestral tradition. I am taking advantage of their absence to raise myself up from branch to branch and dispose over those nest a kind of solid roof of palm leaves that I have attached together.

I had the surprise one morning of seeing and recognizing one of those gibbons suspended from a very high branch. It was devoting itself at sunrise to the trapeze exercises and perilous leaps that Ali the Macassar had taught a few gibbons in my menagerie. I was glad to think that that one had rapidly found a family of its race to welcome it.

I have spent several days going up and down the stream, and have even followed a few rivulets that run into it in the hope of encountering beavers, for I never cease thinking about the one whose death I caused by depriving it of its children. Beavers! Where are there beavers? With what delight I would aid them to hollow out their burrows, to build their huts, to cement their dykes! I have even attempted to dam a small stream at hazard, in order to attract them, but I reflected that they were only builders of dykes by virtue of savant architectural calculations, and to protect their riverside towns from flooding. In any case, the sight of a man would make them flee. I am not sure of being able to pay the debt to the beaver.

I also search for herons and parrots, without knowing to what extent I can be useful to them. I have perceived several of them, but they fled immediately, as if they had an extraordinary horror of me.

And I regret not being a marvelous musician and or possessing all the Chinese musical instruments in order to make resonate at sunset some suave kin, some divine raga, and enchant with a perfect harmony the delicate beos with the iridescent plumage that shelter their inconceivable sensibility beneath the foliage.

Eva told me that this forest is one of the most ancient on earth and that it encloses great mysteries.

One of those mysteries must relate to a strange elephant that I have perceived two or three times, sometimes walking slowly along a path, sometimes detaching young branches in order to nourish itself. It is the color of ash and bears a singular resemblance to Jehovah, whom I killed. I could even believe that it is him, who escaped my rifle-shot, if I had not heard the echoes of various complaints from various property-owners in Singapore that reached the residence, on the subject of the emanations caused by his cadaver.

That elephant is not very fearful. It sometimes prances joyfully, as Jehovah did when he perceived me, and just now he stood motionless a short distance away from me, trunk lowered, with an infinite sadness in his little eyes. I am surprised by the manner in which he glides rather than walks, and in which he suddenly disappears without my being able to tell which way he has gone.

My marvelous faculty of slumber permits me to go to sleep after sunset. But tonight, I have woken up suddenly and am sitting up in the midst of the fern leaves with which I cover my body like a blanket in order to avoid the nocturnal chill. I can hear a voice calling me, coming from very far away but drawing nearer.

It is a voice with terrible accent that I recognize, without ever having heard it, as the one that once called to Eva in the temple of Ganesha. It has a growling and a barking in it, it is sad and low, singularly disquieting, and it dominates the sounds of the wind and the quivering agitation of the trees, which draw closer together. Sometimes, that voice is heart-rending, and at other times it has an alluring lightness that almost obliges me to stand up, to open the door and run outside.

But I sense that if I obeyed that voice, it is not on my two feet that I would start to run, but on four feet, like the beasts. It has just resounded behind the clump of nipas and pandanus, and I almost responded with the long howl of a wolf, and I hesitated as to whether to crawl like a snake or leap in little bounds like a kangaroo. I have stayed where I am, my heart beating rapidly. The voice has change direction, as if it belonged to an errant being, a soul in pain, some supernatural being possessed of a secret magic. There is a power of animal attraction in that voice, and it is that attraction that Eva obeyed.

I resist, holding my human head high and straight. But I surprise myself making a few unhabitual gestures. I scratch the ground with my hand as if with a paw. I sense a grimace on my face that makes me resemble a frightened gibbon.

The voice draws way. I wonder what its significance can be, and what its power is. Has it really resonated in the nipas and the pandanus, or only in my soul? Is there in the delirium of vegetal life that is the forest a disorganizing force that tends to retrograde a human in the scale of beings? Why is that voice perceptible to me tonight, when it was not on the night in the temple of Ganesha? The ascetic Chumbul must not have heard it, but Eve heard it. Perhaps an absolutely materialistic man such as I was then, and a man absolutely disengaged from the material like the ascetic, did not have the senses necessary to be attained by the nocturnal voice? Whereas the young woman who had opened the doors of her soul, and the man who had delivered the animals of the menagerie, had both found, without knowing it, a channel of communication with the unknown world in which the strange voice vibrates.

I am meditating on these things and only interrupt myself to wish ardently for the appearance of the rising sun.

It is finally coming, later than usual, it seems to me.

I take a few steps outside. I perceive the savant ape that is already executing its trapeze exercises, and I utter a cry of surprise. At the foot of the banyan whose trunk looms up facing my cabin, there is a little terracotta statuette that someone must have deposited there during the night.

I look at it, I turn it over in all directions. The statuette represents an unknown goddess, in a pose of meditation. The body is that of a woman, but it has the head of a sow, and that animal had, whose eyes are turned toward the heavens, has a singular expression of elevation and ideal shame.

Did not Mr. Muhcin speak to me about a certain goddess Dorje Pagmo who had exactly that head, on the day when he asked me whether there was not a lamasery of women in the Merapi mountains? Is that statuette protective or menacing, and who can have deposited it there? Who has discovered my retreat? There is no visible trace of footprints.

I have installed the statuette in my cabin and I have even erected a small altar with a few stones.

I have spent the greater part of my day searching for fruits other than mangoes, for my stomach is beginning to wary of that uniform nourishment. But I have not found a sago tree, nor jacks, nor durians. In the hope of encountering some I went a long way into the heights, following the watercourse upstream but without quitting its banks, for I was determined to return to the cabin and the statuette with the sow's head, which constitute a primitive hearth for me.

I marched over a plateau where the vegetation was less abundant, and I suddenly seemed to perceive, in the midst of red rocks, a mass of stones of the same color that gave the impression of a building constructed by human hands. I advanced and I distinguished a circular wall, and a low, square tower.

Is that the lamasery of Buddhist nuns that Eva mentioned to me, and by which she might have ended up on the night of her flight? The wall is inclined over the slope of the mountain and I believe I can see any interior garden with vague designs of avenues. But I cannot distinguish any sign of life, any human silhouette, and I dare not approach, and I go down again the way I have come when the sun is about to set.

I have forgotten the search or fruits and, as mangos sicken me, I have not eaten and I feel slightly dizzy. I go to sleep but I wake up several times. I hear the nocturnal voice, the animal voice, the tempting voice that calls to me. It tells me to come and drink from the stream with the animals, to climb the trees, to search for prey in order to bite into them with teeth, but it seems to me that the voice is more distant, fainter, and diminishes further when I touch the statuette of Dorje Pagmo on its stone altar, with my hands.

A new surprise awaits me at daybreak.

Beside my door there is a sandstone jar filled with an abundant broth of cooked rice. I eat it with an extreme satisfaction, while being astonished by its mysterious origin. I promise myself to stay on watch the following night, in order to know who the being is who is watching over me and has brought me, in turn, the image of a goddess to protect my spirit and a rice broth to nourish my body.

My faculty of sleep is too great. Every evening I deposit outside my door the sandstone jar that I have emptied, and every morning I find it full. But I have not succeeded in staying awake long enough to discover who the silent protector is that does not hesitate to venture into the forest by night and brave its dangers to bring me nourishment.

Almost every day I go back up the steam and contemplate from afar the square tower of the lamasery. Today, by dint of gazing of the mountain slope contained between the walls, I seemed to see a procession of silhouettes in red robes, a slow procession of meditative creatures. Can they be the red lamas of whom I have heard mention—the female lamas whose abbess is a Khoutouktou? What is a Khoutouktou?

In descending the steam, however I thought I say that procession preceding me, and when I turned round it seemed to me that I saw it disappear slowly into a wood of furry mangroves.

Today, I had a fortuitous encounter with the temple of Ganesha and I took account of the fact that it is quite close to the lamasery. That renders more plausible the hypothesis that Eva, in fleeing, was taken in by the lamas.

I have walked in the galleries, descended the stairways, and traversed the interior courtyard. I have seen the statues of animals, the caparisoned elephants, the curled-up marble pythons, the buffaloes half-buried under parasitic plants. The old mystery is still there.

The Ganeshas in their stone cells hold the same objects with their four arms above their fat bellies. Why those objects rather than others? I have racked my brains in search of an explanation. A conch, a disk, a club and a lotus: why is Ganesha holding those objects? Perhaps because abundance, courage, strength and beauty are the qualities that produce wisdom in meditation. But how impressive wisdom is when its symbols are reproduced in a circular fashion and there are hundreds of them! I was suddenly seized by a frisson and a hectic desire to flee.

On the round path that overlooks the monument, a confused red procession was filing through the stones.

I surprise myself having violent regrets with regard to books. There are things that I would love to know and that I would know if I had read. About what can those Buddhist nuns and monks be thinking, who enclose themselves in convents? I know why the nuns and monks of the Occident have retired voluntarily from the world and have renounced its pleasures. They are obeying Our Lord Jess Christ, who has advised them to do it. But those pagans?

I remember that in Singapore the most honest and disinterested men were Buddhists. I made fun of them because they did not eat animals. I said, in talking about the Jesuits of Bukil Timah: those are true priests! They hunt, they kill like me and they eat game with the appetites of ogres. The only Buddhist priest that it was given to me to know I detested immediately and I had him unjustly condemned as a thief. Now the rohi-rohi has sung for me, I would not want for anything in the world to eat the flesh of an animal, and what sacrifice am I not ready to accomplish, in order to rediscover the lama with the straw hat and ask him a few questions?

I would ask him what the animals are, in relation to humans, what is the story of reincarnation of which I have heard talk as a Hindu belief, and which I have always considered as an absurdity of pagans. I would ask him what a Khoutouktou is, what a lama is, and to give me details about the personality of the Manu who has said or written the sentence that I have not forgotten:

"The man who has killed a cat, a blue jay, a mongoose or a lizard must retire to the heart of the forest and devote his life to the beasts until he is purified."

I would ask him whether it is true, as I believe it is, that there are kings, priests and sages among the animals—which is to say, beings more advanced than others in evolution, and if it is them who pass first into the human realm, in the same way that among humans, those who are pure, like Mr. Muhcin, will attain a stage superior to humanity well before those who are stupid, like my cousin, conceited, like Captain Giovanni, or crude, like me. I have known a redoubtable sovereign of beasts, the tiger of Merapi; a magician versed in the science of spell-casting, the toad that killed my mother; and an affectionate and faithful friend, an angel of delicacy, the elephant Jehovah.

I would ask him in what measure there are recompenses and chastisements for animal faults and virtues, and whether it is not us, with our pitiless hatred, who thrust the animals back toward the evil that they would like to escape.

I would ask him whether the solitude in the forest prescribed by Manu is sufficient for purification, and whether the man who has skinned ought not be skinned, and the man who has eaten ought not be eaten in his turn.

I have retired to the heart of the forest and I am beginning to purify myself.

The first that has come is the wild babirusa that captivity had thrown into despair. I was sitting in front of the cabin when it appeared in the bushes. It labored the ground with its tusks. It held itself immobile while considering me, and then it departed with unimaginable swiftness.

But it has come back grunting and crouched down some distance away from me. I sense that it has no terror, and even that it is manifesting the amity for me of one companion for another companion of the forest. But its love of liberty is so great that it prefers to leave a certain distance between us. "One never knows!" it seems to be saying. It never stays for long. It traverses the tangled lianas like a bolide, and at each return its grunts have something more familiar.

I recall the story of Saint Anthony that I was told in childhood. That Egyptian hermit also had a pig for a friend in his solitude. Is it in the destiny of all hermits, or does it me from the relationship that renders the human species and the porcine species so close?

Because of the example of the babirusa, the ape trapeze-artist has descended from branch to branch and has ended up choosing as a domicile the roof of my cabin. It sits there all day and only quits it to go precipitately to swing in the fashion of a trapeze and leap on the banyan, at the same religious hours when Ali the Macassar appeared before its cage, cracking his whip.

Since then, almost at the same time, the opossums, a mongoose, orangs and a tapir from Borneo have come. I recognize the tapir as the one that belonged to me by its zigzag strips, its excessively short tail, its excessively long nose and its white-fringed ears. It looks at me with its little lateral eyes, which are filled with melancholy. There are no tapirs in Java. This one must have wandered through the forest and along the stream, plunging into its waters, for its is slightly amphibious, in the hope of encountering a creature made in its image, with a thick skin like its own, a minuscule tail, and a mobile and excessively long nose. It needs no longer to be alone and it manifests by means of hoarse whistles its satisfaction in encountering me. But it leans against my cabin and I am afraid it might destroy it with its weight. I hasten to make it a little heap of tender cassia leaves, of which I know it is fond, in order to make it change its position.

And other animals are still coming. Peacocks make great stars in the bushes, white salanges fly over my head, a fox shows its curious muzzle, a superb menura with a lyriform tail stretches out its neck not far away from me, and a turtle from the River Tachylga, recognizable by the Tibetan characters on its shell, comes to eat pellets of rice that I knead for it in my hands.

Tonight, there is a full moon. It has risen extraordinarily early and is cutting out the branches of trees, designing the paths, making of the sky, the earth and the forest a huge land-scape of iced marble.

I have taken into my cabin, to sleep there alongside me, a young russet opossum that its family has forgotten while going to search for a comfortable corner in which to spend the night. It has installed itself at the foot of the statuette of the goddess, but from time to time it comes to pose on my breast and scratch it with its paw, as if it wanted to make a hole in it. I wake up and I rejoice in that awakening, which I prolong or as long as possible, in the hope that it will permit me to discover who the mysterious bringer of rice is.

And as I watch the silence through the gaps in my cabin, my wish is finally granted.

The footfalls I hear are very light. They are those of a man who is walking quietly, without trying to disguise the noise he is making. I see him part the lianas with his right hand. His left hand is holding a jar suspended by a strap. He is clad in a red cotton robe belt at the midriff and I believe that beneath that robe he is wearing ridiculously short European trousers. There is no mystery in his gait, He advances like a man accomplishing a simple and quotidian task, and he pours into the jar in front of the cabin the contents of the one he is carrying. He does so meticulously. He turns round as soon as the last grain of rice has fallen and he goes away as he has come, the empty jar swinging at the end of the strap.

It is him. I have just recognized him. It is the lama that I had condemned to prison. But how is that I do not launch my-self on his heels and do not fall at his knees in order to beg his pardon?

I remain where I am, my hand posed on the neck of the little opossum, and a great joy fills my heart. I sense that between us, words are unnecessary, and that there is in the nocturnal gift of the rice a fraternity that has no need of language to be expressed, a silent pardon such as God himself gives none better, and which requires no thanks.

Tonight, I do not go back to sleep.

The pencil with which I am writing is about to be entirely used up and I shall soon have filed up the last page of my notebook. What is the point of writing, anyway? I have learned in writing what has happened to me and what I have experienced everything that I am capable of learning about myself.

I shall deposit these pages here in order that those who are searching for me will find them and will be able to deduce from reading them that their search is unnecessary and importunate. For people are searching for me; I have heard the nostalgic sounds of the tom-tom in which there are memories of childhood fêtes and evocations of lost Eva. This cabin is too close to the places where humans live.

Tomorrow morning I shall set forth toward the summit of Mount Merapi, where there is the crater of a volcano that is reputed to be inaccessible.

I am born of beasts, it is they who have engendered me. They extend beyond my father and my mother, who belonged to the human race and I see them all, making me signs. How much fur, how many feathers, how many fins! My ancestors are gathered around me, raising trunks, snapping jaws, vibrating antennae, cricking mandibles. I distinguish the prayerful gestures of their palmate hands, and I divine beneath the rotundities of skulls the effort of patient thoughts.

All of them have been laborious in their fashion, they have put into the world a hope. The crocodile beneath the mud of rivers, the monkey in its domain of bark and leaves, the bird in the air, the carnivore in its mysterious abattoir, the mole in its subterranean darkness, each has unconsciously formulated the desire to live within a more perfect envelope, with more complicated organs, only two legs, no fur and no feathers, and a human head. I am the child glimpsed in their millenarian meditations, I am the last word of the beast, which terrestrial effort has had so much trouble in modeling. I am the beast itself in its final incarnation.

I love you, my parents bearing shells, you who have four feet to walk, you who have thick fur and cannot take it off when it is hot, you who are naked and have not had the ingenuity to cover yourself in garments, you whose principal concern is daily nourishment, you to whom nature has given heavy beaks, deformed humps, disproportionate necks, I love you for the insouciance, the resignation and the fidelity that are your essential virtues, the present that I have received from you and of which I have made so little.

In order to live beside you I have crossed the gate of tall ebony trees that stands at the threshold of the forest and I have entered the realm of my forefathers. My hatred has changed into love and I understand that which remained hidden from me. I hear words full of tenderness in the chatter of parrots; I see incomparable elegance and a marvelous sentiment of beauty in the slightly mannered cranes with which the blue jay smoothes its feathers; I penetrate the philosophical conversations of immobile marabous and I live full of respect before the sentiment of death that the burials of ants reveal.

O my parents, with hearts so vast and simple, I swear no longer to make use of my intelligence, which is yours, to destroy you. Your life will henceforth be as precious in my eyes as my own. But how difficult the most natural thing is to realize! Now I am filled with scruples. How can I deliver myself to the importunity of a mosquito-net with sufficient delicacy not to give death? My God! Have I not just now crushed an inoffensive mite that was passing over the stone on which I placed my foot? And if I breathe forcefully, are there not minuscule and innocent creatures that I project far from the sun,

into the darkness of my organs, and which perish there unjustly?

The Last Night in the Cabin

It is a regular friction, simultaneously languorous and terrible, which glides over the branch walls of my cabin and which has woken me up during the last night I spend there.

The moon is so bright that one can see almost as in broad daylight, and I wonder at first if it is not some celestial prodigy that has given birth to that light intermediate between night and sunlight.

What is making that noise so close at hand? I look, and I seem at first to see a procession of red lamas. They are moving very softly and what I hear is the rustle of their robes in the wood.

But no. Why did I not think of it sooner? Why has it not come sooner? It is the tiger of Merapi, the one-eyed tiger, the giant tiger, the one that I have martyrized—I, the man.

Through the interstices of the branches I see its enormous snout, its green phosphorescent eye, and it seems to me that the cabin creaks slightly when its back leans against it as it glides. I think that the door is fragile, having only a little knotted liana that forms a hook, and that the lighted thrust of a paw will open.

But I have no terror. I even experience a bizarre delight, that of not knowing exactly what will happen.

Never have I entered the tiger's cage, never have I found myself face to face with it. My rage was only exercised through the bars and it must have accumulated within it, as only beasts can do, an extraordinary sum of unsatisfied vengeance. I know the animal faculty that permits the retention in the memory for years the memory of an offense.

I can hear the tiger growling behind the cabin wall. It is undulating, searches for an opening; it is waiting.

And I, sitting beside the statuette of the goddess Dorje Pagmo, the goddess with the pig's head, think that I have unjustly tortured that savage creature, for the tiger of Merapi had not devoured Eva on the night of the temple of Ganesha. I know that at the present moment with an absolute certainty.

I begin to reflect. The tiger might well circle around the cabin and not evaluate is solidity, not thinking of giving a thrust of its paw to the door. Animals, sometimes so ingenious, are at other times more naïve than little children.

If I suddenly raised my voice severely and gave it an order to depart, perhaps it would go away meekly. It has seen me and heard me command as a master for such a long time. Then too, there is in human speech a rhythmic organization that impresses beasts. I remember an Australian hunter who escaped the wolves that were surrounding him merely by shouting, in an intelligible voice, an order to go away.

But I do not want to intimidate the one-eyed monster that I delighted in torturing for such a long time. There is a confused desire in me—more than that, a necessity—to find myself disarmed in its presence.

Not only have I no hatred against that tiger, which has been the nightmare of my existence, but I have pity for it, because of its blind fury of killing, a sort of fraternal sentiment because of the resemblance I once had with it.

I look outside. The tiger is circling and growling. The imaginary procession of red lamas has disappeared. The radiant night has crystallized the forest and made each tree into a block of sculpted silver. It seems to me that my mind is bathed in the streaming of primal verities and that it is about to launch forth into unlimited space.

I have come to my feet; I have approached the door. A ray of moonlight falls directly on to the forehead of the statuette of the goddess. I examine the liana knotted by Chumbul, which forms a primitive catch. I give it a little flick with my finger and open the catch.

Ordinarily the door opens of its own accord. This time it has not swung. I understand why immediately. The tiger is leaning against the door. There is nothing more to do than give it a little push; the tiger will move, the door will open and we will be face to face.

I have written these last lines by moonlight, and with some difficulty because my pencil is no longer anymore than a ridiculous stub. I shall deposit the sheets on which I am writing at the foot of the statuette of the goddess, and then I shall push the door.

O Lord, I am the beast. Give my soul the necessary fraternity to be understood and loved by the beasts. Enable my body to radiate the love that I finally experience, in order that it expands over my brothers of the forest. Permit me to aid them and guide them in order that they become better, as I have become.

And by way of conclusion, I shall trace once again the prayer that I do not understand, and which I am repeating aloud:

"Om, Mani, Padme, Aum."

Monsieur Charlex's Letter

This is the letter of Monsieur Charlex, charged by the French government with an archeological mission to Java, which I found pinned after the two manuscripts that I am publishing. The first of those manuscripts forms a large notebook from which some pages have been ripped out, and is written in a firm and regular handwriting. The second has been scribbled, rather than written, on the leaves of a little pocket notebook. Monsieur Charlex's letter completes them. One can deduce from reading it that at the moment of his departure for Java Monsieur Charlex was asked by the possessor of the memoirs of the animal-tamer Rafael Graaf to make enquiries about their author in Batavia and Djokjokarta.

Batavia, 1 May 1874.

What I am writing to you is only a rapid summary of my research. I have so many notes to copy, so many sketches and reproductions of bas-reliefs to sort and clarify that I am putting off more detailed explanations until my return to Europe. I have, in any case, only a few things to tell you.

As soon as I arrived in Batavia I questioned all the people in Dutch society that it was given to me to know. All of them were aware of what had happened a few years earlier in Djokjokarta, but it seems to me that after having commented passionately on the affair they had lost interest. All concluded in the same fashion.

"The animal-tamer from Singapore, who has been nick-named the man who lives with a tiger, was a brute whom Juffrouw Varoga knew, to her misfortune. He has gone mad, so much the worse for him. Does he still exist? It's possible but it's of no importance. Juffrouw Varoga is now the Princess of Matarem and she lives very happily in the vicinity of Batam in the domains of her husband, the descendant of the ancient emperors of Java, who is a poet and an erudite man."

People add on speaking of her such phrases as the following:

"What a romantic creature? She's a scatterbrain who has become wiser. She had already had several escapades, notably in Singapore, where she frequented opium-dens. She was one of those women who like poets, animal-tamers and naval officers. But how can one explain that she confined herself in a convent of Buddhist nuns, from which the Prince of Matarem had a great deal of trouble persuading her to emerge? Perhaps Buddhism has a powerful attraction for certain souls."

The captain of a merchant ship that called in at Singapore has told me that a lawsuit has been engaged there between Madame Graaf, installed in Zanzibar, and a cousin of the animal-tamer who lives in Goa. The fortune and property of Rafael Graaf has been put under sequester.

But it has transpired that under the influence of the climate, the gardens in Singapore in the location where the menagerie once was have become a virgin forest. In that forest, crocodiles that must have been forgotten have pullulated and now constitute a danger for the Chinese quarter.

I shall report to you almost word for word something that I heard a teacher at the school of Batavia say, who is reputed to be very well-versed in the knowledge of Buddhism and the religions of India. It is only distantly related to the story of the animal-tamer of Singapore and it was not pronounced in his regard, but it nevertheless permits rather troubling comparisons.

The professor was talking about the powers acquired by certain fakirs in consequence of long meditations.

"Fakirs have a secret knowledge of the power of sound. They can enclose in the vibrations caused by certain syllables influences that act at a distance on those who hear those syllables. They instruct their disciples and claim to render them better, more elevated in the hierarchy of beings, merely by making them repeat what they call mantras. The invocation that is the most mysterious of all, and encloses the most occult power when it is formulated in accordance with a rhythm of which it is necessary to know the secret, is: 'Om, Mani, Padme, Aum.'"

As I promised you, I went to Djokjokarta and stayed there for a few days. The voyage is long and tedious. The railway that will connect Djokjokarta with Samarang is still in the process of construction. The works that are in the process of being carried out are causing an upheaval in the landscape and giving them a physiognomy different from that described in Rafael Graaf's notebooks.

I had several letters of recommendation for the Dutch resident in Djokjokarta. He is a likeable but simple man, perhaps a trifle brutal. He affects to believe that the animal-tamer Rafael Graaf has been dead for a long time and that everything that is said about him has a legendary character.

"A man cannot live alongside a tiger without being devoured by it," he told me—an opinion regarding which I have reservations, since it is a matter on this occasion of an animal-tamer and it is claimed that some men who exercise that profession possess a species of magnetism that reduces the will of animals.

The resident, when I raised that objection, did not hide from me how absurd he found that opinion. It was, he added, that of Ali, the animal-tamer's principal employee; and he recounted to me the difficulties he had had on the subject of the repatriation of the personnel of the menagerie and the searches undertaken to find Rafael Graaf—searches for which Ali wanted to mobilize the entire garrison of the residence.

He was obliged to have him expelled from the territory of Java, for he fell into insensate rages every time he heard the hypothesis of his master's death uttered, and threatened those who were not of his opinion with his kris. It is Ali who found the second part of the journal whose entirety you have in your possession.

"It was a famous story, that affair of the menagerie," the resident also told me, on the day I took my leave of him. "I only look at it from the point of view of the hunter, the only interesting one. One can now shoot game in Java that did not exist previously. I've seen a zebra galloping through a coffee plantation and the same day, an officer of the garrison missed a tapir that was bathing in the river and an animal running on two feet that did not belong to any known species."

It was then that my bargaining commenced with the people of the villages. I will spare you all the difficulties I encountered. The indigenes remain mute and turn their heads away when the word Ganesha is pronounced in front of them. They refuse unanimously to serve as guides for foreigners who want to explore the region of Merapi and Merbarou. The three villages that surround Mynheer Varoga's indigo plantation are almost completely deserted. The Javanese consider that bad luck is a real entity that inhabits certain places that please it more than others. The events that unfurled successively a few years ago have made them think that bad luck has chosen as a domicile the approaches of the Merapi forest. They consider that the best means of warding it off is to maintain an absolute silence on everything relating to the man who lives with the tiger.

That man, the tamer of Singapore, is only seen very rarely. Those who have seen him at a distance have fled in terror. It is known that he lives in the high reaches of Mount Merapi and hardly ever descends into the valleys.

I was only able to collect two items of testimony on that subject, but they are convincing. Here they are:

A woman of the region of Merbarou claims to have seen the man and the tiger sleeping side by side, the head of the man placed on the tiger's snout as if on a pillow. She retains, it appears, from the emotion caused by that encounter, a nervous tremor of which she has never rid herself. She gives one curious detail that she might have had difficulty inventing. She saw a single gibbon suspended from a branch in the place where the sleepers were, carrying out trapeze exercises whose comicality she would have enjoyed, if fear had not caused her to flee.

A Malay who was carrying a sack of flour to the lamasery of Kobou Dalem found himself face to face on a path with the tamer of Singapore. The famous tiger was walking alongside him. When the tamer perceived the Malay he seized the beast by the scruff of the neck, as one does with a dog which one knows to be badly behaved, and made a sign to the Malay to run away, which he did very rapidly.

I interrogated the Malay about the external appearance of the tamer. He affirmed that he had seen on his shoulder two little birds belonging to a rare species, that of beos. He was laughing and singing softly while looking at the birds, and his face reflected the most placid joy.

Perhaps the man who sought purification has also found happiness in the solitude of the trees, among the reconciled animals.

SF & FANTASY

Adolphe Alhaiza. *Cybele*

Alphonse Allais. *The Adventures of Captain Cap*

Henri Allorge. *The Great Cataclysm*

Guy d'Armen. *Doc Ardan: The City of Gold and Lepers; The Troglodytes of Mount Everest/The Giants of Black Lake; The Abominable Snowman*

G.-J. Arnaud. *The Ice Company*

André Arnyvelde. *The Ark; The Mutilated Bacchus*

Charles Asselineau. *The Double Life*

Henri Austruy. *The Eupantophone; The Olotelepan; The Petitpaon Era*

Barillet-Lagargousse. *The Final War*

Barbot de Villeneuve. *The Naiads/Beauty & The Beast*

Cyprien Bérard. *The Vampire Lord Ruthwen*

S. Henry Berthoud. *Martyrs of Science; The Angel Asrael*

Aloysius Bertrand. *Gaspard de la Nuit*

Richard Bessière. *The Gardens of the Apocalypse; The Masters of Silence*

Chevalier de Béthune. *The World of Mercury*

Albert Bleunard. *Ever Smaller*

Félix Bodin. *The Novel of the Future*

Pierre Boitard. *Journey to the Sun*

Louis Boussenard. *Monsieur Synthesis*

Alphonse Brown. *City of Glass; The Conquest of the Air*

Émile Calvet. *In a Thousand Years*

André Caroff. *The Terror of Madame Atomos; Miss Atomos; The Return of Madame Atomos; The Mistake of Madame Atomos; The Monsters of Madame Atomos; The Revenge of Madame Atomos; The Resurrection of Madame Atomos; The Mark of Madame Atomos; The Spheres of Madame Atomos; The Wrath of Madame Atomos* (w/M. & Sylvie Stéphan)

Jean Carrère. *The End of Atlantis*

Félicien Champsaur. *Homo-Deus; The Human Arrow; Nora, The Ape-Woman; Ouha, King of the Apes; Pharaoh's Wife*

Didier de Chousy. *Ignis*

Jules Clarétie. *Obsession*

Jacques Collin de Plancy. *Voyage to the Center of the Earth*
Michel Corday. *The Eternal Flame; The Lynx* (w/André Couvreur)
André Couvreur. *Caresco, Superman; The Exploits of Professor Tornada* (3 vols.); *The Necessary Evil*
Gaston Danville. *The Perfume of Lust*
Camille Debans. *The Misfortunes of John Bull*
Captain Danrit. *Undersea Odyssey*
C. I. Defontenay. *Star (Psi Cassiopeia)*
Charles Derennes. *The People of the Pole*
Georges Dodds (anthologist). *The Missing Link*
Charles Dodeman. *The Silent Bomb*
Harry Dickson. *The Heir of Dracula; Harry Dickson vs. The Spider*
Jules Dornay. *Lord Ruthven Begins*
Alfred Driou. *The Adventures of a Parisian Aeronaut*
Odette Dulac. *The War of the Sexes*
Alexandre Dumas. *The Return of Lord Ruthven; The Man who Married a Mermaid* (w/P. Lacroix)
Renée Dunan. *Baal; The Ultimate Pleasure*
J.-C. Dunyach. *The Night Orchid; The Thieves of Silence*
Henri Duvernois. *The Man Who Found Himself*
Achille Eyraud. *Voyage to Venus*
Henri Falk. *The Age of Lead*
Paul Féval. *Anne of the Isles; Knightshade; Revenants; Vampire City; The Vampire Countess; The Wandering Jew's Daughter*
Paul Féval, *fils. Felifax, the Tiger-Man*
Charles de Fieux. *Lamékis*
Fernand Fleuret. *Jim Click*
Charles-Marie Flor O'Squarr. *Phantoms*
Louis Forest. *Someone is Stealing Children in Paris*
Arnould Galopin. *Doctor Omega; Doctor Omega and the Shadowmen* (anthology)
Judith Gautier. *Isoline and the Serpent-Flower*
H. Gayar. *The Marvelous Adventures of Serge Myrandhal on Mars*
Louis Geoffroy. *The Apocryphal Napoleon*
G.L. Gick. *Harry Dickson and the Werewolf of Rutherford Grange*
Raoul Gineste. *The Second Life of Doctor Albin*
Delphine de Girardin. *Balzac's Cane*
Léon Gozlan. *The Vampire of the Val-de-Grâce*
Jules Gros. *The Fossil Man*
Jimmy Guieu. *The Polarian-Denebian War* (2 vols.)
Edmond Haraucourt. *Daah, the First Human; Illusions of Immortality*

Nathalie Henneberg. *The Green Gods*
Eugène Hennebert. *The Enchanted City*
Jules Hoche. *The Maker of Men and His Formula*
V. Hugo, P. Foucher & P. Meurice. *The Hunchback of Notre-Dame*
Romain d'Huissier. *Hexagon: Dark Matter*
Jules Janin. *The Magnetized Corpse*
Gustave Kahn. *The Tale of Gold and Silence*
Gérard Klein. *The Mote in Time's Eye*
Fernand Kolney. *Love in 5000 Years*
Paul Lacroix. *Danse Macabre; The Man who Married a Mermaid* (w/Alexandre Dumas)
Louis-Guillaume de La Follie. *The Unpretentious Philosopher*
Jean de La Hire. *The Fiery Wheel; Enter the Nyctalope; The Nyctalope on Mars; The Nyctalope vs. Lucifer; The Nyctalope Steps In; Night of the Nyctalope; Return of the Nyctalope*
Etienne-Léon de Lamothe-Langon. *The Virgin Vampire*
André Laurie. *Spiridon*
Gabriel de Lautrec. *The Vengeance of the Oval Portrait*
Alain le Drimeur. *The Future City*
Georges Le Faure & Henri de Graffigny. *The Extraordinary Adventures of a Russian Scientist Across the Solar System* (2 vols.)
Gustave Le Rouge. *The Dominion of the World* (w/Gustave Guitton) (4 vols.); *The Mysterious Doctor Cornelius* (3 vols.); *The Vampires of Mars*
Jules Lermina. *The Battle of Strasbourg; Mysteryville; Panic in Paris; The Secret of Zippelius; To-Ho and the Gold Destroyers*
Maurice Level. *The Gates of Hell*
André Lichtenberger. *The Centaurs; The Children of the Crab*
Maurice Limat. *Mephista*
Listonai. *The Philosophical Voyager*
Jean-Marc & Randy Lofficier. *Edgar Allan Poe on Mars; The Katrina Protocol; Pacifica 1, 2; Robonocchio; Return of the Nyctalope;* (anthologists) *Tales of the Shadowmen 1-13; The Vampire Almanac* (2 vols.)
Ch. Lomon & P.-B. Gheuzi. *The Last Days of Atlantis*
Charles Malato. *Lost!*
Maurice Magre. *The Marvelous Story of Claire d'Amour; The Call of the Beast; Priscilla of Alexandria; The Angel of Lust*
Camille Mauclair. *The Virgin Orient*
Xavier Mauméjean. *The League of Heroes*
Joseph Méry. *The Tower of Destiny*

Louis-Claude de Saint-Martin. *The Crocodile*
Frank Schildiner. *The Quest of Frankenstein; The Triumph of Frankenstein; Napoleon's Vampire Hunters*
Nicolas Ségur. *The Human Paradise*
Pierre de Selenes: *An Unknown World*
Norbert Sevestre. *Sâr Dubnotal: Vs. Jack the Ripper; The Astral Trail*
Angelo de Sorr. *The Vampires of London*
Brian Stableford. *The Empire of the Necromancers (1. The Shadow of Frankenstein; 2. Frankenstein and the Vampire Countess; 3. Frankenstein in London); The Wayward Muse; Eurydice's Lament; The Mirror of Dionysius; The New Faust at the Tragicomique; Sherlock Holmes and The Vampires of Eternity; The Stones of Camelot* (anthologist) *News from the Moon; The Germans on Venus; The Supreme Progress; The World Above the World; Nemoville; Investigations of the Future; The Conqueror of Death; The Revolt of the Machines; The Man With the Blue Face; The Aerial Valley; The New Moon; The Nickel Man; On the Brink of the World's End; The Mirror of Present Events; The Humanisphere*
Jacques Spitz. *The Eye of Purgatory*
Kurt Steiner. *Ortog*
Eugène Thébault. *Radio-Terror*
C.-F. Tiphaigne de La Roche. *Amilec*
Simon Tyssot de Patot. *The Strange Voyages of Jacques Massé and Pierre de Mésange*
Louis Ulbach. *Prince Bonifacio*
Théo Varlet. *The Castaways of Eros; The Golden Rock.; The Martian Epic* (w/Octave Joncquel); *Timeslip Troopers* (w/André Blandin); *The Xenobiotic Invasion*
Pierre Véron. *The Merchants of Health*
Paul Vibert. *The Mysterious Fluid*
Villiers de l'Isle-Adam. *The Scaffold; The Vampire Soul*
Gaston de Wailly. *The Murderer of the World*
Philippe Ward. *Artahe; Manhattan Ghost* (w/Mickael Laguerre); *The Song of Montségur* (w/Sylvie Miller)

Victor Margueritte. *The Bacheloress; The Companion; The Couple*

www.ingramcontent.com/pod-product-compliance
Lightning Source LLC
Chambersburg PA
CBHW030356020726
47493CB00003B/835